Pam Dickens Keeps Christmas All The Year

By Sarah Tipper

Introduction

Pam Dickens will be released from paid employment this year and she is jolly pleased about it. Join her as she gets used to retirement and occupies her time very pleasantly by focusing on her favourite festival. Meet her husband Malc and see what marriage looks like after more than four decades. Meet her family and friends and enjoy the bits of Oxford that locals inhabit.

January

Monday 1st January 2018

Today is the eighth day of Christmas, which is unquestionably my favourite time of year. It has been my favourite time of year since I was seven years old. I remember having a wonderful Friday before finishing school for the holidays and having a party in the big hall in the afternoon. Then in the evening I remember decorating the Christmas tree with Dad and Val, while Mum was in the kitchen making mince pies. When we were finished Mum came into the living room with a big plate of mince pies and admired our efforts. We sat on the sofa with the big light off, eating mince pies by the light of the tree. The tree lights were little golden lanterns. They shone through pink, red, orange, yellow, green and blue shades creating a rainbow hued vision. It was the loveliest thing I'd ever seen and it was in our house and I'd helped make it.

So I am not one of these people that gets fed up of having the decorations on display and takes them down early, like my friend Gail, who says they clutter the place up and interfere with her regular housekeeping schedule. Writing 'on display' makes my decorations sound fancier than they are. We have a six-foot tree, tinsel on the picture frames, the nativity Dad made and various festive ornaments for the mantelpiece and shelves.

Christmas 2017 was better than Christmas 2016 because I worked less. I've been doing four days a week instead of five, getting ready for retirement. My daughter Nicola presented me with this diary on Christmas Day saying 2018 is going to be my year and I'll have more time to plan things like going to London with Aunty Val. It's an A4 lockable diary with a whole page to fill per day. It has a gold cover.

'Pam's got no secrets from me,' Malc (my husband) said and I wondered if that was true.

It's tidy when the year begins on a Monday. We watched the final of *World's Strongest Man*. Eddie Hall won. Malc was pleased.

'Well we did it at last! I remember when Geoff Capes won and that was 24 years ago,' said Malc.

When I think of Geoff Capes I also think of Jaffa cakes, the sounds are similar. Malc is unable to mention Geoff Capes without providing the information that he is an accomplished budgie breeder, which everyone knows.

Tuesday 2nd January

Today is the ninth day of Christmas. Christmas is still here even though I had to go to work this morning. I told myself it's not for much longer and I only have to work three days this week so I should count myself lucky. I shan't tell you which supermarket I work in because I might want to write rude things about it. Also, it doesn't really matter which one it is, I've worked in two branches of the one I work for now and in another one and it's much the same. There's always a colleague who's a shirker, one that obeys the rules to the letter and one that's plain rude. The customers lately act like anything not perfect is the staff on the tills fault.

My resolutions for 2018 are;

1. Don't let work stress me out, I retire in February so there is no point in getting in a flap about things I won't be around long enough to change.

2. Enjoy being retired, really make the most of it, no guilt about not having to go to work, I've got up early for years and done as I'm told, so now it's time to suit myself (and Malc of course).
No-one knows how long their retirement will be. My Dad died just eleven months after he retired. Mum said he had only just begun to relax and enjoy life.
3. Keep Christmas all the year so I don't feel glum when it's over. This diary is going to be my keeping Christmas diary. I shall record my Christmas thoughts and doings.

I had a chat with Lauren at morning tea break. She's one of the good ones. She's studying accountancy part time and working full time. She's got a two-year-old, Daisy, who kept her awake much of last night. Lauren was worried that she hasn't done all the studying she wanted to get through. Also she's been on a diet but has put on weight over Christmas (haven't we all?!) I told her you don't have to strive to achieve all of your ambitions on the second day of the New Year, especially when you've had a bit less than four hours sleep.

Wednesday 3rd January

Today is the tenth day of Christmas. I called in on Mum after work. She has watched none of her new Christmas DVDs because she's lost the DVD player remote control. I looked for it but could only find a universal remote which she says isn't it. It had no batteries in and she had no spares in the house so I couldn't test to see if it works. She said at eighty-eight she doesn't see the point of stocking up on things. I hope I'm as mobile and healthy as her when I'm her age and I haven't inherited my longevity from Dad's side of the family. She's a bit scatter-brained but she always has been, it's got nothing to do with her age. I showed her how to press the eject, play and stop buttons on the DVD player then left her watching *Downton Abbey*. Tomorrow is bin day in her road and loads of people have put out their real Christmas trees for recycling. It's a sad sight, the end of the Christmas tree being indoors. Some people use clear recycling bags and they are filled with empty chocolate boxes, Pringles tubes, gift wrap and gift bags. I always re-use gift bags, until they get too scruffy.

Malc came back from the allotment with some parsnips. The little shed on the allotment has fallen over, storm Eleanor is making the UK windy today. We had a using things up dinner; some Wensleydale and double Gloucester on crackers, a mini Babybel, pickled onions, ham, coleslaw and chocolate log. There is some space in the fridge again.

I went to bed early and read Charles Dickens' *Christmas Stories*. It was a Christmas present from Nicola as well as this diary. She has always been a big reader. I didn't know Dickens wrote four other Christmas stories as well as *A Christmas Carol*. I'm now reading 'The Chimes'.

Thursday 4th January

Today is the eleventh day of Christmas. I quite enjoyed my walk to work even though it was drizzling. Cowley looks good in the drizzle. There is a house by us with a gorgeous spruce tree in the front garden. It's been decorated with simple white lights. Next door is a house covered in garish multi-coloured Santas and snowmen. One of the Santas looks like he's waving at passers-by. Both brighten up the neighbourhood wonderfully.

Mum rang to say she found the DVD remote down the side of her chair, (along with a load of hair grips, Fox's Glacier Mint wrappers and a hair roller no doubt). Mum is the only person I know who still uses hair rollers. Val bought her a curling tong a few years ago but she's never taken it out of the box.

After dinner Malc went on the computer and booked our holiday to celebrate my retirement. On March the sixth I'll be waking up in Bognor! I'll be a free woman! A lady of leisure! I don't work Fridays now so my weekend has begun and I can practice being free from paid employment.

Friday 5th January

I met Val in town for a look round the Christmas sales. Val got me a Y shaped potato peeler from Ocado. She used my peeler at Christmas and didn't get on with it. She said once she got this Y shaped one she's never looked back. I gave her some of Malc's parsnips, which she had complimented highly on Christmas Day. This Christmas it'll be Val's turn to be Christmas Day host.

Val said she came into town on New Year's Day but most things were shut. She had wanted to exchange a cashmere jumper in John Lewis but it was closed, which she said considering it's the Westgate's biggest shop is a bad decision. I'm pleased when shops are shut because I work in one and think they should be shut for longer over Christmas and New Year. We went to John Lewis and Val got a gift card in place of the beige cashmere jumper Henry bought her for Christmas. She already has a beige cashmere jumper. The new one Henry bought was a size too small. We browsed the reduced decorations. There is not a single spare branch on my Christmas tree so I didn't buy anything. I enjoyed looking though. The Westgate shops are very different to how they used to be. As a treat when we came into town as kids Mum used to buy us a jam doughnut from Don Millers. That's long gone.

We went to Boswells and the Covered Market. The cake shop in the market had sugar mice. The florist looked lovely, they had glitter pine cones. Cornmarket Street was full of homeless people shouting at each other. If you took a photo and erased the shop names you'd think it was a Victorian slum area.

I got the bus home from the new stop on Castle Street. I'd got Malc's favourite wild boar sausages from the Covered Market and we had sausage, mashed potato and onion gravy for dinner. He kissed me on the cheek. He loves sausage and mash. We watched the news while we ate. Donald Trump is trying to ban a book about his presidency so far called *Fire And Fury*. Malc said imagine if we'd let Alan Sugar from off *The Apprentice* be our prime minister? A businessman knows nothing of social justice.

Saturday 6th January

Today is Epiphany. I took the Christmas decorations down. It felt very symbolic deflating an inflatable Father Christmas. Nicola phoned me when I was half way through. She said she knows I don't like the day when the decorations have to come down, and she's right, I don't.

It's partly the ending of Christmas and partly the dusting and hoovering. Val has a robot hoover. She says everyone should get one. I have a Henry, which is also Val's husband's name! Henry (Val's husband) never hoovers and nor does Malc.

Nicola went to Coventry for university and never came back. It's only an hour away by train. She asked if I've been writing my diary. I said yes and she sounded surprised. She said she's only ever seen me write shopping lists and birthday cards. I said I'm part way through the Dickens' book she got me too. I said the diary was a lovely Christmas present and I'm going to use it to record my attempts at keeping Christmas all the year. She said maybe Dickens was the catalyst. I said he used the words 'coal scuttle' at the end of *A Christmas Carol* which I haven't heard for years.

The shiny gold cover of this diary reminds me of gift wrap and the gift of gold given to baby Jesus and also Ferrero Rocher wrappers. It has many pleasant associations. It's also gold like my wedding ring. People say when you retire you have to get used to spending more time with your significant other. I'm not worried about that.

When I'd boxed up the decorations Malc put them in the roof as we call it. Our house has a loft conversion, it was one of the first in the street to have one and we did it when I came up on the Premium Bonds in nineteen-eighty-one. Malc says it was a good decision, we'd never afford it now. Sometimes he calls that room ERNIE's bounty. We sat in the empty looking living room, facing where the Christmas tree was and had a mince pie that went out of date a week ago.

Sunday 7th January

We had an Iceland grocery delivery this morning. Our bananas were so green I don't think they'll be ripe until next week. Mum says frozen food was a revelation and a godsend when it first came out. Malc is very partial to a cod fish finger sandwich or a chicken burger. I'm certainly very fond of online shopping, the last thing I want to do at the weekend is walk round a food shop doing my shopping when I've been working in one all week.

Val came round. We talked about my upcoming retirement, about keeping Mum healthy and about the Mediterranean cruise Val and Henry have booked. Henry always says he works in the science area in the science area then he looks pleased with himself. He means he does something in science, down Parks Road in town. Val and I will both be away at the same time briefly in March, which we try to avoid because of Mum. Val said I could ask David to call in if necessary. David is my youngest and he hasn't got the hang of family responsibilities yet. He lives and works in Bicester. He's a shop assistant in a fancy shop at Bicester Village but he doesn't get paid more than you do working in a non-fancy shop.

Malc expected David to follow in his footsteps and work at the car factory but David said it wouldn't suit him. Malc retired from the factory then got a part time job as a handyman in a care home two weeks later! I won't be so quick to rush into anything. Malc's allotment and the garden keeps him occupied too. People keep saying to me, what will you do with yourself when you retire? And I say don't worry about me.

I've got that Sunday night work dread feeling. I'm going to bed to read Dickens. There is a bit in *A Christmas Carol* where he writes 'we could improve our worldly fortune by our patient industry'. I've got to get up early tomorrow and do this. Trouble is I've become a bit impatient with it.

Monday 8th January
Dickens' story 'The Chimes' is about church bells which are haunted. When I think of church bells I think of St James Church where Malc and I got married in 1974.

I had an okay day at work. No-one is buying much. Cupboards are still full after Christmas. We're selling a lot of Ryvita. Despite having a large display of Easter eggs which went out just after Boxing Day no one is buying them. One woman bought four tins of Slim Fast and two reduced price boxes of Family Circle biscuits.

I went to see Mum after work. She's been to balance class at Rose Hill Community Centre. It keeps her sprightly. She likes to tell people she's still bending down to do her shoelaces up at eighty-eight. In some ways she is a marvel.

At work I was looking forward to getting home and reading. I might buy myself another Christmas book. Reading about Christmas would probably help me keep it all the year.

Tuesday 9th January
Today at work there is niggling between people because a supervisor vacancy has come up. There are three people I know of who have applied for it. The one I think would be

best, Lauren, hasn't applied. The people who don't want to be supervisors and don't enjoy being bossy are the people who make the best supervisors. The ones who love laying down the law and being jobsworths make the worst supervisors.

I told Lauren about my resolutions and she asked me what I mean by keeping Christmas all the year. I said I'd like to maintain a mood of cheerful optimism, like I feel in December, and be nice to people. She said I'm always nice to people. I said I don't always feel like being nice to people. She said no-one does, which is very true, we're all a bear with a sore head sometimes. Lauren asked me if I'm any relation to Charles Dickens! I said no. Before Malc I dated George Darwin. Either way I was going to take the name of a famous man! Malc likes to joke that some women get more cross after marriage but I've become less cross (my maiden name is Cross). Lauren said she'll be keeping her own name if she ever gets married. I said it never even occurred to me as an option when I got married.

For dinner we had chicken, parsnips, Brussels sprouts and gravy in a giant Yorkshire pudding. The sprouts made me feel a bit Christmassy.

Wednesday 10th January

I was going to tell you about work today then I remembered that this diary is my keeping Christmas all the year diary. The things I like best about Christmas is seeing people, the food, the entertainment, the decorations and the time off work. I'll try and have little bits of these things all year.

Malc came upstairs while I was writing this and asked if I was really going to write a diary this year. I said I couldn't see why not, it was a thoughtful gift from Nicola. He asked if he'd be in it. I said probably. He asked how much detail I was going into. I told him it's my diary for new hobbies when I retire and for keeping cheerful. He asked if I was going to put anything personal in my diary. I said everyone who writes a diary puts personal stuff in it. Then he asked would it have sex details? I said I hadn't thought about that. He looked sheepish and went back downstairs. I can assure you diary that if there are sex details, they won't be very frequent or especially unusual. This diary isn't going rival anything by Jackie Collins! I wonder if anyone retires and makes sex their new hobby? So far people have suggested I take up gardening, embroidery, knitting, volunteering and jigsaws. I'd quite like people to let me be and just have a rest for a few months. I shall remember that they are trying to be kind.

Thursday 11th January

I went to WH Smith at lunch time and bought a silver and a gold pen for writing this diary with. I can't believe how something so small can give me so much pleasure! I browsed the reduced Christmas cards, they have some lovely designs, it's one of the things WH Smith does well. I bought a pack with Christmas trees on ready for sending this year. I got a warm glow when I thought that this year I'll be able to spend ages preparing for Christmas because I'll be retired. I had a vision of myself curled up in an armchair with a hot chocolate, writing my cards with a gold pen, then sticking the stamps on which is one of my favourite bits. Amazing that a small square of paper acts like a passport for cards, getting them from the post box near me to the houses of friends and relatives as far away as Australia, Scotland and Wales. Last year it was a religious theme for the stamps so this year it'll be something secular. I felt a bit gloomy when I thought of the price of stamps and that I'll have to stick to a budget for the Christmas shopping this year. I do usually, we're not made of money, so we'll have to be a bit more careful when I retire. Already Malc only goes to B&Q on pensioners' discount day. I can buy second class stamps this year and post early.

I went to see Mum after work. She and Bridget are talking about booking a trip to Eastbourne with Shearings' Coach Tours. Bridget is Mum's most capable and least doddery friend. I never worry if I know she's going somewhere with Bridget.

Thursday is the new Friday for me because I only work Monday to Thursday now. Malc offered to go to the chip shop to save me cooking. We had cod and chips. He bumped into the granddaughter of one of the care home residents and she asked if he'd had a good Christmas. We wondered when in January people stop asking each other that?

Friday 12th January

I found a bag of chestnuts in the cupboard that I had meant to use on Christmas day, with the Brussels sprouts. It all got a bit frantic in the kitchen at Christmas, trying to have everything warm at the same time then plate it up. Every year when it's my turn I decide I'm going to cut down the number of different veg I cook, then Malc comes home from the allotment with the finest of his carefully cared for carrots, parsnips, sprouts and red cabbage and I don't have the heart to say let's just have parsnips and sprouts this year. He's spent many more hours growing them than I have to spend cooking them. He's been vigilant for wire worm afflicting the carrots and is always relieved to dodge the scourge of what he calls 'those rust coloured blighters'.

Also Henry always compliments Malc on the veg, and asks how long it's taken to grow, which is nice. They don't have much in common really. Malc works with his hands more than his brain although he could have worked with his brain if he'd wanted. My friend Gail's husband doesn't get on with his brother-in-law at all well and it's a shame. Malc and Henry try to meet in the middle.

We had pork chop, mashed potato and sprouts with bacon and chestnuts for dinner. I like making dinner on a Friday now, I'm not tired from five consecutive days at work. Eating chestnuts made me feel olden days Christmassy.

Saturday 13th January

If I was going to put sex details in this diary there would be some from last night. Maybe it was the chestnuts! I'm writing this up in the roof. I've decided to keep this diary behind the Christmas tree. There is a single bed up in the loft conversion so I can sit on it, look at our boxes of Christmas decorations and write. When David was little he wrote to Father Christmas and ended his letter by telling Father Christmas he could come in the Velux window if he didn't fancy the chimney! We do have a fireplace with an open grate but we never use it, the gas central heating is too good and Malc bleeds the radiators regularly. I've never, in all our years of marriage, put my hand on the top of a radiator in winter and found it cold due to trapped air.

Sunday 14th January
Malc is indoors much more in the winter. Sometimes he's restless and doesn't know quite what to do with himself, like David used to get at the end of the summer holidays. If I don't keep him occupied he'll start thinking about putting up shelves we don't need. He spent an hour on the computer watching DIY videos this morning so this afternoon I suggested a walk.
We walked to Templars Square and gave two bags of stuff to the British Heart Foundation charity shop. It's always me who hands over the bags, Malc doesn't like doing it, but he doesn't mind carrying them to the Centre. Templars Square used to be known as Cowley Centre and most people of my age still call it Cowley Centre. We like donating to the BHF because we've got heart disease in both sides of the family. I bought a book Malc spotted called *Skipping Christmas* by John Grisham and some Christmas cards with robins wearing scarves on. I have started a Christmas book shelf. It only has Dickens and Grisham so far. It's more of a book duo.

We had a look in the Emmaus charity shop (it's been open for ages but because it's part of the new flats and much smaller community centre I forget to look in it). We didn't buy anything but I thought of lots of things I could donate. They have some lovely furniture. I will declutter when I retire.

It's a shame the big old Cowley Community Centre has gone, it was used all the time for parties, dancing lessons, blood donors, all sorts. The Post Office has gone too, it's moved to inside the Co-op and the queue is always long and the number of staff always small. I sometimes wonder who makes these decisions. Certainly not the people who now have to queue for longer and have nowhere local to hold a party. Gail had her engagement party in the Community Centre. Her mother and her mother-in-law did a huge buffet. There was sherry trifle, sausages on sticks, egg sandwiches, ham sandwiches, corned beef sandwiches, pickled onions, a huge spread. Am I going to become one of those old people always harping on about the good old days? I hope not. It's easy to forget that we didn't have microwaves, duvets or women's rights in the old days.

I cooked the first full roast dinner I've cooked since Christmas. Roast potatoes bring me joy I've discovered. I put the Christmas cards I bought up in the roof with the others and thought about who might like a card with jolly robins on this year.

I finished reading 'The Chimes'. It's not cheerful until the very end and the spirits of the bells aren't as easy to imagine as the ghosts of Christmas past, present and future are. There is a posh person in it, Lady Bowley, who comes up with a song for the poor people to sing, which goes 'O let us love our occupations, Bless the squire and his relations, Live upon our daily rations, And always know our proper stations'. It's hard to love your occupation when it makes your feet ache and Mr Barker is swanning around like the big I am, chatting to the shopping centre security blokes and taking ages to bring you the change you asked for hours ago.

Monday 15th January
The car was MOT'd today and cost us £300! It's sat in disgrace on the driveway. I made a lemon drizzle cake to cheer Malc up. Gail popped round for coffee. She is one of my oldest friends, I've known her since I was twelve. My other oldest friend, Carol, I've known even longer, since junior school. I asked Gail how her Christmas was. She went to her sister's. She said her husband Len was fidgety to leave half an hour after dinner. Gail is always on a diet, even at Christmas. She said no to a slice of lemon drizzle. She said she's glad Christmas is out of the way for another year, all the mess, expense and temptation gone. I said I remembered her engagement party yesterday when I was on Barns Road by the new flats. She said her main memory of that party was wanting some trifle but being afraid she'd spill it on her new dress so deciding she'd wait until the end, by which time the trifle had all been eaten. My main memory of that party was Malc asking if we'd have to have an engagement party if we got engaged. We'd only been courting a few months and I thought steady on fella. I hadn't made my mind up about him at that stage. When Gail had gone I asked Malc what he remembered about Gail and Len's engagement party. He said he'd been delighted by how cheap the drinks were and that he was half cut by the end of the night.

We had a boozy coffee. We usually only have this at Christmas but Malc needed cheering up after the MOT shock and we've still got some Baileys left from Christmas.

We only have a little tot of Baileys in the coffee, in the nice smoked glass mugs which are quite small. I said to Malc that MOTs, like Christmas, only come once a year, so that's that for a twelvemonth.

I started reading Dickens' 'The Cricket on the Hearth'.

Tuesday 16th January

I collected Malc's prescription at lunch time. There were mini toiletries in Superdrug for the people jetting off for winter sun. I'll take my normal sized toiletries to Bognor. There was also some reduced-price Christmas chocolates and gift sets. All the boxes are a bit tatty now. Christmas 2017 has run out of steam.

Interviews for the supervisor position were held at work today. As well as the three internal candidates there were three external candidates. A decision will be made by the end of the week but as my last working day is six weeks away I'm not too fussed about the outcome. Part of me doesn't believe that I'm really retiring, even though I've been looking forward to it for years. I keep imagining someone will tell me there's been a mistake and I have to keep working!

Carol sent me a text asking me to save jam jars for a tombola she is running in April. This reminded me that every year I read in magazines or see on telly people making fudge or coconut ice or homemade chocolates as gifts. Then they package them beautifully in glass jars, often with a little gingham hat. I never seem to have time to do this sort of thing. Maybe this year I will.

I told Malc about the jam jars. He said he could probably finish up a jar of mango chutney this week. I found my cook book with the fudge and coconut ice recipes. I added pink food colouring to the shopping list and daydreamed about producing jars of tasty, homemade, well received Christmas gifts instead of handing over something made by Thorntons or Cadbury.

Wednesday 17th January
It snowed in the night! Not much, just a sprinkling, but enough to give me the magic Christmas tingle. I walked to work viewing snow dusted hedges and flowerbeds. Everything looks prettier, even the discarded Carling cans and abandoned ripped up scratch cards that didn't do what the buyer wanted. Just before people buy a scratch card they have bright eyes full of hope. I've seen it many times. We were busy in the shop in the afternoon, people bought tins and lots of milk, the usual response to a smattering of snow. There's an air of excitement. My walk home was cold but I could almost believe it was before Christmas and not January. I suppose it's always before Christmas, even though the Christmas we're before now is eleven and a half months away. We had chicken schnitzel with katsu spices and sweet potato and cinnamon mash for dinner tonight. Malc said it was perhaps a bit much for his tastebuds. I liked it. It requires constant thought when married to cook a dinner that you both want to eat. Left to his own devices Malc would probably eat sausages every day.

Thursday 18th January

Dylan was five minutes late today and Phil told him off for ten minutes on the shop floor because Mr Barker the manager was in earshot. Phil is one of the ones who has gone for the supervisor job. He isn't in charge of Dylan. He should know better than to reprimand someone in front of people. Dylan went a bit red. He's a nice lad in his early twenties who still lives at home and hasn't quite learnt how to always get up on time yet. That comes later in life when the daily grind has had years to seep into your body clock and your eyes ping awake even on days off. When it was just Dylan and I next to each other on the tills I told him not to take any notice of Phil's showing off to Mr Barker. My Dad was a heavy sleeper and I told Dylan about his system of keeping his alarm clock on top of a tin with loads of copper coins on it to make it noisier. Dylan said you can now get an alarm clock with a pressure pad that you have to get out of bed and stand on to switch it off. Dad could have done with one of these. Often it was only Mum's elbow that got him up. I sometimes wonder what he'd make of the world now.

Tracy was also late this morning but Phil didn't say anything to her, not a dicky bird. He knows she'd have told him right where to stick it if he did. Lauren said she'll be glad when the new supervisor is announced so people can go back to normal. She said Phil is acting like a puffed-up pigeon. When I left today the announcement hadn't been made so I will find out on Monday. Not much of a cliff hanger Dear Diary, but that's the life of a sixty-six-year-old woman approaching retirement.

I struggled to think of a way to keep Christmas today so I looked back in this diary to see how I've got the magic Christmas tingle so far this year. It's come from remembering (Christmas 1959 when I was seven years old and Christmas 1985 when David told Father Christmas about the Velux window), reading and starting a Christmas book shelf, eating and drinking (mince pie, chestnuts, boozy coffee), shopping (with Val, and getting Christmas cards and a gold pen), looking at people's outdoor decorations and snow. I went on the big computer and started a list of Christmas books on my Amazon account. Malc came to see what I was doing, he's the computer buff in this house. As well as the big computer we have a tablet, which is such a strange word for a small computer. When I hear tablet I think paracetamol or Scottish fudge. Our computer and our tablet are old ones of Henry's. He likes having the latest thing.

Friday 19th January

In the news today is Prince William having a haircut because he's going bald. All the money in the world can't stop men losing their hair, it's a great leveller, men's hair. I have time to read the paper on a Friday now instead of rushing out of the house for work. I wouldn't bother buying a paper but Malc likes to do the crossword. He's been doing it since he worked at the car factory.

I went round to Carol's for coffee. Carol is already retired. She said Donna is in the doldrums. Donna is Carol's daughter. She still lives at home. She can't really afford to move out but luckily she and Carol get on very well. Donna is full time in the care home where Malc works part time. This time of year they always lose residents to things like chest infections which become pneumonia and Donna takes it very hard. One week she went to three funerals. It's too much sadness for someone like Donna who puts so much care into caring.

I'm looking forward to London tomorrow, going to the theatre with Val, while also feeling slightly like I can't be bothered, which is January all over isn't it? The darkness makes you want to stay at home in your own little corner of the world. I partly packed my bag ready for tomorrow and began to feel excited. I have a new sparkly jumper with beads and sequins from Bon Marche. I love my little escapes with Val. We do things we could never have imagined doing as children and we can please ourselves and do things Malc and Henry aren't interested in.

We ordered Domino's pizza for dinner. Malc likes ham and pineapple and I like Texas BBQ so we do a half and half. Malc always reads the menu for five minutes then gets the same thing. We watched *The Best Little Whorehouse in Texas*. The song 'Hard Candy Christmas' sticks out as being a bit strange. I'm not sure that your brothel being shut down is all that much like a Christmas when you're living in poverty but maybe it is. Burt Reynolds is dishy. It's a shame he can't lend Prince William some of his hair. I bet Dolly Parton's house looks amazing at Christmas. She's never short of a sequin frock to wear to a Christmas party.

I created a section in my wardrobe of all what I think of as my Christmas clothes. The velvet and the sparkle doesn't get worn very often, it's just at Christmas and theatre trips with Val. I could try and keep Christmas all the year by wearing festive things. I could become Littlemore's answer to Dolly Parton! Except I'm only a B cup and the only songs I've ever come up with are nonsense ones when the kids were small and I was trying to get them to eat their dinner. Once David was very put out at having straight Heinz spaghetti in tomato sauce rather than hoops. He liked to hook the hoops on the tine of his fork and eat them first then eat the soggy toast they were on separately. It took ages but it kept him quiet and he ate all his dinner so it didn't matter. I had to come up with 'Hoops or straight it's all the same, let's have yummy spaghetti again' and sing it repeatedly to persuade him.

Saturday 20th January
Val and I left for London after a long conversation about whether to take umbrellas or not. We decided not after consulting the weather on Val's smartphone. We got on an Oxford Tube bus straight away. I like the bit where we just sit on a bus for a couple of hours and catch up. There are some things I'll say to Val when it's just the two of us that I won't say if Malc and Henry are there. Neither Malc nor Henry wanted to come and see *Les Misérables*. Val gave me a book, *The Christmas Collection* by Susan Hill. She saw it in a charity shop and thought I might like it.

We got off at Marble Arch and walked up Oxford Street. Our hotel is on Shaftesbury Avenue. We left our overnight bags, admired the neatness of our rooms and went to Soho for lunch. We looked at a lot of menus, there's so much choice in London. We ate in Bistro 1 on Frith Street. I had beef bourguignon on creamy mash. Val had fish and chips. Then we walked round Chinatown. It was very wet. We went in M&Ms World for a while to shelter from the heavy rain. It smelled of vanilla and chocolate. We didn't have M&Ms when I was growing up, it was Smarties who were the king of the crisp colourful coated chocolates. I used to get Nicola and David a tube of Smarties sometimes on a Friday as a treat. Nicola was always delighted when the plastic lid with a letter on was an 'n' for Nicola. The 'z' and the 'u' also looked like an 'n' so she had three chances in twenty-six. David used to like putting the lid back on and then stamping on the tube to make the lid pop off, like a pop gun. There was always a Smartie lid behind something or on top of something when I did a big tidy up.

We bought an umbrella each from a tourist tat shop. Val said the weather on her smartphone app changes all the time. I said I listen to Tomasz Schafernaker once a day and plan accordingly. We walked to Covent Garden. There is not much remaining in the Christmas sales now but there are little glimpses of Christmas left and tonight's musical is a Christmas gift. Ben's Cookies smelt amazing as usual. The first one was in Oxford and was Nicola's favourite when she was fifteen. They don't have one in Coventry.

We had Mexican for dinner, from Wahaca. I had a very nice burrito, Val had a chilli con carne. Then we went back to the hotel to freshen up. I put on my sparkly jumper. We went back out at seven. There is a light festival called Lumiere on this weekend and there are installations in Leicester Square, Piccadilly Circus and many other places. We saw the Leicester Square woodland type installation with butterflies, a hare and other animals and the Piccadilly Circus installation of a clock projected onto a building.

Then we went to the theatre! We really enjoyed the show. It was a short walk back to the hotel. When we got to our rooms there was a little gauze bag on our pillows with square chocolates and a fancy lip balm! It felt like Father Christmas had been! We took our shoes off and had a hot chocolate in Val's room then said goodnight. Today has felt like a big treat, it's not just the surroundings or the food or the entertainment, it's getting to spend time with Val. I had a text from Malc before bed saying he hoped we had a good time. He doesn't mind me going for a night away with Val every once in a while. He'll have been to the chip shop for his dinner.

Sunday 21st January

I woke up early so I explored the hotel room. There was *GQ* and *Cosmopolitan* to read. I flicked through the *Cosmopolitan*. I wondered if there are women willing and able to spend £400 on a handbag. There must be I suppose.

I ate the complimentary satsumas but not the apples. I'll take the apples home. There were also two types of biscuit (Viennese whirl and shortbread rounds) and four types of tea (English breakfast, green, earl grey and camomile). There was a kettle and a coffee pod machine. There was a mini bar but I didn't touch it. The Skittles in the mini bar cost £6.50! And it was a smaller packet than the one we sell for £1 in the supermarket! No matter how fancy the hotel, the milk is always UHT. I wonder how fancy a hotel has to be for them to give you actual milk?

Val and I met up at eight-thirty for breakfast. It started snowing! Malc sent me a text saying there was snow in Oxford. We looked at a few menus in Soho then decided to queue(!) for The Breakfast Club. We queued for about fifteen minutes. Val had chorizo hash, I had Cabbie's breakfast (bacon, egg, sausage, chips, beans). Usually I'd give Malc my sausage. I'm not fussed about sausages and he loves them. The food was good. The service was friendly. I'm not sure queuing for breakfast will catch on though.

After breakfast we walked round Chinatown and Leicester Square. It was so nice to see London quiet and be able to walk round without the usual crowds. We bought a coconut bun each in Chinatown to eat for lunch. There are such amazing pastries and cakes in the Chinatown shops. One shop makes little pastry fish with custard inside. It was very cold so we decided to go back to the hotel for a bit and decide what to do for the rest of the day. We had a coffee in my room, made eventually with pods. I wonder how long the pods craze will last for? Val says it's bad for the environment. She says she'll stick to her cafetiere. I said I'll stick to bunging some Kenco in a mug and not being fussy.

We decided we'd check out and get a taxi to the V&A. In the taxi we went past St James Church and saw a Tracy Emin neon sign, unlit and small, saying 'Be Faithful To Your Dreams' that is part of the Lumiere Festival. When Val and I were growing up, no-one ever told us to have dreams, they told us to get a job as soon as we left school and to not get pregnant until we were married.

We put our overnight bags in the V&A cloakroom and we went to look for a display about Christmas number ones. We went through gold, silver, jewellery and finally found the Christmas numbers ones display. It was small but informative. There were loads of other great things in the performance gallery including clothes worn by Jimmy Page and Adam Ant, both slim men fond of fancy trousers. There was a replica of Kylie's dressing room. She could give Dolly Parton a run for her money with sequins.

We decided to save our coconut buns for later and went for lunch to L'opera (241 Brompton Road). Val had a falafel sandwich and I had a waffle with Nutella and vanilla ice cream. The toilet had locking doors on both cubicles and was not in the basement which is unusual for London. We went to Harrods and saw Andy Warhol's soup can prints and looked round the food hall. Imagine buying your groceries from Harrods! I looked at the reduced-price Christmas things and got a tingle of festive excitement! Then we got a 74 bus to Marble Arch. We didn't wait very long for an Oxford Tube home. I got in at 5:15. Malc was cooking boiled egg and toasted soldiers for dinner. Malc can cook three things well; boiled eggs, beans on toast and sausage sandwich.

I'm going to go to bed early tonight, after *Still Open All Hours*. I love London but it tires me out! There are chip papers in the bin. There are no chocolates on my pillow. I put the Susan Hill Christmas book from Val on my Christmas book shelf along with Dickens and Grisham.

Monday 22nd January

It was hard to get out of bed this morning. Nowhere is as comfy as your own bed in winter. It's so cold and dark out. As I walked to work I counted the number of working days until I retire. I have twenty-three more days to do, including today, and will have to get out of bed for work twenty-two more times. It's a shame there isn't a retirement advent calendar. As soon as I got into the staff room Lauren told me an external candidate got the supervisor job. Mr Barker announced it on Friday. Phil is sulking. Tracy said Mr Barker already knew the new supervisor from when they worked together in Kwik Save many moons ago.

After work I went to see Mum. I took her some biscuits me and Val bought her in London, from Whittards in Covent Garden. We always go in there and drink the tiny samples of their drinks. We always say how nice it is, whether hot chocolate in winter or mango iced tea in summer, but neither of us have ever bought it. Some people must, or they'd go bust spending all their money on tiny plastic cups and exotically flavoured hot chocolates and teas.

I asked Mum what she'd done today and she said sweet Fanny Adams. I try not to be jealous of the leisure time she has or that Malc and Val have. I will have it myself soon. I read some Dickens. Then I lay in bed thinking about what I'd put behind the doors of a retirement advent calendar.

I finished reading Dickens' 'The Cricket on the Hearth'. Although it's in a book Nicola bought me of his Christmas stories, it's not about Christmas, but it was published just before Christmas. It's one of those books where there is a misunderstanding between husband and wife that eventually gets resolved, the sort of thing that wouldn't happen in real life because you'd just ask 'Malc, what are you up to?' and it would come out. It had a nice happy ending.

Tuesday 23rd January
I had eight minutes for morning tea break today because three people called in sick. Phil was one of them. He rarely has time off ill but he's probably decided he's not going to bend over backwards to be helpful at work since they didn't give him the supervisor's job. He's been doing it to help out and not getting any thanks so I can see his point. I ate my Frusli and drank a glass of water then went back on the till so Lauren could have her break. At half eleven Dylan came in even though it was his day off so we had our proper lunch breaks.

Nicola phoned up this evening to ask how London was. I told her I was still keeping my diary. She said it could become a travelogue! I said I don't know about that but we are looking forward to having a couple of days away at the start of March when I retire. I asked her how's work? There is a selfish part of me that wants to ask why she can't work in a library in Oxford, we have plenty of them, rather than staying in Coventry. She said the library is busy with people booking the computers to apply for new jobs. I don't think Malc and I would have had a computer if Henry didn't give us his old one. Henry says older people who don't use a computer are at a huge disadvantage. He gets quite a bee in his bonnet about it. Mum is also using an old computer of Henry's.

I browsed the January sales on the computer. There are a lot of reduced decorations now. I didn't buy anything, sometimes it's nice just to look. When you get to my age you realise that the important thing about Christmas isn't what you buy. That needn't stop you from enjoying a browse though, especially when shiny things make your heart glad.

I started reading Dickens' 'The Battle of Life'.

Wednesday 24th January

Work was quite dull today. I spent a lot of time reducing the price of our own brand mint chocolate assortments. I think that most people don't like mint chocolates much because it reminds them of brushing their teeth, but at Christmas when they see adverts for after dinner mints they give mint chocolate another go. Then they decide they aren't that fussed and don't eat any mint chocolates until next Christmas. Ask yourself honestly, would you rather have a box of mint chocolates or a box of milk chocolates? Wrapping mint chocolates in green foil makes them seem festive and attractive but when all the Christmas decorations are down there's less green and the mint chocolates fade back into the background. This is what I've concluded after many years of seeing the mint chocolates left over in January.

I didn't have to cook dinner tonight. We went to The Tandem Hungry Horse pub and restaurant. Malc made his usual joke about he could eat a horse so it seemed the best place to go. There was an offer on big plate specials, two for ten pounds. Malc had the gigantic gammon and I had jumbo cod and chips. We didn't eat it all. I knew we wouldn't, but Malc's eyes were bigger than his belly and he likes the gigantic gammon because you get egg and pineapple instead of just egg. They used to call the jumbo cod and chips good cod almighty.

A boy at the table next to us got a toy from the claw machine and played with it for no more than a minute then watched SpongeBob SquarePants on his Mum's phone and picked at his food. We never ate out when Nicola and David were that age, we'd have liked to, but it was just so expensive. The Tandem wasn't a Hungry Horse then, it was just a pub that did jacket potatoes. It's lovely to be able to afford a meal out to cheer up January and we've got one on Sunday too.

Thursday 25th January

I had a good day at work today, it was quiet. People are waiting for January pay day before doing a big shop. Malc had a good day too. He does Tuesdays and Thursdays at the care home, doing a bit of painting, then mainly gardening in the summer, he's Jack of all trades really. He can swap his days if he needs to, they're quite flexible. Today he fixed a rabbit hutch for one of the residents. The rabbit who lives in it, a big white one who goes by the name of Snowball, kept wiggling the catch free and going for a wander. Malc fixed the catch but also built a bigger run for Snowball. They like to try and create a bit of interest for the people who live there. They've had a giant tortoise visit before. It's not all plonk them in front of the telly and wait for death. One of the big challenges with retiring is not thinking of yourself as too old to enjoy life. None of us know how many Christmases or summers we have left.

Nicola phoned. She has entered a competition to win a year's supply of malt loaf. She asked if I was still keeping my diary. I said yes and she said it's probably a habit now.

I finished reading Dickens' 'The Battle of Life'. It was about two sisters and the younger one of them went away for six years so the other one would marry Alfred. It only had one mention of Christmas. The longest I've ever gone without seeing Val is about three weeks when she's been on holiday.

I flicked through the Christmas catalogues rather than start reading Dickens' 'The Haunted Man and the Ghost's Bargain'. I find I need to let the end of a story settle in my head before I start a new one. Malc asked on Tuesday if he could put the Christmas catalogues in the recycling bin but I wanted to hang on to them for a bit. I read the George at Asda one, the M&S one, the Wilkinson's one, the B&M leaflet and part of the Boots one before I went to sleep.

Friday 26th January

The Christmas cupboard is a thing I've started in the kitchen today. It's actually the corner of a big cupboard. It's got the bottle of Baileys, an unopened rectangle of fruitcake (the bottom has got a wiggly pattern I've also seen on bricks), a jar of mincemeat and two reduced price Christmas puddings that expire in August. I wondered if you only need to get two out of the three of Christmas cake, Christmas pudding and mince pies because they all taste similar. I suggested this to Malc but he said we need all three. He said you have to have Christmas pudding on

Christmas Day for dessert, you have to have a slice of Christmas cake on Boxing Day at about four o'clock and you need mince pies and a cup of tea many times in December.

I've spent forty-five Christmases with Malc and only just realised he always has a slice of Christmas cake on Boxing Day afternoon. I did the usual Christmas cake this year. A round eight inches in diameter, decorated with white icing to represent snow and a collection of plastic decorations I bought in Boswells when we were first married; two snowmen, two robins (on opposite sides of the cake as Malc always points out they're very territorial), a post box, a gold 'Merry Christmas' and a sprig of holly. Some years I've deviated from this and done a cake decorated differently. I did a square one made to look like a parcel once with ready rolled icing and one year I decorated the cake with fruit and nuts but we missed the marzipan. Marzipan is very Christmassy.

Saturday 27th January

I went round to have coffee with Carol. She opened a box of M&S extremely chocolatey biscuits to go with our coffee. We had some at Christmas but they didn't last long. A fancy box of biscuits is something we only had at Christmas when I was growing up. Carol is a best biscuit friend, I'd open my best biscuits for her and she would for me. One of the things I like best about Carol is that she's an encourager. If I was planning something big and scary that I wanted to do, like get a new kitchen, I'd ask Carol what she thought first then mention it to Gail. If I was thinking about something big and scary that I wanted to be talked out of, like a new job, I'd ask Gail what she thought first and then mention it to Carol. I love both my best friends dearly but they have very different personalities. Carol has always been a cheery sparky one, Gail has always been able to spot a downside at ten paces, even aged thirteen. I need them both.

I forgot to take the jam jars I've collected so far for Carol's tombola. She said not to worry, it isn't until April. I gave her her sponsorship money for dry January. She is ninety-nine percent sure she'll get to the end of the month without cracking. She considered asking me to take her Tia Maria home for safekeeping but then said she'd use her willpower. She said she didn't drink last January so she thought it'd be easy to do dry January this year, but by doing it for sponsorship money it feels much harder and she's thinking about it much more. She's not going to do it next year.

In the evening I started reading 'The Haunted Man and the Ghost's Bargain'.

Sunday 28th January

We went out for Sunday lunch to the Prince Of Wales pub with Mum, Val and Henry. I wore my sparkly jumper from Bon Marche and Malc asked if we were going out night clubbing! Malc never usually notices when I have new clothes. Henry had a tie on, Malc didn't. Malc keeps his ties for funerals and weddings. Henry gave Malc a bag of *New Scientist* magazines, he always passes them on when he's read them.

I had beef, as did Val and Henry, Mum had chicken and Malc had pork. Conversation over lunch was about feet

(Malc's corn, my verruca, Mum's toenails, Malc instigated this topic and I tried to steer him from it), the new Westgate shopping centre, the cruise Val and Henry are going on and what Mum is doing this week.

Mum and I agreed that the roast potatoes were not as good as the ones Malc did on Christmas day. He did the potatoes and I did everything else and as usual when a man cooks it's a wonderful novelty that requires continual comment and when a woman does it, it's just expected. I remembered my resolution to keep Christmas all the year and smiled politely. I'll have calmed down by Christmas 2019 when it's my turn again.

We decided to have pudding, Mum said we might as well be hung for a sheep as a lamb. She had rum and raisin ice cream, the rest of us had sticky toffee pudding. As we were leaving the pub I noticed Mum was walking slower than usual. She'll be eighty-nine at the end of March. We have lots of family birthdays in March, there's Mum, Val and Nicola.

When we got home I asked Malc if he'd noticed how slow Mum was walking today? He hadn't but said he spends two days a week surrounded by slow walkers at the care home, it's not the speed that matters, it's still having the will to do it he said.

We had a lovely lazy rest of the day. I lost myself in Dickens (Charles) while Dickens (Malc) snoozed gently in front of the telly, waking briefly at intervals to do a bit more of his crossword. Today has had three of the best bits of Christmas in it, despite being the end of January, it's had family, good food and time to relax. At about eight o'clock

I began to get the gloomy weekend almost over feeling. I wish I was retired already.

Monday 29th January
After work I went to see Mum and helped her order a new cooker on the computer. It took ages. I like to try and teach her how to do it rather than tell her how to do it but she isn't really interested. She has been to balance class today and is walking better than yesterday. I hope I'm as active as her when I'm her age. You hear stories about people retiring then dropping dead. There is balance class for the body of old people but not for their mind. When I was twenty I thought people were old at forty. Then when I reached forty I thought people were old at sixty. Now I think people in their sixties are middle-aged and people are old at eighty.

Mum gave me some hand cream. She got given loads at Christmas and already had loads. She said when you're her age you get either a tin of biscuits or a set of three floral scented hand creams. It's always lavender, rose and one other. She would rather have the biscuits. She has a big collection of empty Christmas biscuit tins on the top shelf in the larder. One is musical and shaped like a Christmas tree, it was from M&S. She says it's too nice to throw away. It's this attitude (which me and Val have picked up) that means me and Val are destined to live in cluttered houses.

When I got home Malc made me a cup of hot chocolate in one of the Christmas mugs that I haven't put away in the roof yet.

Tuesday 30th January

When Malc came home today he said 'You'll be pleased to hear I've decided to increase the size of my rhubarb patch.' When someone says 'You'll be pleased to hear' it doesn't give the person hearing any choice about their reaction to it, they are expected to be pleased. Once, early in our marriage Malc came home and said I'd be pleased to hear he'd bought a salmon off a man in a pub. I thought he'd been had but it did get delivered the next day, uncooked, and I had to work out what to do with it. Malc's mate Ken from the allotments has offered him a rhubarb crown he's got going spare.

I finished reading 'The Haunted Man and the Ghost's Bargain'. It's the last story in my Dickens book. It was about how we have to remember our sorrow and trouble, or we lose compassion for others. The last line is 'Lord, keep my memory green'. This is a thing people of my age worry about. When people jokingly say 'Senior moment!' when they can't remember a thing there is often a little bit of panic behind their eyes. We ask ourselves what is normal, not to be concerned about forgetfulness and what marks the unable to return from start of dementia?

To cheer myself up from thoughts of decline and death I browsed the M&S sale on the internet. It's mostly Christmas gift wrap and decorations.

Wednesday 31st January

Work dragged today. The new supervisor got Tracy's back up by asking her why she'd gone on the till rather than continuing to put reduced price stickers on the stollen. The queue was ten people long and the last six were tutting, so

Tracy was right to go on the till or we'd have had baskets abandoned. This never used to happen, but nowadays, if the queue is really long, sometimes people just give up on it and walk out.

I had a shower as soon as I got home. To stop feeling cold in the shower I pretend I'm Wim Hof, a man who can withstand low temperatures. For dinner we had cod fish finger sandwiches. Malc likes gherkin added for a bit of crunch and tang. If there's too much gherkin he makes the same face as when there isn't enough sugar in a rhubarb crumble. By this stage in our marriage I've calibrated my cooking to match Malc's tastes fairly successfully.

I started reading John Grisham's *Skipping Christmas*. I could never agree to skip Christmas, it's the reward for slogging through another year of work!

January reckoning, have I kept Christmas all January? If the ghost of Christmas present appeared before me now (although I think he can only operate at actual Christmas) would he show me things I'd want to see?
I sponsored Carol for dry January and I took some things to the BHF shop. I feel I could have done more to spread the Christmas spirit to other people. I kept it in myself though, with the Christmas cupboard, Christmas book shelf and Christmas section of my wardrobe. I liked it when it snowed, that was the weather helping me to keep Christmas.

February

Thursday 1st February

There's a big change coming for me and it can't come soon enough. This is my last month of work! It's such a relief not setting the alarm on a Thursday night now I have Fridays off. I wish I'd gone down to four days a week sooner. I'm tired out by the end of Thursday. Mr Barker moaned about having to do the paperwork for payroll so I could change my hours but if he doesn't want to do the paperwork he shouldn't be the manager. Anyway, enough moaning, this is my diary of keeping Christmas.

I remember the first Christmas I was earning my own weekly wage. It was 1968. I bought Dad a bottle of cherry brandy, Mum some apple blossom perfume and Val a box of Weekend chocolates. I've loved going Christmas shopping ever since then.

Friday 2nd February

I went to the dentist in Greater Leys first thing this morning. It cost £20.60 for a check-up. I didn't need anything done today which is a relief. There was a while in the early 1990s when you couldn't get an NHS dentist for love nor money in Oxford and we had to pay £50 for Nicola to have a filling. That was a lot of money then.

On my way home I walked past Nash's bakery and admired the vanilla cream meringues. They still sell Mr Blobby biscuits even though he hasn't been on telly for years. I went to the Nisa shop and bought Garibaldis to take on the journey to Bognor. There was a lot of smoking of funny cigarettes by the shops as usual.

I went to see Mum. She has got her new cooker. She showed me how fast her rings heated up. She's only ever three minutes away from some hot soup. Malc asked if my choppers got the all clear. He knows I don't like the dentist. For dinner we had quiche, new potatoes and marrowfat peas. Malc said it didn't seem like quiche weather.

Winter feels different when Christmas is over, now it's a thing to be slogged through. I will try instead to make it a thing to be cosy in, like it is during Christmas. I think Malc was right, it's not quiche weather. It's not new potatoes weather either.

I listened to Greg Lake's 'I Believe In Father Christmas' and it reminded me of shopping in Woolworths for stocking fillers for David and Nicola. I always used to get some of their stocking things in Woolworths and some in Fred's market hall on the Cowley Road. Both are gone now. Nicola was always delighted with felt pens and David always played with the Plasticine first. He once modelled an accurate looking Curly Wurly while eating the Curly Wurly from his selection box.

Saturday 3rd February

We went to Shoe Zone this morning, Malc is in the market for some new slippers. Shoe Zone smells very strongly of plastic today. It reminded me of the old blue rectangular paddling pool from Argos with triangular corner seats that David and Nicola loved. None of the slippers met with Malc's approval. While we were in Templars Square there was an announcement that pickpockets are operating in the area. Malc said it was like Dickensian London, but it wasn't really. He meant Charles Dickensian London. Having the surname Dickens since I got married means that sometimes people ask me if I'm any good at writing. I always say I have my moments. I suppose technically anything Malc and I do could be described as Dickensian since that's our name.

We went to the Co-op and got a loaf of olive bread. It was Henry and Val that got us liking olive bread. We had it for lunch with tomato soup. I always feel cosy when I eat tomato soup. I haven't put the Christmas mugs away yet. I made us hot chocolate in them. Malc put his feet up on the foot stool (I could see the soles of his slippers are going in places) and said 'This is the life.'

Maybe I'll keep the Christmas mugs out all year.

Sunday 4th February

We went over to Bicester to see David today. We picked him up from the house he shares with two other lads. He hopes eventually to start buying a place of his own but he'll be forty this year so if he wants a twenty-five-year mortgage (and round here he'll need it), he'll have to get his skates on. He's never been much of saver, whereas Nicola learnt to be thrifty at university.

We took him to Bicester Avenue garden centre for lunch. We all had the chicken roast dinner. David said the potatoes weren't as good as the ones Malc did on Christmas Day. Malc smiled modestly. David told us about the goings on in the shop he works at in Bicester Village. He had to stop two women coming to blows over a reduced dress, which still cost six hundred pounds! No-one local shops at Bicester Village, but tourists get bussed in from all over. I wore my sparkly jumper from Bon Marche to lunch. I'm glad I bought it now, I ummed and ahhed about it but it's had four outings already. I didn't have to fight anyone for it in Bon Marche, they had plenty. After lunch we looked round the shops. I got some reduced-price clear gift bags in Lakeland with a poinsettia print. I'm going to have a go at making homemade sweets this Christmas.

Making sure your uniform is washed clean and dry on a Sunday ready for Monday steals a tiny bit of your non-work time. When I first began work the uniform was a blouse and skirt. Now it's a polo shirt with the company logo on it and you supply your own black trousers. You only get two polo shirts so have to wash them often. Lauren says you can claim money back from the tax man for doing this, but no-one does, no-one wants to risk attracting his attention. The younger ones, like Dylan, change into their uniform when they get to work. I don't remember who first started having polo shirts, it might have been Woolworths.

Monday 5th February
The new supervisor got right on Mr Barker's wick today. She kept telling him how they did things in her old job. You could almost see him thinking that if her old job was so bloody brilliant what was she doing here? Mr Barker likes things staying the same. He was very resistant to the fresh bakery items coming into our store and was against the self-service checkouts from day one. We actually got rid of the self-service checkouts after less than a year, which Lauren said was a backwards step and Mr Barker said was a triumph of common sense.

After work I went to see Mum. She has got a magazine prescription (her actual words) to *Yours Retro* magazine. She said she'll lend it to me if I like. I said once I retire I'll only be looking forwards, not back. She said suit yourself. Today she has been to the Longwall for lunch. She told me not to slow down too quickly when I retire. She also told me it was my time to take it easy. I hadn't realised that retiring was one of those things, like getting married, or having children, that people just can't help giving you advice about, even though you didn't ask for any.

I listened to *The Andy Williams Christmas Album*. I like 'It's The Most Wonderful Time Of The Year' best.

Tuesday 6th February

It's very cold today. I'd have liked to keep my woolly hat on at work. Malc and I went out for dinner this evening. We got the bus to the Cowley Road to save Malc the worry of parking.

We met Val and Henry, Henry's visiting colleague Peter and his wife Shirley outside Mario's. Neither Malc nor I have ever eaten in Mario's. I had a chicken, mushroom and tomato risotto which was very good. Malc, Peter and Val had pizza, Shirley had a spaghetti dish and Henry had penne that had sausage in. Conversation was about travel, Brexit, Oxford, Coventry (which I said was an overlooked gem of an English city), Washington (where Peter and Shirley are from), food we ate as children and the best ways to relax. It was a nice evening.

When Henry first started inviting us to this sort of thing I hated it. I never knew what to say to people, I thought his work people would want to talk about things I didn't understand and I'd show myself up. Mum used to be always on at me and Val about not showing ourselves up, or showing her up. I tried not to tell David and Nicola the same when they were growing up. It was only a couple of times a year Henry had colleagues to entertain so I just sighed and got on with it for family harmony. After a few dinners where I was uncomfortable I went to the loo at the same time as a woman called Beth. She confessed that she detested this sort of thing and she never knew what to talk about. I said well, we could hate it or we could make the best of the opportunity to eat something we haven't cooked ourselves with some people who are fellow humans and might be feeling awkward too and we could talk about the food if we got really stuck. Once I'd told her that I had to take my own advice! I realised that in the back of my mind was the feeling that I wasn't as smart or interesting as other people then I remembered some of the dull things I'd politely nodded at over the years. Everyone has their dull moments and their brilliant moments.

I think of Beth whenever I go to the loo in a restaurant I've never been to and I go back to the table and make myself take an interest and then I find out all sorts of fascinating things about people. Shirley used to be a cheerleader and she loves to go to yard sales. Her favourite ever find was a Barbie jewellery box made especially for Avon like one she had when she growing up. I didn't know they had the Avon catalogue in America too. I'm not a remarkable woman. I'm very average. Husband, two children, shop worker, size fourteen to sixteen, but I've got an ability to listen to and also to share little parts about my life with strangers and I feel it's a privilege to meet new people rather than a chore.

When we left Mario's it was snowing outside! It made me feel suddenly Christmassy. Malc and I flagged a taxi. I watched the snow fall on the short journey home. I wished it were Christmas Eve. I looked at the clock before turning out the light knowing it'd be a struggle to get out of bed in the morning. Good company and risotto makes it worth it.

Wednesday 7th February

I woke up tired and wondering what time Mario gets up. It was a very cold walk to work this morning. I slipped twice on the way and my heart lurched both times. When I got into the staff room Lauren was warming her bum on the radiator. She moved over to let me have a go. Lots of customers remarked on the weather. There's an old couple who've been coming in for years, he's getting increasingly frail. Today he said 'It'd freeze the brass off a balls monkey out there.' I knew what he meant.

The new supervisor found us some bodywarmers with the old logo to wear. We put them on and Tracy said we looked like hot water tanks. Mr Barker came downstairs a bit later and asked where we'd got them from. Lauren overheard him and the new supervisor having a bit of a barney, he was saying they aren't part of current uniform, she was saying they're only a gilet and will only be worn on the coldest days.

I checked to see if I need to buy any toiletries to take on holiday to Bognor. I'm holding Bognor in my mind as a wonderful prize to get me through the next few weeks of work and winter. I don't buy travel size toiletries, I just take a mostly used bottle of whatever I need so my suitcase isn't too heavy. Malc says the beauty of Bognor is you don't have to fly there.

I finished reading *Skipping Christmas*. I was looking forward to reading about the cruise the main characters went on but that's not how the book ended. It was very good though. I had an early night. I dreamt I was cooking a risotto and Malc was telling me to put sausages in it but I didn't want to.

Thursday 8th February

I met Val in town after work for some late-night shopping. She bought two jersey maxi dresses from Debenhams. She said she hasn't got her long-haul flight outfit properly sorted yet. She collected US dollars from M&S. While Malc and I are in Bognor, she and Henry will be in Miami and then on a Caribbean cruise. Mum's friend Bridget has lent Val her Florida travel guide from twenty years ago. Val said she didn't like to say she's already been to Florida six times.

When I got home Malc was on the Pavers website looking at slippers. He has won £25 on the Premium Bonds this month and he's keen to blow it on something. He made us a hot chocolate in the Christmas mugs. We ate the last of the Christmas cake. I got a cheery festive feeling knowing that I don't have to get up for work in the morning. Christmas is about magic and presents when you're a kid, then when you're a teenager it's about parties, new records and new clothes, then it becomes about time off work. It's always about family and friends, even if you don't realise it. I started reading a story called 'The Glass Angels' in Susan Hill's *Christmas Collection.* Malc bought the iPad to bed and carried on looking at slippers. I wish I'd got him some in Marks and taken the decision out of his head. He gets stuck in a loop of comparisons when buying things.

Friday 9th February
Today I'm wearing a thermal top and leggings indoors! It's lovely to not have to go out to work and stand at a till point by automatic doors that let blasts of cold air in. Going down to four days a week instead of five is one of the best decisions I have ever made. Other good decisions I've made are marrying Malcolm, not having a fifth glass of wine on the first night of the holiday in Weymouth in 1972 (Gail did and she was as sick as a dog all the next day) and stopping having my hair permed (it's a very dated look, it didn't suit me, and it's not good for your hair, plus the smell is terrible).

Malc and I had a lazy day pottering about the house. We had cheese on toast for lunch with the last of the Christmas double Gloucester. Nicola phoned. She has entered a competition to win a year's supply of toilet roll. I told her I enjoyed reading *Skipping Christmas*. She said she will give it a go, she's sure she's seen a copy in her library. We don't often read the same books.

Saturday 10th February
Malc requested bacon to be cooked at 10:30, which is an hour earlier than usual. He wants to go to the allotment today and think about what he's going to grow this year. We had an early lunch. I walked round to Cowley Centre

and browsed the Christmassy bits left in the sales. I spent ages upstairs in WH Smith, trying to decide whether to buy gift tags or just do what I usually do and use parts of old Christmas cards. I didn't buy the gift tags but I did buy some heart shaped glitter baubles in the BHF shop. It's hard to see the detail of Christmas in December when you're right in it. In February when you catch sight of baubles or crackers in a shop it's lovely and you really have time to appreciate it.

Malc brought Brussels sprouts, leeks and celery home from the allotment. The celery was grown by his mate Ken, he swapped some sprouts for it. He and Ken often swap seeds and produce. I have met Ken a few times and he has consistently the hairiest ears of any man I have ever seen. It's a wiry kind of hair which reminds Malc of a type of worm that attacks carrots. Even Malc has noticed Ken's ears and Malc is not big on noticing people's physical features. I once went from sandy blonde hair to warm copper and Malc took two weeks to say anything, and even then Nicola had to prompt him.

We had Domino's pizza for dinner, paid for with Malc's Premium Bond winnings. Malc got the hiccups before going to sleep. I used to try and startle him out of hiccups by saying I was pregnant. This no longer works when you're as distant from the menopause as I am.

Sunday 11th February

I decided that the glitter heart baubles I bought yesterday are too nice to just sit in their packet until December. I've put one in the downstairs loo in amongst a vase of bronze painted pine cones and peacock feathers that is hiding a crack in the wall. I've put one in the Christmas cupboard in the kitchen, one on my Christmas bookshelf and one hanging off the Christmas tree box in our loft conversion. I like popping up into the roof when I get a quiet moment to write this diary. Sometimes Christmas is having a minute to pause and take a step away from your busy workaday life and responsibilities and just look at some lights or some glitter for a moment and remember there is loveliness shining in the world.

Monday 12th February

If Saturday nights are the icing on the cake of the week then Monday mornings are the empty cake board with rips in the silver foil. There are the work things that exasperate you but never change. The new supervisor came up with the idea of having a suggestion box during the five-minute weekly catch up we had before opening the doors. Everyone laughed. Then Lauren yawned and then everyone yawned. A few years back we tried having a suggestion box. It only lasted one week. Mr Barker was the assistant manager at the time and he said he'd never seen such filth written down. There were only two suggestions, both about the ex-manager, one questioning his parentage and the other suggesting he take a course of action not repeatable in polite company.

Also today there was a milk spillage in the dairy cabinet. No-one ever wants to be the one to clean this up. Mr Barker asked Dylan. This isn't really fair because Dylan did it last time, but Mr Barker knows that Dylan will do it with the minimum of fuss and back chat. Last time Tracy did it she huffed and puffed throughout and said she hadn't got this job to be a cleaner. I might never have to clean a spill in the dairy cabinet again, I have just ten working days left! Just two Monday mornings to slog through despondently and then freedom from March onwards. I've moaned about work in this diary again when it's meant to be my keeping Christmas all the year diary. I'm going to go and get a hot chocolate and browse the We R Christmas sale on the iPad.

Tuesday 13th February

Today is Pancake Day. We sold a lot of eggs, flour and milk but even more packets of ready-made pancakes. I decided to buy ready-made for the first time. I was on till with Lauren and she said ready-made pancakes are fine and life is too short for making batter or pastry. By the time I had my lunch break we'd sold out of ready-made so I had to go over to Iceland. I got ham and Kinder Maxi bars to put in the pancakes (not both together, Malc likes Ham and Lauren said she puts a Kinder Maxi bar in a pancake then microwaves it until it melts). I helped a woman and her daughter carry their shopping to their taxi from Iceland. The trolley that customers are allowed to use for this was not brought back by the previous customer! I was a few minutes late back onto the shop floor but I got away with it.

Malc made no comment about our pancakes being ready-made. I don't think he noticed. I had a pancake with golden syrup first, while Malc had a couple with ham and cheese. Then we both had a pancake with a melted Kinder Maxi bar.

Val phoned after dinner. We are going to see *Lady Windermere's Fan* in London in April! Henry has bought the tickets as a birthday present for her (her birthday is March the tenth but she and Henry will be in the Caribbean then). I have never seen an Oscar Wilde play. I told her Malc is on the lookout for slippers. Val said to get some Mahabis. She and Henry think they're the best slippers.

Wednesday 14th February

I don't think I kept Christmas yesterday. I kept the very start of Easter. Today is not an obvious day for honouring Christmas in my heart and trying to keep it all the year, but it is a good day for hearts, being Valentine's Day.

I was on till with Lauren again. I said I'm sticking with ready-made pancakes from now on. I like how thin they are and how fast they warm up in the microwave. On her way to work Lauren saw two people yarn bombing a tree by the bus stop on The Slade with knitted hearts. They also put up a happy Valentine's Day sign. Decorating to give other people pleasure is a very Christmas thing. We sold a lot of flowers and chocolates today. Lauren bought herself a heart shaped box of Ferrero Rocher. She said she's too busy studying and working and bringing up her daughter to engage with the whole romance side of life and she'll meet a better class of bloke when she's better qualified. She sounds like she's got it all worked out.

I came home from work and had a quick pancake. Then Malc and I went to the Littlemore chip shop and got two small fish and chips and took them round to Mum's (me and Mum always share a portion). Mum asked if the chip shop was busy (it was).

We ate in the front room. Malc admired Mum's placemats (scenes of Cotswold villages, I sit at Stow on the

Wold, Malc at Bourton on the Water and Mum at Burford, there are three more in a box on top of the glass display cabinet). Mum had run out of ketchup. She said at her age she doesn't see the point in stocking up. Malc said she was in rude health. This pleased her. She told him that me and Val used to go through a bottle of ketchup a week when we were both living at home and she thought she should have bought shares in Heinz. For dessert we had Viennetta. I had three ridges worth, Malc had five. Mum always serves men with more food than women. Conversation was about holidays and Mum's friends. When I went upstairs to the loo I paused on the landing and added a heart shaped bauble to the vase of fake flowers Mum has on the windowsill there. I wonder how long she'll take to notice it?

Thursday 15th February
Today is what we in retail think of as Half Price Heart Shaped Chocolate Day. Anything mentioning Valentine's Day or with a short date gets reduced in price, anything heart shaped but not specifying Valentine's Day and with a far-off use by date gets added to the Mothers' Day display. The new supervisor started the Mothers' Day display today. I showed Dylan how to change the till rolls. The new supervisor keeps promising to show him then not getting round to it. She likes some bits of the job, but isn't interested in the basics like restocking the swiftly emptied shelves (bread and milk) or jumping on the till when the queue is long.

At lunch time I went to Peacocks to see if I could find something I liked for wearing to Bognor. I found nothing but I did enjoy browsing the last bits of the Christmas stock. I used to leave my shop every single lunch time for a change of scene but lately I've just sat in the staff room resting my tired feet. I'm getting very impatient for retirement. I like the shop name Peacocks, it sounds like it would sell fancier clothes than it actually does.

After work I browsed knitwear in Asda but bought nothing. I'm still dithering about my travelling outfit which needs to be comfy, stylish and have layers for cold and hot environments. I don't want to arrive in Bognor looking like a dog's dinner. Why do dogs get used so much in sayings? You can be a dog's dinner or sick as a dog or dog tired, or the tail can be wagging the dog. I once worked with a woman from Canada and she found the phrase 'not a sausage', meaning nothing, baffling, which I suppose it is, if you haven't grown up with it.

Malc was sad this evening. The care home have lost a resident. Her name is Dotty and she has been there for the whole time Malc has worked there. She was fond of custard creams and watching the birds on the bird feeder, but of course there will be so, so much more to her than that. I tried to take Malc's mind of it by looking online with him for slippers. You will not believe how much Mahabis cost, Dear Diary, Malc made a sort of spluttering noise. He said for that kind of money he'd expect them to be gold plated and take the bins out themselves, without you in them. He said you can't take it with you, but if you spend it like that you won't have anything to take with you. So that's a no to slippers costing almost eighty pounds!

Friday 16th February

I feel a sense of relief and a bit of a holiday tingle when I wake up on a Friday morning now I don't have to rush off to work. I had a cup of tea in bed and read my Susan Hill book for ten minutes! Malc asked if I fancied a run out. We went to the Root One garden centre late morning. It has incredibly local greetings cards (an example is pubs of Wallingford) and the least amount of non-gardening stuff of any garden centre round here. They still had a few Poinsettias from Christmas reduced in price.

They have a café and also a picnic area if you want to eat your own food. A pigeon was sat on the picnic table but there were no humans. The Victoria sponge looked good in the café. I suggested we have lunch in The Bell Hungry Horse pub on our way home. At the back of my mind was Malc talking about Dotty yesterday, and the thought that we should live a bit and enjoy things together in case we get split up by one of us needing round the clock residential care in later years. I think more about the years to come now I'm close to retiring, it forces you to, you have to think about if you'll have enough money to last until you die and then you have to think about when that might perhaps be. I hate thinking about who will go first so my brain just skates across it, like a needle on a record that won't play. It's not a song I ever want to hear.

We both chose the gammon and chips for dinner, which is on the two meals for £8.99 offer on a Friday. We looked at some of the local photos while waiting for our food. I liked one of the local boys' football team taken in the 1960s. All these boys will now be men. I wondered where they ended up. I looked around the pub, in case a fully grown one was present. I also liked the photos of local Christmas pantomimes. One of them showed the audience all wearing hats. Our food came quite quickly. Malc swapped his egg for my pineapple (Malc is funny about fried eggs, he'll only eat them overcooked and he sometimes forgets to ask at the till for that to be done or to ask if he can have double pineapple instead of egg, then the egg comes and he says that it isn't egg-xactly how he likes it and I offer to swap my pineapple).

Today felt Christmassy because I read a bit of a Christmas book, spent time with Malc and ate food I didn't cook myself. Gammon is a festive food, its salty deliciousness feels celebratory.

Saturday 17th February

We went to Val and Henry's for dinner this evening. Val cooked chicken chasseur and creamy mashed potato. She did a lemon cheesecake for afters. She makes the base with a mixture of ginger nuts and digestives, it's very good. Then we sat round the table chatting and eating Elizabeth Shaw orange chocolate crisps. We all have a holiday to look forward to so conversation was mostly about that. Henry said he can tell Val's looking forward to it because she's had her suitcase on the bed in the spare bedroom for weeks. He said he couldn't take a whole winter now, he's got used to having a cruise somewhere warm early in the year. Val agreed with him. Malc said maybe our Bognor trip will become an annual event rather than a retirement celebration one off. Henry said he thinks I'll adjust well to retirement and that it will be nice for Val when we can do more days out. Henry and Malc are the kind of men who don't need all of their wives' time, which is a relief. Gail's husband blows hot and cold. I wouldn't like that.

When we left Val gave me some tea from Holland & Barrett in a lovely box which is called Yogi Tea Christmas Tea. She got it when she was getting Henry's chopped apricots, he likes to add some to his muesli, to sex it up a bit he says.

We went to bed with a hot chocolate when we got in from Val and Henry's. I finished reading 'The Glass Angels'. It was everything a Christmas story should be, some kind neighbours helped a little girl and her mum out of a sticky situation.

Sunday 18th February

We got the bus into town late morning. I got a coral with white star print jumper in M&S. I thought coral was a nice colour to wear to the seaside, although Bognor has no coral reefs as far as I know. Malc got a new coat with a really sturdy zip. The zip has gone on his old coat and he didn't mention it. I noticed when we were leaving Val and Henry's last night. I had a Sparks 20% off clothing voucher which was useful. We haven't got money to burn so it's nice when you get money off a necessity. I'm thinking more about money now I'm retiring. We'll have a bit less coming in. I put my new jumper on the bed in the spare room next to the suitcase. We're not going until Monday 5th March but I'm ready to go tomorrow!

We tried the Yogi Tea Christmas Tea Val bought me. Each teabag is individually wrapped, like a little present and has a red tag with a message. Mine said 'You will always live happy if you live with heart'. Malc's said

'Experience will give you wisdom'. It's hard to describe the taste, it smells like when Nicola had a phase of incense burning (which Malc disapproved of because of the fire risk) and has a bit of a liquoricey after taste. I drank the whole mug but I can't say for sure if I like it or not. David once drank a two-litre bottle of dandelion and burdock and wasn't sure if he liked it, we're not a decisive family, drinks-wise.

Monday 19th February

I had a very busy day at work today (Tracy is off sick and the new supervisor has a day off for an appointment that no-one knows what it is) but I was quite grateful for it because the day went fast. I have six working days left now! Three this week and three next week. I feel like I'm in a kind of personal advent.

We had jacket potato and cheese for dinner. Malc packed Viagra for Bognor. He said 'I've budgeted for having it off twice.' Is there a more romantic sentence in the English language? He's being a bit ambitious with twice but I didn't like to discourage him. I'll be happy with once.

I've done a bit of a sock inventory and have a lot of pairs of Christmas socks, probably too many to only wear in December so I will start wearing them when I get back from holiday. Also, I'm going to be a bit careful about buying new things until I see how far my pension goes.

Tuesday 20th February

The new supervisor lost the key to the fags and tobacco stockroom cage today. Luckily Lauren found it on the floor in the ladies' loo when she went for lunch. It must have fallen out of the new supervisor's pocket. We had a scandal a few years back with a supervisor who was nicking fags and blaming it on part time staff.

I watched *Elf* after dinner. Nicola always enters competitions for New York shopping trips. Val and Henry have been. Nicola has never won the actual shopping trip but did once win a runner up prize of some anti-fatigue insoles.

Wednesday 21st February

I am now the proud owner of a three-foot-tall cardboard Santa and a three-foot-tall reindeer! The new supervisor was having a tidy up of the office and found some Christmas display materials that should have been binned years ago. She was taking them to the recycling area in the stockroom but Lauren suggested she offer them to me as a souvenir of my time here! The new supervisor said it was a bit irregular but since they should have been thrown out years ago she didn't see the harm in it. I brought them home today and they are standing next to the box the Christmas tree is in, looking at me and smiling as I write this. Malc said it makes a change from being given a carriage clock when you retire!

Thursday 22nd February

I told one of my favourite customers that I'm retiring at the end of the month. I've worked my last Thursday! I'll miss the polite people and the cheerful people. I won't miss the rude woman with the almost non-existent eyebrows who won't have a loyalty card because she thinks we'll spy on her or the man who smells overpoweringly of stale cigarettes, always has greasy hair and never makes eye contact.

I'll be glad to be out of little arguments about who didn't stack the cardboard neatly in the stockroom and big arguments about who is slow to jump on till. I'll be very glad to not have to do anything about shoplifters ever again. We had a code 100 today (Code 100 is what Mr Barker or the supervisor says over the tannoy when a shoplifter has been spotted). I once accidentally helped catch a shoplifter, I was rolling a big stock cage of economy size washing powder to its aisle, and I could see round the cage but not over the top of it. I blocked the end of an aisle that the shoplifter had just run up and Don the security guard caught him. Don worked here for years but when he retired we stopped having our own security guard and now we have to radio for the shopping centre security guards. Today's shoplifter ran off.

Malc has been humming Tom Jones' 'The Green, Green Grass of Home'. He put up a shelf in the music room at the care home today and one of the residents was in there playing *The Best of Tom Jones*. Malc asked him if he was from Wales. He said no, he was born in Walsall.

I watched Delia Smith make some Christmas party nibbles on YouTube. She did some mini scones with cream cheese and olives. It's amazing what's out there to be watched if you have the time and inclination. I went to bed thinking of all the lovely buffets I've ever had at Christmas. I asked Malc what he thought was the best buffet item ever. He's still thinking, but he said it might be mini pork pies or potato skins filled with cheesy potatoey bacon mixture.

Friday 23rd February

I did some ironing this morning. Now I have Fridays off I can do chores on Fridays and leave the weekend clear. If not working on Fridays makes me this glad, what will actual retirement be like? Will all the days smoosh together and be like months on end of Fridays?

I went for a walk before lunch. There are still beautiful fir trees to be seen even when it isn't Christmas. The best local ones are in Florence Park but there are also some big ones on Bartholomew Road and a fine example outside Littlemore chip shop. I stood by the chip shop tree today and I imagined how I'd decorate it if the council suddenly gave me a big budget and put me in charge of it. I decided it would have yellow lights to reflect its proximity to the chip shop (chips are golden yellow), white tinsel to honour the lovely flaky cod, red baubles to symbolise ketchup and a small number of pink baubles to represent spam fritters.

Malc heated us up some mulligatawny soup for lunch. It is his default soup. Mine is tomato. We always have both in the cupboard. This evening Val and Henry came round for a pizza night. Val gave me a book she got in the Scope shop, *A Very British Christmas* by Rhodri Marsden. It's lovely to have a present when it isn't even Christmas or my birthday.

We ordered Papa John's pizza. Henry likes The Greek, he says feta reminds him of his student days. I didn't have any student days, unless you count school, and I only had feta about ten years ago in little parcels at a buffet Val did. I bet there's other cheeses I'd like but I don't know about. My life is a bit cheddar when I look back on it.

Val and Henry told us all about their cruise. People without kids seem to be able to see themselves as young and energetic for much longer than people with kids. Tomorrow Val and I are getting the bus from Gloucester Green to Milton Keynes to go shopping! She wants some new evening wear for her cruise. I've never got the bus to Milton Keynes before.

Saturday 24th February

The bus to Milton Keynes was a National Express one (Val booked our tickets in advance). The seats were comfy and we went through some lovely villages. There was a couple on the bus behind us that were Irish, she talked all the way, with very little input from him, apart from when he saw a Rolls Royce. Twice she said to him 'Remind me to put some sucky sweets in my bag for tomorrow.'

Val and I saw every sparkly cardigan in Milton Keynes this morning. Then we stopped for lunch in Ask Italian. We both had pasta. Malc will be eating left over pizza from last night for his lunch. After lunch Val bought a gold cardie in Monsoon. She got a white dress with silver sequins in House of Fraser. I tried on the same dress in red, just for fun. It'd be a bit much for Bognor Pier. I stopped having white in my wardrobe when Nicola was born. We looked in an American sweet shop and the Lego shop. Both Nicola and David were mad keen on Lego. I got them both a Santa keyring. This is the earliest I've ever got a Christmas present but I'll have to budget carefully when I'm retired. Val said she misses Past Times, I agreed but said we have so much to look forward to, she looked at me a bit quizzically (we were actually walking past Quiz) and said she meant the shop that sold reproduction Victorian cards and nighties and similar. We laughed.

The same Irish couple was on the bus on the way home, sat behind us again. She said they should eat at the hotel because she was bollocksed. I wasn't sure if she meant tired or drunk. He said he wanted steak and chips.

According to Val's smartphone we walked 17,892 steps/8.45 miles today! Val said the shopping centre is quite good, but as a city Milton Keynes has the kind of personality that if it was someone from school you wouldn't keep in touch. It isn't as beautiful as Oxford with our magnificent buildings dripping with history and our lovely big Asda Living at the John Allen Centre.

Sunday 25th February

When I woke up I wondered if the husband of the Irish couple on the bus behind us yesterday reminded her to put some sucky sweets in her bag. Then I wondered why they stopped making fruit Polos. Maybe it was because they all fused together in the tube and they were too small to individually wrap. Malc and I had a lazy day. I feel a bit impatient, knowing I retire on Wednesday, it's so close I want it to be done now, I'm absolutely ready to be retired and pull down the shutters on that chapter of my life. It was a long and repetitive chapter and I must have sold the milk of a whole herd of cows in my time. Probably a whole wheat field of bread too.

I finished reading Susan Hill's Christmas book. I loved 'Lanterns Across The Snow', it's about a country

Christmas. I have never had one of those, but it's lovely to read about. We're not one of those families that dreams of an escape to the country, we like to be within a short walk of the Co-op, on a decent bus route and not requiring wellies very often.

Malc has decided what he thinks is the best buffet item ever, he thinks it's pork pie. He also considered sausage roll and chicken goujons with barbecue dipping sauce. My absolute favourite is cheese on crackers but we are both agreed that the thing that's good about a buffet is the variety, you'd never have just one thing.

Monday 26th February

I cleared my locker today. I'll have to hand the key back at the end of the day on Wednesday. I've brought home old pay slips, a spare umbrella, some cereal bars (with the receipt to show I haven't nicked them from the shop), headache tablets, my work mug and a paperback of Sue Townsend's *The Woman who Went to Bed for a Year* (I'll re-read this, it was wonderful). I was telling Dylan today that when I stared work women got paid less than men for doing the same things. He looked shocked.

I started reading *A Very British Christmas*. Val said she'll look out for Christmas books for me when she's in the charity shops from now on. Val has always encouraged my enthusiasms, and I hers, she's a good sister. We've never had any truck with jealousy or competition. She's like another version of me, I'm not happy if she's not happy, same with Mum and Malc, we're all so tied up in each other's fortunes after so many years.

Tuesday 27th February

Today is my second to last working day! I only have to get up early for work one more time! I feel very tired when I look back on all the years I've got up, turned up, put up and shut up. When I got to work Mr Barker said 'Ah! The penultimate good morning Pam. This place won't be the same without you,' which was quite nice. I won't be the same without it, but in a good way. Dylan told me 'You'll miss the people but not the work.' He is barely in his twenties and even he has retirement advice to give! The new supervisor has ordered the wrong type of till rolls.

I cooked chicken goujons and mashed potato for dinner. We watched the *Still Open All Hours* Christmas special while we ate. Granville claimed that his French custard makes men irresistible to mature women for two hours after eating it. There has never been so much telly available to stream. When Malc and I were kids a stream was a thing you paddled in or jumped over in the park. When I think back to when we had just three channels I feel rich with choice. Malc says he sometimes has too much choice, that's when he asks me 'What shall we watch on the box?' and from now on I'm going to suggest a Christmas special. You don't have to wait for something Christmassy to happen, you can make it happen. Malc thinks there is too much choice in crisps too.

Wednesday 28th February

Today is the last day of my working life! There was a small presentation for me before the shop opened. I was half expecting it but still somehow was surprised it was happening to me. Mr Barker made quite a good speech. He got how long I'd been working in the shop wrong, but no-one noticed because none of them have been there as long as me! The new supervisor said I could always come back part time if I get bored. I thought no chance but I said thank you. There's no need to burn bridges you've got no intention of crossing. Later on, when it was just me and her she said she wouldn't make that offer to most of the staff. She was trying to be nice, not to make me feel like I was being sucked back into a job I'm really rather keen to finally escape after all these years. I am now the owner of a cut glass vase and a bottle of prosecco. Tracy said don't drink it all at tea break!

Lauren gave me a lovely gift just from her. It's a glass which says 'Merry Christmas' in curly red writing and a pack of chocolate biscuits from a competitor (they aren't just any old chocolate biscuits). Also, she took some photos on her phone of me being presented with the vase and prosecco. She wrote down my email address so she can send me the photos. Malc and I each have our own email address. Gail and Len share one.

February reckoning, have I kept Christmas all February? If the ghost of Christmas present appeared before me now would he show me things I'd want to see?

I've thought a few uncharitable thoughts about the new supervisor. But I have also tried to be helpful and showed her the knack to getting the shutters to open on the fags shelves behind the front till point.

I've read two- and a-bit Christmas books. I've seen some snow early in the month which always brings a little frisson of Christmas. We've finished off the Christmas cake and cheese and kept the Christmas mugs in use. I've got a new Christmas glass too, thanks to Lauren. I've had a little bit of Christmas in February but I can probably do better in March when more of my time is my own.

March

Thursday 1st March

Today is the first day of my retirement! I don't feel any different yet. It just feels like Friday, even though it's Thursday. I waved Malc off to work at the care home at a quarter to nine. He'll be back at about a quarter past five. I have a strange kind of freedom. It's not that Malc stops me doing anything when he's at home, it's just that there are some things I tend to do when he's out, like hoovering. I'm not going to do that today though. Today is my day.

It started snowing just after Malc left for work. I put the telly on and watched it and the snow. I had another cup of coffee, slowly. I went for a walk round our Crescent, feeling like I was in a snow globe. I had a slight twinge of guilt, like I was bunking off school and had to remind myself that I am legitimately retired. I had a chocolate biscuit from the pack Lauren bought me and I thought about them all at work, serving panic buying customers (snow always causes bread, milk and tins sales to sky rocket).

I had tuna mayonnaise in a jacket potato for lunch which makes a lovely change from a cheese sandwich I made the night before and transported to work with me. It is blissful to not have to do much, to be alone with my thoughts for a day. I read after lunch, *A Very British Christmas,* which is a lovely book. It's got people's memories of their Christmases. I decided to cook a roast dinner. My feet don't ache.

When Malc got in he asked how my day was. I said blissful. He has been checking and bleeding radiators today. When I told him we were having roast dinner he said that was just what he fancied. He gets lunch provided at work, today he had cottage pie.

Nicola rang. She has entered a competition to win a sponge cake on Twitter. They have snow in Coventry too.

Friday 2nd March

We woke up to a fresh dusting of snow. Malc and I will be at home together now on Mondays, Wednesdays and Fridays. It's only Tuesday and Thursday he'll go to work and we'll not be together. This is a new chapter in our marriage.

I finished packing the suitcase this morning. We go to Bognor on Monday! The hardest things to pack were a book for bedtime (what will I feel like reading?) and clothes. I don't know if we'll go anywhere smart or what the weather will be like. When we booked we thought it could be mild and damp or cold and dry. I can't wait to breathe in the sea air!

This afternoon I met Carol for coffee in Asda cafe. She showed me a Christmas countdown she has on her phone. It is 298 days until Christmas and we don't have to work on any of them! Carol loves being retired. After coffee we had a big browse. I was very tempted by an Easter egg.

Saturday 3rd March

Mum's heating malfunctioned today. I only found out by mistake when I popped round with a leek and half a stalk of Brussels sprouts. Her house was a chilly nine degrees Centigrade and she had an EA56 error on her thermostat.

Luckily I know what this is, it can happen when the plastic pipe at the left of the boiler that leads to outside has condensation in it that freezes. I reset the boiler then went outside to pour hot water on the outside section of the white pipe. Mum has the same boiler we do, fitted by the same heating engineer. She doesn't like making big decisions about this sort of thing so copies us if it's a thing we've done. I made me and Mum a hot drink and phoned Malc to ask him to bring round our old fan heater and the electric radiator from the spare room.

Malc was round in a flash and we sat Mum in front of the electric radiator in the back room to warm up. Malc said the boiler should purr, not gurgle. He went to listen and it was purring. He said something which made me sad, that he's glad I can reset a boiler so I won't be stuck if he goes before me. He means dies. I don't want to think about this on day three of our long-awaited retirement together.

We all had a cup of tea. I noticed Mum had Cravendale milk instead of Co-op's own brand. She said she had to buy the more expensive Cravendale, there was nothing else left. It has been snowy in Oxford this week and so the milk panic buyers have been out in force. Mum told us about when she once saw Wesley Smith from Central News buying Cravendale milk in Abingdon Waitrose.

We looked at the thermostat and it had gone up to eleven. We persuaded Mum to come round to ours for lunch and the afternoon and Malc would drive her home later when her house has warmed up. She said she didn't want to be a bother. I said we were only having soup for lunch, it wasn't a bother. Mum brought an unopened M&S

Christmas cake with her and we had it for pudding. A neighbour gave it her for Christmas. We sat and watched a couple of old *Carry On* films; *Carry On Henry* and *Carry On at Your Convenience*. I felt a bit Christmassy, with the cake, the snow outside and having Mum round.

When we took Mum home the temperature indoors was eighteen and it got up to twenty before we left. Mum said we were making a fuss. She said she used to wake up with ice on the inside of her windows. I said that was decades ago. I tried to persuade her to have the heating on all night when it's really cold and snowy. I'll get Val to have a word too, we back each other up on this sort of thing so Mum is more likely to listen.

Sunday 4th March

There is still snow on the ground and snow on the news. The weather lady showed us snow pictures sent in by viewers. Mum insisted on leaving us half her Christmas cake yesterday so we had soup and cake for lunch again. A large cake always provides a feeling of celebration and plenty.

Val rang to wish us happy holidays. Malc and I are off to Bognor tomorrow! Val said she checked when she can next get an Ocado shop and there's nothing available until Thursday morning. She said people are online shopping more due to the snow. Val will keep an eye on Mum for the three days Malc and I are away, then it'll be my turn when Val and Henry are on their cruise. I told Val about the boiler yesterday. Before she rang off Val said she was going to help make my retirement a lot of fun. I'll take her up on that offer!

I had an email from Lauren, with the pictures of my presentation. It's my last day in that work uniform and I look pleased as punch. I'm mainly pleased about leaving, not about the vase and the prosecco, nice though they are. In her email Lauren said to keep in touch and to have a wonderful retirement.

Tomorrow will be a very different Monday to my usual Monday!

Monday 5th March

We left for Bognor at half past ten, when I'd usually be going for tea break. Malc's car is a little Citroen Saxo. He bought British until he was involved in making Rover cars and then he went off them. Sometimes he pats the Saxo and says 'Above all, it's not a Rover.'

It took two hours to get to Bognor. We passed snowy fields. We wondered if we should have waited until our wedding anniversary in June to book a couple of nights away. 'Sudden snow is like a new toy you weren't expecting' is something Nicola said as a ten-year-old. She's always had a poetic turn of phrase.

We were a bit early checking in but they didn't mind, a room was ready and the hotel isn't fully booked. Our room has a sea view and is on the second floor. George V has stayed in our hotel! We had a complimentary cup of tea and biscuit (individually wrapped Viennese finger). We wrapped up warm and walked on the beach. We got chips for lunch and ate them on the pier, watching the grey ocean churn. I thought of all the grey hours I've worked over the days, weeks, months, years and decades being washed away to sea, leaving me to enjoy my retirement unencumbered. I don't want to be one of those retired people who is always going on about when they were at work. That's done now.

We took a stroll round the town centre. The Iceland is smaller than ours. We spent a long time browsing in Heygates Bookshop. We found a sweetshop at the end of a little arcade. Malc got a liquorice pipe. I got a sugar mouse. Both of these were things we got at Christmas when we were kids. I bought postcards and we walked back to our hotel.

We went to an Italian restaurant five minutes away from our hotel for dinner. I had a wonderful risotto and Malc had spaghetti and meatballs. It was very cold when we came out of the restaurant. Back in our room I made us instant hot chocolate I'd brought with me and we sat in bed enjoying our liquorice pipe and sugar mouse.

Tuesday 6th March

We got chatting to some nice people at breakfast who are here on a coach trip from Bolton. Breakfast was a self-service buffet of full English and Continental items. We took our time. Malc had two types of sausage twice. I had most of a full English (except sausages and fried bread) and some cheese and a Danish pastry. We had two pots of fresh coffee.

We walked to Hotham Park and admired the flower beds and rose garden. We played a round of crazy golf. It beats being at work! The people from Bolton we chatted to at breakfast started a round of crazy golf as we were finishing ours. We all agreed that the breakfast had set us up for the day.

I had a knickerbocker glory in Macari's. It was heavenly. Malc had a hot dog. I said he'll look like a sausage by the end of the day. We went back to the bookshop, which is not just a bookshop, it's a paperback exchange, so you can get new books for old. This made me think of Aladdin and the sorcerer who exchanged new lamps for old as a trick, but this bookshop isn't a trick, it's a labyrinth with highly patterned carpets. I got two books, *Trade Secrets Christmas* by Annie Ashworth and Meg Sanders and *A Treasury Of Christmas* by Frank and Jamie Muir. I used to like watching Frank Muir on *Call My Bluff*.

Malc found some slippers he liked, in a shop that sells a bit of everything. They are burgundy corduroy. We went to the arcade on the pier and spent a pound each on the 2p falls. I got a thimble for Mum from The Rock Shop. She collects them. We took our shopping back to the hotel and had a cup of complimentary tea and a biscuit (individually wrapped fruit shortcake). We sat by the window, watching the sea. For us Oxford people the sea is a huge novelty.

We went to The William Hardwicke pub for dinner. We both had fish and chips. It's lovely eating food someone else has cooked.

Wednesday 7th March

We had a leisurely breakfast. There were three types of eggs available. We have to check out at midday. Our two-night break has flown by. Malc doesn't like to leave the allotment for very long. I didn't want to start my retirement like a spendthrift and have a whole week away. We're much more comfortably off than at the start of our marriage when we really were scrimping and saving. I have to remind myself of this. When you've had to think hard about spending in the past that caution doesn't leave you when you're a bit better off.

After breakfast we walked up as far as the Butlin's compound. We said goodbye reluctantly to the sea and checked out. We called in at Manor Nursery garden centre on the way home. Malc bought a lemon yellow kniphofia, we haven't seen anything like it in garden centres round our way. I browsed the reduced-price Christmas bargains. I was looking at a snow globe with a Christmas tree inside and woodland animals gathered round it when the assistant tidying up the area said she'd reduce it further if I liked. She stuck a £2.99 price sticker on it and said it was the last one, and as I could see the box was damaged. I said thank you, I'd take it. It's a lovely souvenir of my snowy Bognor retirement holiday at the start of my new life as a retiree. I shall use it as a bookend on my Christmas books shelf. Malc and I smiled at our frivolous purchases.

We stopped in Ringwood to stretch our legs. The freedom of retirement means we don't have to rush home. I asked Malc if he minded being semi-retired while I'm fully retired. He said no, he doesn't mind his two days a week at the care home, he's glad he's doing something useful and that he's physically able to still work. I said his gardening keeps him fit as a fiddle. He flexed his arms and winked at me.

Thursday 8th March

This morning I weigh eleven stones and seven pounds. I have put on two pounds in Bognor. I did enjoy a lot of chips so it was worth it. I waved Malc off to work. This is a novelty. I used to leave for work before he did. Today is the start of my second week of being retired. I'm full of glee at not having to wash my work uniform or set an alarm clock. I feel like I've won a lottery where the prize is time not money.

I finished reading *A Very British Christmas* and put it on my Christmas bookshelf. I have four Christmas books I've read now and two I haven't read yet. I put my Christmas tree snow globe on the end of the shelf. If I don't know what to do with myself over the coming months of not being at work I will read a Christmas book.

We had mulligatawny soup and olive bread for dinner, something light after our Bognor excesses. We decided we'll go back to Bognor in the summer, or maybe venture to somewhere new! Malc and I watched the first in the new series of *Still Game.*

Friday 9th March

Malc went to the allotment today and I went to Cowley Centre. I browsed books in the British Heart Foundation shop and had a chat to the woman behind the counter. She was having a conversation with the previous customer about how Ramipril gives you a tickly cough. I used to be able to hear Malc's cough clear across BHS, before they went bust. Recently Toys R Us and Maplin went bust. Malc will miss Maplin. We once took David and Nicola to the Toys R Us in Birmingham, before we had one in Oxford. Their eyes were out on stalks!

I began reading *A Redbird Christmas* by the wonderfully named Fannie Flagg. I bought it in the BHF shop this morning. Malc came home with a present for me! He was cycling past a skip on his way back from the allotment when he spotted an almost pristine (the corner of the box is dented) box of Christmas crackers still in their cellophane wrapper so he brought them home for me. I shan't need to buy any Christmas crackers this year (it will be Val's turn to host Christmas dinner) and so I can use the ones Malc has brought home at Christmas 2019.

We have a Rover biscuit tin of spare cracker novelties that I get out on Christmas Day. It's so that if people get something they don't want they can swap it for something else. It all started when Malc got a hair slide and swapped it for some mini screwdrivers.

Saturday 10th March

Today is Val's birthday, but she's floating round the Caribbean. We'll catch up when she's back on home soil. In April we've got her late birthday trip to London for *Lady Windermere's Fan*. I'm not sure I'd like to be away for my birthday.

I cooked our usual Saturday lunch of bacon sandwiches. I did an online grocery order with Sainsbury's because we had a good voucher. Whichever supermarket gives me the best money off wins my custom that week. Malc calls me a supermarket tart! I say it's my economies that leave room for treats like takeaway pizza and fish and chips. Then Malc says I should be Chancellor of the Exchequer and I say I don't like the hours but wouldn't mind the salary or the residence.

I took Mum her thimble. I noticed she's already got a Bognor one. I wonder if you can get a souvenir thimble in the Caribbean? We both said we hoped Val was having a good birthday. I asked Mum if she was looking forward to her birthday (she'll be eighty-nine on March 27th). She said that it's just another day and that birthdays come around faster when you're her age.

Malc and I watched two episodes of *This Country*, about Kerry and Kurtan, young people living in a Cotswold village. It seems very real. It is quite rude, but it is things you'd overhear at a bus stop or in B&M.

Before I went to sleep I thought about Christmassy places I could visit and get Mum a thimble from. There's Lapland, Cologne Christmas market and Winter Wonderland in Hyde Park.

Sunday 11th March

This morning we went to Asda and got tumblers for Malc's morning aspirin, two pasta bowls for rice and salad dinners and two bright light bulbs. Malc says the early versions of energy saving bulbs are all a bit dim. He likes being the one who chooses our light bulbs. We had a bit of a barney about it once and I said I don't know the difference between a lumen and my arse so you can be in charge of light bulbs from now on. We went in The Works and I got a book which Malc spotted called *Haynes Explains Christmas*. It's like the car manuals Haynes do, but for Christmas. Malc got some wooden lolly sticks which he will use to label plants in pots.

We had chili con carne for lunch in the new bowls and neither of us spilled any rice on the carpet. In the afternoon we went to the Royal Mail parcel collection office (they were unable to deliver a tiny funnel to fill

Malc's hip flask. Malc said other couriers would have managed, he has a long running gripe about Royal Mail for sneaking red cards through the door claiming he was out when he was most definitely in and they didn't even ring the bell). When you're a wife for a long time you learn to soothe the pressure points of your spouse's existence and know what will set them off. Royal Mail and dim light bulbs can really unsettle Malc's equilibrium, as can reports of thefts from sheds, bruised bananas in our online shop and inconsiderate parking.

Monday 12th March
Ken Dodd has died today, aged ninety. Mum saw him in Oxford on a school night and he went on until 11:30 p.m. She said people were leaving because if they lived out in the sticks they had to get their last bus home. Malc and I are very lucky in that our last bus home from Oxford is way later than we would ever want to stay out.

I browsed Christmas thimbles on eBay. There are 1,109 Christmas thimbles for sale! I saw some lovely Royal Worcester, Spode and Wedgwood ones. I'm going to get Mum one for Christmas this year, once I've narrowed down the type I want.

Malc's new seaside slippers are broken in. Val and Henry fly home today.

Tuesday 13th March
The novelty of not having to get up and go straight out on a weekday has not worn off yet. Having the time to lie in bed and collect my thoughts is a great gentle start to the day,

much better than wrenching myself upright and rushing off to work.

I've decided I'm going to go for a walk most days now I'm retired. I can go local or I can get a bus somewhere further afield. I might branch out to Headington or even to Witney in the summer.

I had a good walk to Iffley Lock today, it was dry and sunny all the way. I stood on the little stone bridge just up from the lock and watched the swans and ducks. I thought about when royalty used to eat swans. I thought about a glass swan Mum has on her dressing table, a rare frivolous Christmas gift from Dad when they were first married, before Val and I were born. Usually gifts for Mum were really gifts for the house.

On my way home I called in at Greggs and got cream doughnuts. As I queued, looking at the pre-packed sandwiches, I thought that Christmas is the tasty filling in the bread of our normal lives every year. It's the glass swan in amongst the new irons, curtain tie-backs and hand blenders.

Malc asked what the occasion was when we had cream doughnut for pudding. We don't usually have pudding. I said we should bestow some good living upon ourselves when we get the opportunity. He nodded, satisfied with that answer. Men are generally better at accepting life's bounty than women. Jammy creamy sugary doughiness is wonderful.

Wednesday 14th March

Stephen Hawking and Jim Bowen died today. Both brilliant men in their own way.

Snow is forecast for the weekend. I booked an Iceland grocery delivery for Saturday morning. Last time it snowed it was hard to get one. I'll get some of their frozen custard slices and a Black Forest gateau for when we fancy a pudding. I hope Stephen Hawking and Jim Bowen got plenty of puddings. Life is short and you do tend to get distracted while you're living it. I would like to sit quietly with a slice of Black Forest gateau and savour every piped rosette of cream and every mouthful of cake and cherry. Slow down Pam, slow down and enjoy the now, I will tell myself more often in future. I do wonder how many more Christmases Malc and I have together. I hope it's a great many. He thinks I'll be okay because I know things about the boiler but…

Thursday 15th March

Val met me at Cowley Centre, or as she calls it Templars Square for a look round the shops. Older people and very local people call it Cowley Centre, younger people and less local people call it Templars Square. Val is jetlagged. She wanted to do something today to keep her awake. I got four individual Christmas puddings for twenty-five pence each in the Co-op. Val spotted them. I'll put them in the Christmas cupboard in the kitchen with the two big Christmas puddings that go out of date in August. These little ones are in date until September.

We heard Bob Marley being played at Templars Square. David had a Bob Marley phase. Malc didn't approve but I liked a few of his songs. There is a new café on Upper Barr and they've spelt sandwiches wrong (as sandwhiches). Val says this wouldn't happen in North

Oxford. She buys her kitchen roll in Cowley because it's cheaper. Henry jokes that he's going to set up a barrow on the Banbury Road selling kitchen roll at knock down prices.

Val and Henry had a super holiday. They're going to come round on Sunday lunch time and show us their photos. Val promised me that when she is fully awake again she'll make sure I have a fun retirement.

Friday 16th March

I went to see Mum. She is going to Florence Park Community Centre with her friend Bridget tonight for a talk about the Florence Park area. Bridget is good at getting Mum out and about. Mum has got some new big Bon Marche pants for her holiday to Eastbourne. They have a floral pattern. They are going in June for three nights. We like to get our money's worth out of holidays in our family by looking forward to them for a long time. It would be nice if holidays had advent calendars like Christmas does. A holiday advent calendar could be full of things like sun cream sachets, sunglasses, stamps for postcards, a notebook for writing holiday memories in and sweets for the journey.

Saturday 17th March

It was snowing when I got up at 7:30 a.m. I got toast and coffee then went back to bed and finished reading *A Redbird Christmas*. It was a bit soppy but I liked it. I am not one of those women who read pastel covered romance books. Gail loves them but I think they all have the same plot. I never took to Mills & Boon. I added *Redbird Christmas* to my Christmas book shelf and took down *A*

Treasury Of Christmas by Frank and Jamie Muir to read next. Frank Muir looks very dapper on the cover in a pink bow tie.

I read the meters. Isn't gas and electric amazing? We use an energy supplier that isn't one of the big six for both gas and electric, we can't afford not to shop around. I have to read the meters every month so we get a real bill not an estimated one.

For dinner Malc and I had chicken Kiev and potatoes left over from yesterday. We had a nice day indoors with it snowing all day outside.

Sunday 18th March

There is a couple of inches of snow on most things outside. I like the way snow changes what you do and you don't have to feel guilty for not going out and doing things (this is fine for a couple of days, but when we've had it for longer it's got annoying). Today feels a bit Christmassy due to the snow, it's like the year has been shuffled.

Val and Henry came over and showed us their holiday photos. They aren't printed out, they're on Henry's iPad. The cruise ship looks very plush. There's so much choice of food. Henry bought us some rum cake and Val gave me a book she'd got in a Goodwill shop (which is like our charity shops, but bigger Val says). It's called *The Holly And The Ivy A Celebration of Christmas* by Barbara Segall. We ordered Indian food from our favourite place on Rose Hill. It was lovely being in the warm eating spicy food and talking about Miami, the Caribbean and Bognor. Val and I shared a Peshwari naan. Malc and Henry think it's too sweet but we love it.

Monday 19th March

There is still a little bit of snow on the ground today. It's a great day for doing some Christmasing. Christmasing can be anything that makes you feel Christmassy. It can be reading a Christmas book. It can be looking at Christmas decorations on the internet. It can be cooking mince pies. It can be thinking about what fun you'll have at the next Christmas or looking at old photos from previous ones. I treasure the small number of Christmas photos I have with Dad in.

Bits of Christmas are in all sorts of places. I walked past the VCR Food & Wine off license today. They have a big box of red and gold baubles on a shelf that I can see through the window. This is an odd name for a newsagents/off license now I come to think of it.

Tuesday 20th March

Frank Muir's Christmas book starts with olden days Christmases and Halloween then goes through December, the start of January and ends at plough Monday. I'm reading the Christmas Eve bit at the moment. There is a tradition from the Cotswolds I've never heard of where women who want to know who their husband will be bake a cake on Christmas Eve with their initials on top and at midnight their intended husband will come in the door and put his initials on top of the cake. If this ever happened in real life I bet the woman had to drop some pretty heavy hints, or maybe it was a thing people did for their friends, like saying 'My mate Brenda will be making a cake with her initials on, on Christmas Eve and she doesn't bolt the front door, so if you were to pop along with a clean knife and carve your initials next to hers you could be getting wed by Easter.'

For dinner I cooked roast chicken, roast potatoes, marmalade glazed carrots, honey glazed parsnips, Yorkshire pudding and gravy. Being retired makes a week night roast dinner a viable option, we don't have to wait until the weekend now. Malc loves a roast dinner.

Wednesday 21st March
I met Gail for a coffee in Costa this afternoon. She gave me a book, *Quartet in Autumn* by Barbara Pym. I've not read anything of hers. Gail still has to work so I didn't go on about how lovely it is to be retired. She and Len have two years left on their mortgage. There were some years when he had moved out, but then he came back. Gail doesn't like her job, nowhere is life more unfair than in the world of work. It's unfair in health too. And love.

Malc was flicking through the Screwfix catalogue when I got in. Listening to Gail talk about Len I realise that Malc is everything I want in a husband. We had cheese on crumpets for dinner. I like dipping mine in salad cream while Malc favours a light spreading of Branston pickle.

I decided it would be pleasant to have something Christmassy in every room of the house. Downstairs we're open plan, we've got a lounge, then a big table in the dining area, then the kitchen. I have to remember to use the extractor fan when cooking strong smelling food or the whole house smells of onions. I have the Christmas cupboard in the kitchen and the Christmas book shelf in the dining area but nothing Christmassy in the lounge.

Thursday 22nd March
I've had the most peaceful morning reading *Quartet in Autumn* by Barbara Pym. I had to put it down when my stomach was growling for lunch. I had a small cheese and tomato pizza with cottage cheese. I love cottage cheese. Malc hates it.

I have found something Christmassy for the lounge. On the windowsill I have put a round tin with snowmen dancing on it (the lovely Raymond Briggs ones from the animated film). It originally contained chocolate chip cookies and was a gift from Nicola to Malc. I am unable to throw away even the most un-decorative of tins. Every time I get an idea for a present to buy someone this Christmas I'll note it on a bit of paper and put it in the tin.

In the evening Val phoned to ask what Easter egg Nicola, David, Malc and I would like this year? She said she'll add them to the Ocado order she'll get on Saturday morning. I'm getting Mum a Wispa egg, David and Malc Yorkie eggs (I like the boxes shaped like trucks), Nicola a Mini Eggs egg and Val and Henry Green & Black's butterscotch milk chocolate eggs. I used to like stacking the Easter eggs on the shelves in the shop. You can fill up a display nice and fast. Foil wrapped chocolate eggs are fragile though. I once saw a toddler punch through a Smarties egg when his mum was distracted.

Easter and Christmas go hand in hand. They're both opportunities to see family, to enjoy some chocolate and to think about what your life was like last Christmas or Easter. As well as recording my keeping Christmas efforts this diary should record high days and holidays, the highlights of my life. Some people think you can't afford highlights when you're retired but some people think all sorts of things. It doesn't feel like I'm retired yet. I'm still finding my feet, and deciding to give them excursions.

This weekend is going to be a highlight, Nicola and David are visiting.

Friday 23rd March

Today is Nicola's birthday. She is forty-two. We spoke on the phone, but it was one of those phone calls that never really got going, all pauses and short sentences. She'll be over tomorrow. She told me it is 276 days until Christmas, she said she follows a Twitter account that tweets a countdown.

I got a bargain this morning. I got some old-fashioned Christmas gift wrap from the little shop on Phipps Road for fifty pee. The shop is mostly used by people on their way to work at the car factory. Malc used to get his paper there, when we got a daily paper. I haven't seen the sort of gift wrap I got this morning since the early 1980s at the Sunday market at the speedway stadium.

I finished reading *Quartet in Autumn*. I loved it as a book, but will hopefully have a very different retirement to the characters in it.

Saturday 24th March

David has a rare Saturday off today, part of me wishes he hadn't followed me into retail. Nicola picked him up on the way to us. Then she picked Mum up and we had a houseful! David bought Nicola a leather handbag from the Vivienne Westwood shop for her birthday! It looked very expensive but he played it down by saying he knows the girls who work there. David is more interested in fashion than Nicola. Nicola always looks nice, in a bright cardigan, chunky jewellery sort of way. She doesn't have to wear a uniform in the library, just a badge. We didn't have any arguments about clothes when she was a teenager, not like Carol and her daughter Donna did.

David told us tales of all the difficult customers he's had lately. He had a cheeky woman trying to get a refund on a dress she'd clearly worn, it had make-up on it and smelt of perfume.

We got fish and chips for lunch. Malc took the orders and went to Littlemore chip shop. Everyone except David had fish and chips, David prefers steak pie to fish sometimes. Mid-afternoon Val and Henry popped in and we had chocolate cake and sang 'Happy Birthday' to Nicola. Val and Henry bought Nicola a lovely necklace with a teapot pendant. Malc and I bought her some books she wanted and I got her some malt loaf because she didn't win the competition for a year's supply. Val and Henry took Mum home when they went, she finds too much time out of her own house tiring she says. She'll be eighty-nine in three days but she says she doesn't want any fuss. David and Nicola wished her a happy birthday in advance.

Even though it was Nicola's birthday she bought me a book, *The Country Diary Christmas Book* by Sarah Hollis. She also gave me a little robin pin badge. She said there is a craze of RSPB pin badges at the library. Her senior librarian's son is selling them to raise money for doing his Duke of Edinburgh award. She got a seahorse for David and a leatherback turtle for Malc. She has a kingfisher on her bag. She said she would have got one for Aunty Val and Uncle Henry but there were only killer whales left on Friday.

We had pizza for dinner and then David left to meet a friend in Oxford. He'll be forty in September. We watched the telly with Nicola. She said Ant And Dec's *Saturday Night Takeaway* isn't on this week because Ant has been arrested on suspicion of drunk driving. We watch the other side so wouldn't have noticed. Malc nodded off in front of the news so we went to bed. Nicola stayed up and watched *Guardians of the Galaxy*. She said she'd turn the plug off at the wall before she came upstairs. This is usually Malc's job.

Sunday 25th March

British Summer Time begins today. Malc changed all the clocks at 9:30, which is now 8:30.

Nicola got up just after 9:00 (new time) and said suppose the hour that's been nicked from her weekend by British Summer Time was the one in which she became a best-selling novelist and didn't have to go to work tomorrow? She has started six novels but not finished any yet. I told her I still write this diary and she said that was great. Actually it is great, it's lovely to put my thoughts somewhere and remember my big plan of keeping Christmas all the year. Yesterday had a Christmassy feel.

I felt a bit sad when Nicola left but she'll be back on Easter Sunday. Every time she leaves after an overnight stay it reminds me of the time she went off to university. David's leaving home was less of an event, he kept moving out for a bit then having to come back again.

I finished reading Frank Muir's Christmas book which cheered me up. It claimed that bees sing a song to praise Christ at midnight on Christmas Eve. Only people who have led blameless lives can hear it. I doubt anyone my age can hear it.

Nicola talks about affirmations a lot, which are things you tell yourself. I am Pam Dickens, lady of leisure, keeper of Christmas all the year, grateful for the time I spend with my now adult children.

Monday 26th March

It is a Monday morning but Malc and I are not at the beck and call of an employer. This is still a huge novelty for me. Today is my fourth Monday of being retired.

Malc went to the allotment. I wrote Mum's birthday card ready for tomorrow. I wrapped her presents; a bag of Murray Mints and a bottle of Badedas bubble bath. I think I can imagine being eighty-nine, but can I really? Mum seems to have distilled her life down to the essence of necessity and the small number of things she enjoys.

If I am not horribly unlucky like Dad was, I may have lots of time to be retired and to do what I really enjoy. I felt a bit gloomy and under pressure to make good use of my day so I got a cup of tea and read some of *Haynes Explains Christmas*. I've noticed that reading seems to reset my mood.

Tuesday 27th March

Mum is eighty-nine today! When Malc finished work we went round with fish and chips for dinner. I took tartare sauce and tomato sauce in case Mum had run out (she had, she seems to view tomato sauce as non-essential). I gave Mum her birthday presents. She smelt the Badedas (it is a strong no-nonsense smell which reminds me of Mum's bathroom) and she put the Murray Mints in the cupboard behind an already opened bag of Murray Mints. Every handbag and coat pocket of Mum's has a couple of Murray Mint wrappers in it. Val had been round earlier in the day and taken her a cake (M&S Victoria sponge) and some flowers. We had cake for pudding.

Bridget bought her a lovely bone china William Morris mug in the golden lily design (Val told Mum this earlier, she knows a lot about William Morris, she likes his wallpaper). According to William Morris 'The true secret of happiness lies in taking a genuine interest in all the details of daily life.' Our local Wetherspoons is called The William Morris but it's a different William Morris who founded Morris Motors and made cars.

I borrowed a *Woman's Weekly* from Mum. I was intrigued by 12 Great Cheese Recipes and Joan Collin's Secrets To Looking Your Best (I reckon it'll be plastic surgery and a lot of make-up).

I feel like I haven't done enough for Mum's birthday but there's no point buying her expensive gifts she doesn't want. She said she'd rather have dinner at home than out somewhere because then she can save what she doesn't eat and have it tomorrow. When we got home I made a note for the snowman tin to buy Mum something in William Morris's golden lily print for Christmas.

Wednesday 28th March

Malc drove us to Heyford Hill Sainsbury's so he could stock up on compost. They have an offer that Ken told him about, three bags for a tenner. Malc said Ken always keeps an ear to the ground for gardening bargains and I thought of Ken's big hairy ears. We put the compost in the boot then went back into the shop and we pootled round thinking about what to get to eat for Easter weekend. We chose a Cadbury Mini Eggs Chocolate Gateau. Isn't the word gateau wonderful? I've baked a cake but I've never baked a gateau. Maybe I will now I'm retired. We got all sorts of exotic sounding hot cross buns.

David once met Mr Cadbury's Parrot. We still have the photo. Nicola was on a school trip to France and so to give David a treat me and Val took him to Cadbury World. It was a great day out. We bought Nicola some chocolate from the gift shop and promised to go again with her. David still says he'd rather go to Cadbury World than France.

I've been retired for a whole month! It still feels like a long holiday, I can't quite believe I never have to go back to work. Life feels lovely and full of possibilities today, like my stocking is stuffed with as yet unseen delights! I can sort of discern the shapes my life could be. Malc is happy too, he's always relaxed when he has a stock of compost. I made a note for the snowman tin to check how much compost Malc has in November.

Thursday 29th March

I had a phone call from Mum this morning, she has won the Coventry Building Society Easter hamper! She said come round and eat some chocolate! I didn't need telling twice! We had a cup of tea and a Cadbury Crème Egg. Mum gave me a Crunchie egg to bring home and share with Malc.

In the afternoon Carol and I met at the John Allen Centre shops. She's after a new duvet cover and there's Matalan, TK Maxx and Asda to choose from. We looked at all the options then went to Asda café and had a drink. Carol gave me a lovely Easter card. The woman running the café gave us a portion of free wedges each to take home, otherwise she'd have had to throw them away. Carol said it was a free potato bonanza! Today has been really rather good. I told Malc all about it when I got in. He had a good day too, it was corned beef hash for lunch which is one of the chef's specials at the care home. I showed him the Crunchie egg from Mum and he said thank Crunchie it's Thursday!

We watched *Still Game*. It's nice there are programmes about retired people.

Friday 30th March

Good Friday. When I was falling asleep last night I thought about how nice Mum's hamper looked, all the Easter goodies sat in a basket surrounded by cellophane and topped with a bow, like a hot air balloon of joy. This morning I made a note in the snowman tin to make some hampers to give as gifts this Christmas.

Nicola rang, she wanted to know if she should bring anything on Sunday? We're having our Easter family get together. She's going to drive and get David and Mum/Nan on the way to us. She told me she's bought some fairy lights in the shape of rabbits. It costs Nicola much less to rent a flat in Coventry than it would in Oxford. She's squirreled away a deposit to buy somewhere but not taken the plunge yet. She and a friend from uni are planning on buying a house together.

For elevenses Malc and I had orange and cranberry hot cross bun with lemon curd. For lunch we had apple and cinnamon hot cross bun with butter. I have more time to plan what we'll eat now I don't go to work.

Val rang, she wanted to know if she should bring anything on Sunday? The women of this family are very good at ringing up to ask if they can bring anything. The men of this family are very good at eating whatever's there. I don't suppose we're much different to any other family. Nicola says that women do most of the work of creating a family Christmas. Easter is similar but on a smaller scale. I like all of it apart from trying to get all the bits of a roast dinner hot and plated up at the same time, it's a frenzy of draining saucepans and spooning things onto plates.

Saturday 31st March

Easter Saturday. I finished reading *Haynes Explains Christmas*. I looked on Amazon to see if there is a Haynes Explains Easter but there isn't. There is holidays, pets and the British. Then I watched *Classic Mary Berry*. She did a Spanish tortilla. I might have a go at it one day. Weekends are more relaxed now I don't work during the week. I can have a lazy Saturday morning instead of trying to catch up on things I've been too tired to do.

In the afternoon I hoovered just over half of the stairs. I do it in two sessions, it's one of my least favourite jobs. I made a beef casserole for dinner. I put in carrots, celery, potato and plenty of red onion. Malc and I both think that celery is best in a casserole. Malc would eat a casserole over a salad any day. We watched David Attenborough talk about eggs on BBC Two. He is marvellous.

It's been an odd month, not working has made it feel like a holiday, and Bognor was a super treat. I don't have any solid routines yet. Mum's friend Bridget told me you need to establish good routines when you retire, while also doing something new every once in a while.

March reckoning, have I kept Christmas all March? We've had snow, I have six read and three unread books on my Christmas book shelf. I've felt a bit unsure what to do with myself for the first half of the month, what with Val being away. It was lovely to meet up with Carol. We've had lots of family events in the second half of the month. It can be hard to feel Christmassy slap bang in the middle of Easter but the good things about Christmas (seeing family, food you don't eat all year round) are also things you get at Easter. I will endeavour to make April a festive month and keep Christmas in my heart. It can be in your mind, but not reach as far your heart, when it's in your heart you know because you get a feeling like the world is a wonderful place and that there is more joy on the way.

April

Sunday 1st April

Easter Sunday. Next weekend Val and I will be in London for her late birthday theatre treat of *Lady Windermere's Fan*. Today we're having Mum, David and Nicola, Val and Henry to lunch. I hoovered the other half of the stairs.

Everyone arrived at eleven-thirty. Mum brought a simnel cake from the hamper she won. She said you don't get that kind of perk if you do your banking online. She told Henry the tale of her winning the hamper. It has got longer since Thursday and now includes a premonition that she was going to be lucky. Val brought some chocolate hot cross buns. Nicola brought some Tunnock's Tea Cakes. Malc loves these. I had told them all they didn't need to bring anything but women like to.

David helped Malc extend the dining table to comfortably seat seven. This only gets done a handful of times a year. Christmas and Easter are the big occasions. We tend to eat takeaways on our laps in front of the telly. My roast dinner got a lot of compliments. Everyone loves a roast dinner. Chat was about religion (no-one in our family is big on it), shopping (there are a lot of flavours of hot cross buns now) and the EU/Brexit (everyone except Henry is sick of hearing about the EU/Brexit). Val said Henry wants to talk about the EU/Brexit way more than she wants to listen about the EU/Brexit.

Val and Henry took Mum home mid-afternoon. Then David did his quite good impression of his Uncle Henry. He says 'I merely mention it as a source of conjecture' and 'Could someone pass the crostini?' This always gives Nicola the giggles. Nicola has been known to describe the food served at Aunty Val's as Aunty Val's middle class swanky bollocks. She says that on the rare occasions when me and Val do a buffet together she can tell the parts of it each of us has brought. She says I do pork pies, sausage rolls, cheese and pineapple on sticks and Black Forest gateau. Aunty Val does olives, houmous and crudites, filo parcels and a lemon tart. There is some truth in this.

We all went with Malc to drive David home to Bicester. He has to work tomorrow. Nicola is staying over tonight, she doesn't have to be at work until Tuesday. I sometimes wonder if Nicola and David's generation is as happy as they say they are, with their feeling that they should be happy? I truly hope so. My generation didn't expect to be happy, at least not all the time, but often is, in a quiet sort of a way. When you've retired it's like you've climbed a big hill. Financially we're okay and that makes a big difference to the ability to be happy. It was hard for me and Malc to buy a house but it's much, much harder for Nicola and David's generation. My generation made decisions about who to settle with in our twenties, by and large, but Nicola and David's generation seem very reluctant to get started on the adventure of marriage. It was Gail who I first heard using the phrase 'the adventure of marriage'. Sadly hers has been a bit of an assault course.

Monday 2nd April

Easter Monday. Malc went to the allotment when Nicola left after lunch. He's planting his carrots today. I went to bed for a while and read *The Holly And The Ivy*. What absolute luxury it is to read in bed on a Monday afternoon! Other peoples' paradise might look like a sandy beach with palm trees and cocktails but mine looks like an uninterrupted afternoon under a duvet with a good book, a cup of tea in a Christmas mug and a hot cross bun. I love being at home with Malc but I do also love knowing that I have a little bit of time when no-one will be asking me for anything. As an example, on Friday between eleven and midday Malc asked; where are the bulldog clips? Have we got any more marmalade? What happened to the sponge I use for washing the car? Have you seen the Scotts of Stow catalogue?

Mum phoned to tell me that *Flog It!* is from Oxford today. She is always very pleased when daytime telly is from somewhere she knows.

Tuesday 3rd April

I went to six shops this morning to try to get Malc's favourite spicy mango flavour Walkers Sensations crisps and the shelves were bare in all of them. Two of the shops were Co-ops but they have different things because one is a Midcounties Co-op and the other is different kind of Co-op. They each have their own reward cards. Like most shoppers I'd prefer no reward cards and prices to be cheaper.

While I was looking for Malc's crisps I thought about the times I've bought Christmas presents that are just right. There is a real satisfaction in getting the exact thing you know will delight someone. We managed to get Nicola a Cabbage Patch doll in the year they were the bee's knees. One year David was mad keen on Transformers and we got him an Ultra Magnus. It doesn't matter that you think it's just a load of overpriced plastic tat if it's the thing your child has set their little heart on.

In the evening Malc had Lucy round to do his corn. She does the care home too. She's a lovely lady, self-employed, she once cured a verruca I had and said I had nice feet. Feet can be tricky when you get older. This theme has been captured by my favourite poet, Pam Ayres.

Wednesday 4th April

Malc and I went to Lidl. We got goat's cheese and pesto focaccia and an iced cinnamon bun for lunch. We had a really good browse of the middle aisle but didn't buy anything. It is a luxury to be able to go to Lidl during the day on a week day, it has a different, more relaxed feel to the frantic evening trips we did when I was working.

I had an email from Lauren asking if I'd like to meet up on Lauren's lunch break one day? She always has to go straight home after work and pick her daughter up from the childminder. It is lovely that Lauren wants to keep in touch, I replied saying I could do any lunch time that suited her.

I typed 1980s Christmas into eBay and spent a cheery half hour looking at photos of decorations. I had forgotten those metallic balls made of small foil cones which have silver outsides and red, gold and green insides. I'd love to know who invented them.

Thursday 5th April

I went to Gail's for coffee this morning. She has a week off work but she and Len aren't going away because they couldn't agree on where to go. She put a plate of biscuits out and I ate two and she ate none. She asked how I was adjusting and it took me a moment to realise that she meant to retirement. Even though she doesn't like her job, Gail doesn't seem to be looking forward to retiring. She said she and Len will be rattling round the house with nothing to say to each other like a long winter evening. I said when she retires perhaps we could take up a new hobby together, or do an evening class, anything she fancies. I said I'd like to learn how to knit so I could make some handmade Christmas gifts. Gail doesn't like Christmas because it was at Christmas that Len left her the first time. She doesn't eat biscuits because he left her for someone two stone lighter and ten years younger. If I were her I'd eat the biscuits and kick Len out but of course it's not that simple.

I walked home and had an individual Christmas pudding from the Christmas cupboard with coffee ice cream for my lunch. It would be nice if Gail felt she could treat herself sometimes. She tries to keep puddings and Christmas out of her world. If only Christmas spirit were like Oxo cubes and you could open a foil corner and sprinkle some on where it was needed.

Malc and I watched *Still Game* this evening which is very funny. Sometimes we don't have anything to say so we just watch the telly for a bit.

Friday 6th April

We had the longest chat we've ever had with our next-door neighbours, Tom and Tamsin, today. They are in their early thirties. They moved in three years ago. We always say hello but not much else. Today we talked about gardens.

They are trying to get pregnant and they moved three years ago so they would have a garden for their as yet unborn children. We don't know the neighbours of the house that adjoins ours, it's rented out as rooms and the people come and go like shadows without speaking. Tom and Tamsin are a bit more solid. She wears the same sort of clothes as Nicola.

I'm going to tell you about a thing I do on my walks round Littlemore. You might think it's silly but it helps keep me cheerful. I leave myself messages by the tallest fir tree opposite the chip shop and in the ivy in the underpass. What I mean is I think of a message I'd like to leave myself for the next day (or the next time I walk past), something like 'Pam remember to enjoy being retired now you've got here' or 'Try to get a Christmassy tingle today' and I imagine the words on a piece of paper. Then I imagine myself tucking the piece of paper into a hollow in the fir tree or underneath the ivy (people often tuck their empty beer cans into the ivy under the underpass). When I walk past next I remember what message I left for myself and collect it.

Malc and I had Louisiana blackened chicken pizza from the Co-op (Midcounties) for dinner. For the record Malc likes his chicken browned but not blackened. We won't have it again. They had put it upright and lengthways on the shelf so most of the filling had slipped to the bottom and had to be redistributed. Having worked in a shop for so long I notice this sort of error despite being retired now. I will never again know the satisfaction of a neatly stacked shelf.

A new series of *Have I Got News For You* starts tonight. Malc used to tell David he should be a satirist because he's so cheeky.

Saturday 7th April
Trip to London with Val for *Lady Windermere's Fan* at the Vaudeville Theatre.
Val and I got the Oxford Tube coach to London. We got off at Marble Arch and walked up Oxford Street, pausing to taste things in Selfridges' Food Hall (red pesto, cucumber and passion fruit juice, chocolate houmous) and to look in their Wonder Room. We also looked in Monsoon (Val's wardrobe is like a small branch of Monsoon) then we walked down Carnaby Street, through Soho and Chinatown. I love the bustle of London. We had lunch in Wahaca, a Mexican place. I had a chicken tinga burrito which is served with tortilla chips on the side. We checked into our hotel at two. We're staying at the four-star Strand Palace Hotel, on The Strand. It's pricier than Bognor! Our rooms were nice, small as you'd expect in London but well designed. My radiator was very responsive and came on quickly.

We walked over Waterloo Bridge and past the National Theatre and walked along the South Bank. We had a walk on the little beach. We saw the *This Morning* TV studios. I waved at Philip Schofield. Val said Henry gets wound up by Eamon Holmes. We walked along to the OXO Tower and looked in the shops. Then we went to Trafalgar Square and saw a Pikachu, two Yodas and a busker that was actually quite good. He was playing a blues song I sort of recognise called 'Boom Boom Boom' (or similar). We had dinner in Wagamama (both of us had chicken katsu curry) then we freshened up at the hotel before the theatre. I wore a black lace dress and tried not to feel provincial.

The Vaudeville Theatre is small and lovely with lots of gold paint. *Lady Windermere's Fan* was splendid. Jennifer Saunders was wonderful in it. Kathy Burke the director was sat two rows behind us! She should be very proud of herself. There was a musical interlude with a song written by Kathy called 'Take Your Hand Off My Fan'. Val and I giggled like schoolgirls. There was a standing ovation at the end. It was great hearing actors speak Oscar Wilde quotes like 'We are all in the gutter, but some of us are looking at the stars.'

We had a drink in the hotel bar then went to bed, arranging to meet at nine for breakfast. It was hard to get to sleep so I imagined I was doing Christmas shopping at Cowley Centre shops and had to pick two Christmassy things from each shop. This usually helps me feel calm and fall asleep.

Sunday 8th April

I slept as well as possible in a strange room. I had a bath this morning (the shower head was an unadjustable height and I had plenty of time. The cold bath tap squealed like a banshee). For breakfast we went to Dishoom, an Indian café. I had bacon naan. It was very good. Val would make a good food critic, she knows all the interesting places to eat. There is an ice cream shop called Milk Train that sells ice cream with a candy floss cloud around it. We're going to get one next time.

After breakfast we went to the National Gallery and saw loads of paintings belonging to the nation. I saw Constable's The Haywain (which reminded me of my favourite Monty Python sketch; 'Dad, it's the man from Constable's The Haywain'), and Van Gogh's Sunflowers and many more. I got virgin and child fatigue. There were a lot of religious paintings. Although I love Christmas, I'm not a religious woman.

We had lunch at the hotel (burger and chips for Val, fish and chips for me, both very good). We talked about little foibles our husbands have. For instance, Malc always leaves the tea towel on the kitchen worktop, not on the hook (and it was him who put up the hook for it!). He uses more kitchen roll than is necessary to mop up spills. Henry rearranges things Val has put in the dishwasher. If he takes in the Ocado delivery he forgets to give back the carrier bags for recycling at five pee each despite saying at parties that he thinks all plastic should have a deposit on to make us reuse it in perpetuity. Henry complains that Val doesn't understand fluid dynamics or the Navier-Stokes equations. Despite all this we'd miss them if we were away too long.

After lunch we went to Covent Garden and looked at the shops and stalls. We collected our bags from the concierge and got a 23 bus to Marble Arch. We had a quick look at Speaker's Corner (lots of men with beards, loads of police) then came home. It is now seven o'clock and I'm tired but happy. I love spending time with Val and I think London is a beautiful city.

Monday 9th April
I've got a lazy day planned today. London takes it out of you when you're my age. Malc is out in the greenhouse planting seeds. I finished reading *The Holly And The Ivy*. I've noticed so much holly and ivy on my walks round Littlemore while I've been reading it. There's also loads in the little alleyway that runs along the back of Rose Hill cemetery at the top.

I had some lovely post from Nicola today, a metal bookmark with a snowflake hanging off it. She has started making bookmarks and jewellery. She's very creative is our Nicola. I rang her in the evening to thank her for the bookmark.

Tuesday 10th April
When Malc goes to work I sometimes feel guilty and think I should get a part time job too. Then I think sod that for a game of soldiers, I've worked since I was fifteen. His Tuesdays and Thursdays at the care home and his time spent at the allotment and in the garden keep him occupied. Then there's his crosswords and browsing the internet. He's got retirement sussed because he's been doing it for years. Even though he works two days a week he considers himself retired because he could stop at any time he likes, he doesn't have to work, he chooses to. I think I'm doing okay at getting used to being retired, I just need to quiet the nagging voice in my head telling me I should be doing something useful.

I met Lauren for lunch. We went to Boswell's Café in the middle of the shopping centre. Lauren's studying is going well. Her daughter will be three in the summer. She filled me in on the work gossip. Dylan has got a girlfriend. Tracy got caught skiving, she phoned in sick but was seen by Phil in Wetherspoons looking a picture of health and vitality. Mr Barker and the new supervisor had a disagreement about where to put the special offer display baskets and the new supervisor moved them when Mr Barker had a day off. It's all carrying on without me, in its usual way. I still wake up at the time I needed to when I was working. I told Lauren about some of the Christmas books I've read and about how nice it was to go to London with Val.

On Saturday there is a spring fayre at the care home and I've said I'll make some cakes for a stall Carol's daughter Donna (who works there with Malc) is running. I flicked through my cook books looking for recipes. I'll do the actual baking on Friday morning. I think I'll make mince pies and millionaire's shortbread. I'll make a bit extra for Malc and I. I don't think we've ever eaten a mince pie in April.

Wednesday 11th April

I have decided that turkey is not just for Christmas. We had croissant filled with turkey slices, cheese and cranberry sauce for lunch. Malc said it made a nice change.

I read a bit of *Trade Secrets Christmas*. Part of it is how to pack shopping in a supermarket, something I'm a bit of an expert on after my long career. The book says 'Baguettes are a real nightmare' but they aren't really.

Thursday 12th April

I went shopping for ingredients to make mince pies and millionaire's shortbread. Shopping when you're retired is a totally different activity to shopping when you work full time. I browsed. I got ready rolled pastry for the mince pies. This is not cheating. A woman in the queue behind me noticed my ready rolled pastry and pointed at it and said wasn't it marvellous? I agreed it was. I tried on a lacey cardigan in Peacocks. When did cardigans stop coming with buttons as standard? Is this so they are cheaper to make?

Friday 13th April

I spent the morning making mince pies and millionaire's shortbread for the care home spring fayre tomorrow. I took them round to Carol's this afternoon, packaged in plastic Chinese takeaway containers that I don't need back. I knew it was worth keeping them. Carol has just had her hair done. It looks lovely. Carol has blonde highlights and her hair is longer than most women our age have it. I told her Malc and I will pop along to the fayre at about half two tomorrow.

Nicola phoned. She's entered a competition to win a year's supply of tea bags. She has been invited to go on holiday with Letitia to Spain. She has declined, having previously holidayed with Letitia in Newquay, when all Letitia wanted to do was sleep late then go out drinking and looking for boys. Nicola has known Letitia since they went to school together. It is a source of delight to me that Nicola tells me things. I've had much less trouble boys-wise with Nicola than Carol had with Donna.

Malc and I had a mince pie and watched *Gardeners' World*. There was a man on it who likes growing exotic plants. Malc said mince pies are perhaps slightly nicer in April when you've not had one for months than in December when they are ubiquitous.

Saturday 14th April

This afternoon we went to the spring fayre at the care home where Malc works two days a week. The money raised will go towards a day at the seaside for the residents. There was a book stall, a cake stall run by Carol's daughter Donna, a handicrafts stall (mainly knitted things and jewellery), and a tombola (run by Carol). I bought something from each stall. I love going to the seaside. Us Oxford people really appreciate the change of scene.

From the book stall I got a little book called *Keep Calm At Christmas* which I read as soon as I got home. It's a series of quotes about Christmas. I liked one from Calvin Coolidge; 'Christmas is not a time nor a season, but a state of mind. To cherish peace and goodwill, to be plenteous in mercy is to have the real spirit of Christmas'. I also got a book called *A Berkshire Christmas*. I got a lemon drizzle cake, a knitted snowman and I won a tin of corned beef on Carol's tombola. I chatted to one of the residents who used to come into the shop where I worked.

Carol's daughter Donna has the perfect temperament to be a care assistant, she's very patient. She says of the residents that often they're just rubbed a bit raw by life, by their aches, pains, sadnesses and frustrations, they don't mean to be short with you some days. Malc says when he's at work he always remembers that he is in their home, so asks how they want things. If he's leaving their room after fixing something he asks if he should leave the door open or if he should shut it.

When you retire, you can't help wondering if one day you will end up in a care home, and that's how people say it; 'end up' like you've been washed up on a beach of infirmity, without your own volition. I thought of Dickens; 'Keep my memory green'.

Sometimes this afternoon there was forced cheerfulness, sometimes genuine cheerfulness, and sometimes the forced cheerfulness gives way to genuine cheerfulness. All the mince pies I made were sold before Malc and I got there! I had forgotten to sprinkle them with icing sugar.

Sunday 15th April

I finished reading *Trade Secrets Christmas.* It recommended ripening bananas by putting them in the microwave. I've never heard of that before. I am writing this in the company of the knitted snowman I bought yesterday. He's sitting on the bed in the roof. I haven't named him yet.

Monday 16th April

I felt restless this morning. Sometimes I get the idea that I'm not living my life in the best way I can and not helping other people to be happy as much as I could. Being in the care home on Saturday has made me think that I'm in the autumn of my life. Now I'm retired I don't have any excuses not to be having a good time and making the most of being alive and healthy. I told Malc I was bored, I couldn't quite put into words my particular malady. Often when I write this diary things come into sharper focus for me and I get a little closer to what's really the crux of a situation. It is a Monday and I don't have to work. I should be happy. I should not be wasting my time worrying that in future Malc or I might go separately to a care home or that I might get only a short retirement like my Dad did.

This morning Malc said we should go to the garden centre at Yarnton. He said there's enough stuff there to interest non-gardeners. We had a lovely day out. We had lunch there, chicken and mushroom pie and chips. We looked at the tropical fish. We went in the antiques bit and they were selling some poppy pattern plates that we've already got for £40! They were only from Argos. Malc said we'll have to be more careful when we're washing them up.

My snowman is still unnamed. Maybe I'll call him Purity. It sounds a bit pretentious, but he's my snowman so I can call him what I want. Malc suggested I call him Woolly Willy or Frank Flake.

Tuesday 17th April

I woke up feeling joyful. I cooked bacon, eggs, mushrooms and toast for Malc and I's breakfast then waved him off to work. He'll be doing some pruning in the care home garden today. I went to B&M and got some condensed milk. It's ages since I've used a tin of condensed milk. I made some coconut ice. I used fresh sieved raspberries to colour the pink part. I'm letting it set overnight then I'll cut it into squares. If it's nice I'll make some again at Christmas as presents for people.

I've decided my new snowman will be called Woolly Willy.

Wednesday 18th April
I cut the coconut ice I made yesterday into squares and put it in little plastic bags. I'm saving the clear gift bags with a poinsettia print I got in the Lakeland sale for Christmas, by then I hope to be good at making homemade sweets. I wrote coconut ice on a slip of paper and put it in my snowman tin of present ideas.

I've been reading *A Berkshire Christmas* for the last few days. The compiler of the book continually makes reference to the county boundary changes in 1974, as if afraid of an unseen reader continually piping up 'That's not in Berkshire'.

Thursday 19th April
I met Val in town today. On the bus a man with a tattooed head got on and sat in front of me. Among the pictures on his head was Betty Boop's head in a Santa hat and the message Merry Christmas. It's not often the back of someone's head makes me feel jolly.

Val and I had lunch in Zizzi (pasta della casa for me, salmon tortellini for Val and we shared a side of chips). Then we looked round the shops. It was so warm I had to take my cardigan off. I gave Val some coconut ice. We looked round the market at Gloucester Green. I bought *The Christmas Book* by *Good Housekeeping* magazine (even though my style is more adequate housekeeping. I don't intend to spend my retirement doing housework).

At the bus stop on the way home a lady whose husband is in the care home Malc works at chatted to me. She recognised me from the fayre on Saturday. She'd had a disappointing mushroom risotto for lunch with her friend, who had a voucher. She'd have preferred something nice with chips. I agree, something nice with chips is much better than mushroom risotto, it's the worst risotto. I like getting the bus to Oxford. It's free if I go after nine o'clock now I'm a pensioner.

Friday 20th April
I took some coconut ice round to Mum this morning. She said she couldn't tell me when she last had a bit of coconut ice. She sometimes used to get a bar of coconut ice from St Giles Fair when she was a kid. She would make it last as long as possible because sweets were few and far between. I don't remember exactly when chocolate and sweets got cheaper but Nicola and David ate more sweets than I did growing up, suddenly a multipack of Chewits was inexpensive. I vividly remember the year Mum's friend Bridget bought Val and I a chocolate selection box each for Christmas. It had a game of snakes and ladders on the back and was a big deal. We even played with the plastic trays from inside the box, sorting coloured buttons from Mum's button tin into them. Nicola and David have a selection box every Christmas and I'm sure they enjoy it but it's not the event it was for Val and I. There is a temptation at Christmas now to buy a stuffalanche of gifts rather than one or two well-chosen things.

Malc smells of Deep Heat, he overdid the gardening a bit at work this week and has an achy shoulder. He groans if he has to lift his arm as high as the top cupboard where we keep the ginger nuts.

Saturday 21st April

We had our Iceland delivery which contains mini Viennettas on a stick. They're calling them Viennas so they don't get sued but they are clearly trying to copy the success of the Viennetta. We got a box of vanilla flavour and a box of strawberry flavour. Malc and I tried the strawberry flavour. They were very good. Malc smells very strongly of Deep Heat again today but says his shoulder is slightly improved. We had a lazy day in front of the telly. We watched a bit of *The Queen's Birthday Party* then turned over for *Dad's Army* when we didn't like the music the Queen was getting. Malc wondered if she'd rather be watching *Dad's Army* too.

I think I would like to see a Christmas music concert this year.

Sunday 22nd April

Malc's shoulder is only twinging with certain movements today he says. There is still a whiff of Deep Heat every time he moves or when I come back into the room he's in. I did a roast dinner to cheer him up. He said his shoulder used to be able to cope with a long day of rigorous gardening and then he sighed. Preparing food for people is a good way of quietly showing your interest in their continued healthy and happy existence. Christmas dinner is the ultimate expression of this but all the smaller examples of cups of tea or bowls of soup are cumulative proofs too. Even a fruit pastille on a bus sends a heartening message.

Monday 23rd April
Everyone I know thinks today should be a bank holiday because it's St George's Day. I went to the library with Carol. The librarian told us that today was Shakespeare's birthday. She pointed at a display of his books. I borrowed *The Enchanted April* by Elizabeth Von Arnim. Carol borrowed Coleen Nolan's *Upfront & Personal*. The librarian said 'April hath put a spirit of youth in everything'.

William and Kate Middleton had their third child, a boy, today. I hope they name him Malcolm. Malc could do with a boost. He's having a day off the Deep Heat today. My nose is relieved. He hasn't said, but I think he's a bit worried he might not be able to go to work and be useful tomorrow.

I made butterscotch Angel Delight for a mid-afternoon treat. The fifteen minutes while you're waiting for it to chill is a long fifteen minutes. David used to get very impatient waiting for Angel Delight or Instant Whip. His favourite flavour is chocolate but the rest of us like butterscotch best. I used to get a packet of each sometimes and use the trifle bowl and do a chocolate bottom layer and a butterscotch top layer. I made a note in the snowman tin to get David some chocolate Angel Delight as a stocking filler. They don't make Instant Whip now. It wasn't strictly instant, you had to wait for it to set or it was just gloop. I remember having raspberry flavour once.

Tuesday 24th April

Malc went to work this morning. He's only been off work sick twice since he's been working in the care home, both times in winter, both times when they had a bug. I made millionaire's shortbread because it's one of Malc's favourites and he only got one piece of the batch I made for the spring fayre. Malc says it's like a very fancy Twix, which I suppose it is. I had to pop out for some light muscovado sugar from the Co-op. I got some reduced-price sushi for my lunch. I can have something different for lunch every day now I'm retired, I have plenty of time to shop for it and prepare it. I feel like I'm discovering food all over again. When Malc and I were first married I was an adventurous cook.

I read half of *The Enchanted April* by Elizabeth Von Arnim this afternoon. I had to pull myself back to the here and now when Malc got home. I asked how he got on with his shoulder at work. He said it was fine. I told him he was doing well to still be working at his age and he smiled. He said sometimes he can't see much difference between him and the residents. I said there's a good couple of decades between him and the residents.

Wednesday 25th April

Malc and I had millionaire's shortbread with our mid-morning coffee. He said it had the perfect ratio of chocolate to caramel. I was pleased with how buttery the biscuit tasted. Malc went out to the allotment. I didn't think about Christmas yesterday, I was a bit preoccupied with Malc. I'm so glad his shoulder has stopped bothering him. Sometimes in our small concerns and preoccupations our bigger ones are revealed. All of us will become gradually less able physically and mentally as we get older but we don't know when or how, what bits we'll escape and what will finally do for us.

Today I've been reading *A Berkshire Christmas* and am nearly at the end of the book. There's a bit about Didcot and it's pointed out that it used to be in Berkshire but since 1974 has been in Oxfordshire. I almost wish the boundary changes had never happened just for the peace of mind of the man who put this book together. Reading about Christmas in Berkshire reminded me of a day's shopping Val and I had in Reading. We saw Keith Chegwin turn on the Christmas lights, there was quite a crowd. I love being in a buzzy, excited Christmas shopping centre.

I can tell Malc's shoulder is better. He came into the room eating a ginger nut and I didn't hear him groan when reaching for the tin in the kitchen. Ginger nuts and Fox's Ginger Crunch Creams have their own tin on top of the cupboard because of being spicy and potentially transferring their flavour to gentler tasting biscuits.

Thursday 26th April

I got the bus into town on a whim and got new undies. My old ones will be used as dusters. They started life a sort of delicate lilac colour but are now undeniably grey. I don't want to spend the rest of my years in grey undies. I spent a very long time in M&S trying on bras, the longest time I've ever spent, but I have got the time now and it's rather liberating. Pants are easy to choose, I always get a bikini brief or a high leg. Bras are tricky but I found a comfortable, flattering one. I went for festive red, the sort of thing I always look at in the Christmas catalogue but have never yet got. Malc is not a buyer of lingerie and that's fine by me. Sometimes you have to be your own Santa.

I looked in the American sweet shop on Cornmarket Street. Cornmarket Street has changed so much, it used to have Gordon Thoday's, the big Co-op, Thorntons, Littlewoods and Woolworths. I'm going to try not to be one of those oldies who are so busy looking back that they don't notice the wonder of now. We have amazing things now, shopping deliveries, statins, the internet and ready-made pastry.

I finished reading *The Enchanted April* by Elizabeth Von Arnim. I enjoyed watching the people in it relax into happier versions of themselves. I am relaxed today because Malc's shoulder is fine. It had a lot of flowery language, by which I mean stuff about flowers, and I know what they all are, so could imagine them. It was like reading a Thompson & Morgan catalogue, in a good way. The holiday version of you and the Christmas version of you are the you it would be good to be a mix of all year round but daily chores and stresses get in the way.

Friday 27th April

I'm wearing my brand new, matching, red lacy bra and fancy pants today. I feel like I have a firm foundation of luxury for my new retired life. Mid-morning Malc and I had a strawberry Vienna ice cream. He went to the allotment. I put my feet up and finished reading *A Berkshire Christmas* then started reading *The Christmas Book* by *Good Housekeeping*. It still feels a little bit surreal at times that I'm retired. I don't feel old enough, although I did this time last year by the time I'd got to the end of a week. I've had a couple of dreams where Mr Barker has rung up to ask where I am! In the dream I'm worried I'm going to get told off and then I wake up and realise I'm retired!

Nicola rang this evening, I told her about the strawberry Viennas (she has an Iceland in Coventry) and then we talked about what used to be everyone's favourite ice cream, Gino Ginelli's tutti fruitti ice cream. We could not get enough of the stuff but they stopped making it. We bought loads when it came with a colour changing spoon, David and Nicola thought that was the bee's knees and the cat's pyjamas all rolled into one. When I got off the phone with Nicola I wrote tutti fruitti ice cream on a slip of paper and put it in the snowman tin of Christmas ideas.

Saturday 28th April

I painted my nails gold this morning. I usually only get round to doing my nails at Christmas or on holidays or if I'm going somewhere special with Val. I'd just finished when Malc pointed out a goldfinch in the garden. Its red face reminded me of my new undies. Being retired, I can transform myself into a more exotic specimen! It feels like when I was a teenager, before I began work, when I could spend all day putting an outfit together and practising doing my hair. I've been retired for two whole months now.

Val and Henry came for pizza this evening. We considered our three local pizza options and discussed their relative merits; Pizza Hut (good dusty garlic crust, unless they put too much on), Domino's (what Henry calls the ITV of pizza, and Val complains that they do not cook their bacon crispy enough) and Papa John's (the most recent pizza provider to these shores, Val approves of their crispy bacon, Malc dislikes their garlic sauce, they often have quite exciting sides). We ordered from Papa John's in the end. We had a lovely evening just chatting and watching telly. There was a thing on with Mary Beard called *Civilizations on Your Doorstep* and it had the Pitt Rivers Museum on it. Val and I are going to go soon, we haven't been for ages.

Sunday 29th April
Sunday evening work dread is no longer a part of my life. My Sunday evenings are free of thoughts of having to get up early and slog through a day of work. My Mondays are my own. My alarm clock is just a clock now. Every Sunday night feels a tiny bit like Christmas Eve.

Monday 30th April
When I worked in the shop I noticed people buy more bags of salad on a Monday and Tuesday than on any other day of the week. Chocolate is a common purchase on a Friday, as is cheesecake and expensive ice cream. People treat themselves for getting through the week. On Mondays people resolve to be other than their inclination. Why do we repeat these cycles? I suppose they must be comforting in some way. I'm trying to have good retirement habits. Going for a walk every day is one of them. Today I walked to Nash's Bakery. I got a white bloomer and a Mr Blobby biscuit each for Malc and I. We had the bloomer with some spicy parsnip soup for lunch. Parsnip is one of the vegetables I always cook for Christmas dinner.

April reckoning, have I kept Christmas all April?
It's been quite a festive month. It began with Easter Sunday and a lovely family get together much like we do at Christmas. I've seen Lauren, Gail and Carol. I've had Christmas pud for lunch. I've been walking past my favourite fir tree and under the bridge ivy and leaving myself cheering thoughts. I've been to London with Val which was fab and luxurious. I've made mince pies for the spring fayre and I bought Woolly Willy the snowman and some books to help the oldies go to the seaside. I've made coconut ice and I'm writing this while wearing festive red undies. My gold nails match my gold gel pen. But, I didn't think of Christmas on the one day it might have been really helpful when I was worried about Malc's shoulder. I will endeavour to make May a jolly month for me and others.

May

Tuesday 1st May

Today I had a go at making marzipan fruits. Marzipan is undeniably Christmassy. I started with a lemon. I used the smallest holes part of the cheese grater to texture the surface and a clove for the stem. I was pleased with the lemon. I did an orange, pear, apple, strawberry and banana. The size of the strawberry was the same as the rest of the fruit, even though in real life a strawberry would be much smaller. I looked online and this seems to be what all marzipan fruit makers do, even Fortnum & Mason. Their marzipan strawberries have a sugar coating and they also sell a marzipan vegetable patch. I made a note in the snowman tin to make Malc a marzipan vegetable patch this Christmas.

The Labour candidate came round this evening. We are likely to vote for him. He said it was a disgrace that David and Nicola don't have affordable housing where they grew up. After the Labour chap left Malc and I had a rare political discussion. Malc said he wanted freedom. I asked why did he get married then? He said I'd got him there.

Hugh Fearnly-Whittingstall and Jamie Oliver have been lobbying government to tackle the obesity epidemic. Val has got all their cook books. There's one where Hugh is holding a piglet under each arm. Nicola calls Hugh Fearnly-Whittingstall Hugh Firmly-Whipping-Cream.

Wednesday 2nd May

I've been reading Lady Violet Bonham Carter's thoughts on relations from *Good Housekeeping* in 1927 and it made me feel very, very grateful for my lot. It's about time I gave

David a ring. If I ring him today he'll call me back in about a week.

Thursday 3rd May

Gail came round for coffee this afternoon. She prefers to come round when Malc is out. She thinks husbands eavesdrop. Isn't eavesdrop an odd word? Malc is not an eavesdropper. Sometimes it's hard to get his attention when you actually want to tell him something. I got skimmed milk and the smallest, plainest biscuits I could find (rich tea fingers). Gail will only drink skimmed milk and rarely eats a biscuit but she did have one today. She said Len is being quite attentive at the moment so she's wondering if he's up to his old tricks.

Gail once had an affair, which is why she feels she can't be too hard on Len when he strays. She said everybody does it and I said not everybody does it. Malc and I don't do it. Life isn't a Jilly Cooper novel. I sometimes feel unsettled after talking to Gail. We've been friends for a long time, but I sometimes think we might not have much in common other than living in Oxford and having been to the same school.

Sometimes I want to say to Gail why are you thinking something negative when you could be thinking something positive? But I don't. Nicola thinks it's okay to gently challenge people but I'm not sure it's worth the effort when they are so set in their ways. Gail being a pessimist is like the ebb and flow of the ocean. She was a pessimist at school.

When Gail left I came up to the roof and sat on the bed and looked at my Christmas things; the cardboard Santa and reindeer, the boxed Christmas tree and Woolly

Willy. I found the Christmas tree lights and switched them on for a minute, still in their box. Then I went back downstairs, had a chocolate biscuit and looked forward to Malc coming home from work.

When Malc got home we went to vote (Labour as usual, up the workers!) then we got fish and chips from the chip shop.

Friday 4th May
Malc and I had a day out in Reading. It was cold and wet but we made the best of it. They have a bigger M&S than ours. Malc got a new work shirt. I have no work clothes now. This makes me very happy. We had lunch in Zizzi. Since BHS closed Malc dithers over where to eat in Reading. Malc had a calzone with meatballs in it. I had a pizza with artichoke, sun dried tomato, black olives and goat's cheese. Malc looked at my lunch and said 'That doesn't look like the lunch of a Labour voter!' It was very tasty. On our way back to the car we went to M&S again to get something easy for dinner. I picked things I'd usually only get at Christmas. We got smoked salmon and soft cheese to have on brown toast and blackcurrant sundaes for afters. The first time I had smoked salmon was at Val's. Before then I'd only had tinned, and that infrequently. We didn't grow up eating fancy fish. Just because you didn't grow up doing something, doesn't mean you can't take to it later in life.
I gave David a ring this evening but he didn't answer.

Saturday 5th May
The first thing I saw when I opened the curtains this morning was a robin on the bird feeder.

Sunday 6th May
I've got to the wartime part of *The Christmas Book* by *Good Housekeeping* so it's about using potatoes rather than bread. The book covers 1922 to 1962. It's got adverts included. There's one for Pyrex from 1932 saying 'Your women friends will love it'. I do love Pyrex. It can't rust like metal baking tins, it's easy to clean and it lasts for years. I'm still using Pyrex we got given as a wedding present.
David rang. He's fine. I know so much less of the detail of his life than Nicola's.

Monday 7th May
Early May Bank Holiday. Malc and I went to Witney for a day out. He wanted some lightweight summer trousers but we didn't find any despite going round M&S menswear twice and asking in Debenhams (I had to ask, Malc doesn't like to). If Malc had decided he wanted summer trousers last week we could have looked in Reading's big M&S.

We treated ourselves to lunch in Huffkins. I had Burford afternoon tea which is a scone and a classic sandwich (I had chicken and bacon in black pepper mayonnaise and I chose fruit scone out of plain, fruit and cheese. I wasn't expecting the cheese option). Malc had a brie and bacon baguette, followed by a millionaire's shortcake. He said it wasn't as good as the ones I made. This reminded me of when everyone praised his Christmas roast potatoes to high heaven when we were at the Prince Of Wales in January and I felt bad for having got grumpy then. Malc only started eating brie about five years ago at Christmas when he won a cheese selection box in a raffle. He used to not trust cheeses that oozed a bit and he never knew if you could eat the outside bit on a brie. When he won the cheese selection box he got a bit more adventurous with cheese. It's occurred to me that I should buy cheese as a gift this Christmas.

We looked in a few shops after lunch. I got a sugar thermometer from the fancy kitchen shop. I'm going to have a go at making fudge. I've made it before but I didn't have a sugar thermometer, I just did the thing where you test if it's ready by dropping a little bit of the fudge mixture in a glass of water.

Today has been the warmest Early May Bank Holiday since we started having this bank holiday in 1972. We had quiche, sweetcorn and green beans for dinner. It's been a lovely day. Malc says he can feel summer coming. Can you feel summery and Christmassy at the same time? I suppose people in Australia and New Zealand must do.

Tuesday 8th May

I made fudge this morning using my new sugar thermometer. It went well. I made plain fudge and cherry fudge. I spent a very pleasant five minutes eating the last little vestiges of it from the saucepan with a teaspoon after I'd left the majority of it to set.

I went for a walk after lunch (egg mayonnaise and tomato sandwich) and saw that the horse chestnut tree is flowering outside the catholic church with the pointy roof in Littlemore. It looks fabulous.

I browsed fairy lights on the George at Asda website. Then went I upstairs and switched our fairy lights on for a minute. I love both the natural candles on the horse chestnut and the artificial fairy lights. Illumination is a big theme of Christmas.

Wednesday 9th May

I went round to Carol's this morning. She gave me some strawberry bonbons and some pink champagne truffles from her Approved Food order (Approved Food is an online shop that sells short date and out of date food plus the sort of household and beauty stuff that ends up in Poundland, Carol is the only person I know who uses it, she loves it). Carol is a very generous soul, it's rare to leave her house without something she's seen and thought of me. Without even knowing it, Carol keeps Christmas in her heart all the year. I took her some of the fudge I made yesterday. We talked about everything and nothing, the way old friends can.

I walked past some trees shedding their blossom on my way home from Carol's. For a moment it looked like it was snowing and it gave me that feeling of Christmas joy you get when you see something beautiful and otherworldly. Because snow is infrequent here in Oxford it seems magical.

Malc was quiet after dinner (chicken and mushroom pie and green beans). His tomato plants aren't as far along as usual but he's done nothing different this year. I tried to cheer him up but he was having none of it. Sometimes in a marriage you have to let each other be grumpy for a while.

Thursday 10th May

Malc is over the tomato plants disappointment. He got some biggish plants from a house by Donnington Bridge for twenty-five pee each. His smaller ones can now take their sweet time he says. He is considering the purchase of some Silent Roar lion dung to keep cats off the garden. He keeps reading me snippets of the Amazon reviews. My favourite is the man who wrote 'I gave a packet to my brother and so far so good for him too' because I wonder how you return that kind of favour. I also liked the very specific detail one reviewer gave of 'Put down two boxes on a garden. 25x12 feet. Within 30 mins 2 cats left a mess' because it sounds like a maths problem and infers that within 60 minutes 4 cats would make a mess. In a 50x24 foot garden you'd have double the trouble too.

I read about what canapés to serve with cocktails in the early 1950s in *The Christmas Book.* What me and Malc call party nibbles Val and Henry call canapés. You can't beat a puff pastry sausage roll or slice of pork pie in Malc's opinion. I like a bit of quiche and a cheese board.

Friday 11th May

I met Val in Summertown and we looked in the charity shops. I got three books; *Debbie Thrower's Christmas Handbook* (she is a BBC radio presenter), *Christmas A Biography* by Judith Flanders and Desmond Morris's *Christmas Watching*. We also looked in the cake shop windows. There is no Greggs in Summertown but they do have alternatives. We saw a couple who live in Val's road arguing outside Farrow & Ball (swanky paint shop). We heard her say that French Grey would absolutely depress her if she had to look at it every day and Verdigris Green was the only sensible choice. He said maybe they should compromise and get Arsenic. She gave him a very poisonous look then saw Val and said hello.

We went back to Val's for lunch because she was waiting for a Waitrose delivery. Dave from Waitrose was waiting for her when we got there (we weren't late, he was early). He was an absolute delight and told us all about the posh houses on Boars Hill he delivers to. The order had no substitutes. Val told Dave she does occasionally use other supermarkets but Waitrose is her favourite.

For lunch Val warmed us up a chicken, asparagus and courgette risotto (from Waitrose of course). The asparagus wasn't as chunky as Val would have liked. I thought it was fine. Malc came and picked me up from Val's. He gave Val some spinach and spring onions from his allotment and we had a cup of tea before we left. The ring road was snarled up because it's Friday but Malc keeps a cool head in the car. Being a gardener encourages patience.

Nicola rang this evening. I told her about my book finds. She said she is reading *The Diary of a Bookseller* by a Scottish man called Shaun and it's very funny. She says the library is a book supermarket and your own bookshelves are your book larder. When I got off the phone with Nicola I made a note in the snowman tin to buy her a book token for Christmas. I know she'll love spending it.

Saturday 12th May

Malc and I went to the big Heyford Hill Sainsbury's for compost. There were drifts of white blossom petals from the trees by Ashurst Way. It looked like snow at a glance. We had a leisurely browse. I remembered that now I'm retired I don't have to rush to squash things into weekends because I have all week too. It's such a freedom. Malc got some summer trousers. We got some fresh crusty bread for our usual Saturday lunch of bacon sandwiches. There was an old couple in the bakery section who used to come into the shop I worked in. She asked him twice to get a baguette but he just looked at her confused and then she said French stick and he caught on.

After lunch Malc went out into the garden. If I know Malc he'll be out of compost again before the day's out. I did an Iceland online shop for delivery tomorrow morning. I looked to see if they had asparagus. They didn't. They did have a lemon roulade so I ordered one. I have time now to browse the online shop as well as the real shop!

I decided to begin decluttering the spare room. I'm sure this is every woman's retirement project. I took three bags of stuff to the Emmaus charity shop, including a never used foot spa which neither Malc nor I can remember buying or being given. Maybe if a room is used as a spare room for long enough a foot spa will spontaneously appear in it.

Malc ordered us Papa John's pizza for dinner. I like it when he takes charge of a meal.

Sunday 13th May

I finished reading *The Christmas Book*. I loved the old adverts for Oxo, Fox's Glacier Mints and Cinzano. I took two bags of stuff to Emmaus including an infrequently used facial sauna. I do remember where this came from, Nicola won it in a raffle and has taken it to none of the places she's lived since she left home. For a while Nicola was so keen on entering competitions that she entered competitions for things she didn't especially want. She once won a disposable barbecue that sat in the shed for years.

Monday 14th May

I went to Mum's for coffee this morning. Mum has stopped going to balance class which is what she used to do on a Monday morning. She says she knows all the exercises and can do them at home so it's a waste of a morning. I'm not sure she does do them at home though, watching her get up out of a chair is quite a performance now.

Mum got out a pack of mint Viscounts and a pack of Drifters. You never stop attempting to feed your children. David and Nicola always leave with something from the food cupboard. I no longer need write mint Viscounts since the orange ones were discontinued. We still get customers asking for them, I mean we did, before I retired.

I had a Drifter which used to be David's favourite thing to get out of the vending machine at Temple Cowley pools after I'd taken him and Nicola swimming in the summer holidays. When I got home from Mum's I made a note in the snowman tin to get David some Drifters. My

Christmas shopping will be easy this year with all these little inspirations!

Tuesday 15th May
Debbie Thrower's Christmas Handbook said dried cranberries should be available in a good supermarket and are a new ingredient! It was published in 1997. It has recipes from Mary Berry, before *The Great British Bake Off* started. People go cake baking crazy nowadays when *Bake Off* is on. I won't be working in the shop this autumn to see it. I can be baking along at home instead. I made some butterfly cakes. I'd gone off cooking before I retired, having to rush home from work and get dinner on, but now I can take my time.

Wednesday 16th May
Malc has had an argument with someone on the internet! He is in a Facebook gardening group and someone said that rhubarb is poisonous in August. Malc put them right (the leaves are toxic all the time, the stalks are not, but won't taste as nice in late summer) and they got the hump with him big time. Why can't people on the internet have good manners? It is very rude to call someone a smug dickhead just because they know more about rhubarb than you.

Malc went out to the allotment. He said vegetables don't argue with you. I cleaned the kitchen while listening to Trans-Siberian Orchestra's *Christmas Eve And Other Stories* album. I find it incredibly stirring and energising. While I cleaned the kitchen I thought of all the delicious Christmas food I've cooked in it. I love opening the fridge on Christmas Eve and seeing everything ready for the next day. I love it when the crisps cupboard also has nuts, Ritz crackers, Twiglets and KP Cheese Footballs in.

Thursday 17th May

I met Carol for a coffee in Wetherspoons. It's nice to have room for more Carol in my life. When you retire you can spend more time with people. You sometimes find yourself wondering if they want to spend more time with you? I don't wonder this with Carol or Val or Mum, but I do with Gail. Carol and I had planned to meet just for coffee today but we were busy chatting until lunch time and then we saw someone having chips so we decided to stay in Wetherspoons for our lunch. Carol said if we don't enjoy ourselves now, when will we? Carol is good at enjoying herself.

Malc is not having a good week. He had to come home from work on the bus. The car has conked out. It's safe for now in the care home car park and he's going to see to it tomorrow. I felt a bit guilty that I'd had such a lovely day and had fish and chips at lunch. My generation of women feel guilty more easily than men do, we've been trained to be unselfish and to put the needs of others, especially men, before our own needs. I reminded myself that Malc chooses to still work. I reminded myself that my life is what I make it and if I'm happy I can help others be happy. I cooked Malc sausage, mash and peas for dinner.

Friday 18th May

When I went to fill the kettle this morning something went ping and now the lid won't lift unless you prise it up with a knife. Malc got the car seen to. It cost £220 and had a faulty starter motor. It's been a day of sitting about waiting for the garage to ring. We got it back too late to go and buy a new kettle. While we waited to hear about the car we watched some DVDs. We watched the Christmas episode of *One Foot In The Grave* in which Victor gets hundreds of garden gnomes delivered by mistake. We have no gnomes. Malc says flowers should be the star of the garden.

Nicola rang in the evening. We got talking about holidays and she said her favourite machine in the games arcade at the seaside was the lucky egg machine. You put in ten pee and a mechanical chicken would cluck then lay you a plastic egg with a small toy inside. You always got something for your money, unlike other machines which would just swallow it up.

Saturday 19th May
We went to the big Currys in Botley this morning for a new kettle. The assistant asked us if we wanted to take out an extended warranty. Malc said no, for a thirty quid kettle he'd take his chances. We test drove it (as Malc says) as soon as we got home. It's see through and lights up blue. Malc says it's like our own aurora borealis in the kitchen. I said maybe we'll come down in the middle of the night and find a circle of polar bears sitting round it, like in the Christmas Coke advert. Malc said polar bear poo might keep cats off his flower beds.

Some Saturdays I used to feel tired from the week at work but feel I had to do something or I'd wasted a day off. Now I can have a lazy Saturday and know I have plenty of time to go somewhere in the week. I made myself a hot chocolate this afternoon and I browsed eBay for Swarovski crystal Christmas things. I use eBay for window shopping when I don't want to go and stand in front of windows! There is a lucky egg machine for sale on eBay. This is probably an impractical Christmas gift for Nicola but I'm watching it anyway.

Sunday 20th May

Malc and I went to Wyevale Bicester Avenue garden centre. We looked at garden furniture. We've got some old folding chairs Mum gave us that she and Dad bought in the fifties. Malc has a romantic ideal of playing his guitar outside on summer evenings. This is a bit like when we were first married, he thought of us reading the papers on a Sunday morning and eating crumpets at a pine table in the kitchen but what we mostly did was be in bed knackered from the week at work. In later years the kids got us up early demanding to be fed, watered and entertained.

At Wyevale they had royal wedding themed cardboard cut outs and lots of Union Jack plates, cups and napkins (yesterday was Harry and Megan's wedding). I thought her dress was boring, I'm sorry but there it is, I've said it.

We've got our eye on a bistro set; two chairs and a table in cream wicker effect plastic that can be left outside all year round, but it's five hundred pounds so we're going to think about it for a week. I think Malc is still getting over having to pay to get the car fixed. I browsed the Christmas sale stock (I love doing this!) and got some Christmas pudding flavour fudge.

Monday 21st May

I went to see Mum this morning. She's going to The Tree in Iffley tonight with her friend Liz Strange. It's a great name. Mum's friend Bridget has given Mum a leaflet for her to give to me about the Cowley WI which meets at the St James Church centre once a month. I asked Mum if Bridget goes, Mum said no. A lot of people are trying to fill my time at the moment, their intentions are good but I'm the expert in what I want to do with my retirement. Sometimes I pretend to myself that I'm in a Jane Austen novel and have never had to work, this gets me in the right mood for choosing what I want to do with my time.

This afternoon I made Christmas cinnamon sugar star bread. It takes hours because of all the having to let the bread dough rise stages. Luckily I have hours and can read my book while I wait. When Malc came in from the allotment he said the house smelt nice. We had bread and cheese for dinner and star bread for dessert. It tasted wonderful but could have been neater. It was good for a first attempt.

Tuesday 22nd May

I made chili non carne for dinner. It's non carne because it's made with Quorn mince not animal mince. Malc didn't notice.

I finished reading *Debbie Thrower's Christmas Handbook.* It had a whole section on mail order shopping. When it was written in 1997 we didn't have internet shopping!

Wednesday 23rd May
I said gladioli to Malc because yesterday he asked me to say gladioli to him. He is going to plant some this morning. I went to buy digestive biscuits for Malc. There is now a huge variety of McVities digestives; thin, with caramel, with banoffee flavour caramel, with coffee flavour caramel and lemon sandwich creams. I got dark chocolate digestives. On my way home I saw Tamsin from next door and we walked home together. She looked a bit sad. After we'd talked about which is the best Poundland in Cowley she said they had had no luck yet on the baby front. She had thought she might be but then her period started. I told her to give it time, she's only young. She said 'Am I?' and I reassured her that she was indeed young. I said to think of a year as twelve chances to win the baby lottery, and think of the fun of buying the tickets. Then I blushed because I'm not very good at being bawdy. She was smiling weakly by the time we said goodbye.

When Malc came in from the garden for lunch (beans on toast) he asked if I wanted to go to the Christmas shop at Lechlade for an afternoon out. I said yes please. This is very unusual, I'm generally the one who suggests excursions and I tend to suggest them a week in advance to give Malc time to get used to the idea of not being in the garden or at the allotment. We parked easily in Lechlade and I had a wonderful browse of the Christmas shop. They have a lot of imported German decorations and a lot of Gisela Graham items. I saw a wonderful glitter lantern with Victorian carol singers inside. The woman running the shop gave me a leaflet and said she could post things to me. I bought a lovely white paper honeycomb angel.

After the Christmas shop we went to Hillier's garden centre. Malc is like a boy in a sweetshop in a garden centre. It's lovely to see. I think still finding things to be enthusiastic about in your sixties keeps you young in the head. I think in a marriage you have to give each other's hobbies your full support and also leave each other room for interests that aren't especially shared. Malc has no interest in cooking. I like flowers and vegetables but hay fever stops me getting really stuck in outside. Malc bought some white pumpkin seeds called Polar Bear F1 that I said looked Christmassy.

When I got home I wrote this diary and put my paper angel on the little bookshelf up in the roof. I've created a sort of Christmas nook for myself up here. It made me think of Jo in *Little Women* who loves to take a big bag of apples and read in the attic.

Thursday 24th May

I had coffee with Gail in the Asda café this afternoon. I told her we'd been to the Christmas shop and she asked if I'm becoming a bit obsessed with this all-year Christmas lark? Then she asked if I'm using it to fill a void left by work? Then she said how are things with you and Malc? She didn't really listen to my answers and went on to tell me how things were with Len. She said Len is so handsome and such a charmer it's not surprising he's got a wandering eye. This is not my experience of Len. He is of average attractiveness at best and he barely speaks when I see him, although that might be due to him knowing Gail is one of my best friends and him being ashamed of his past behaviour (but I doubt it). I wanted to ask Gail when Len was last charming to her but I listened instead. If you have a good imagination, you can weave such magic around a man that he can never possibly live up to it. Gail thinks he's become more surly in the mornings. Does this sound like the actions of a charmer to you Dear Diary?

I went to bed early and read *Christmas Watching* by Desmond Morris.

Friday 25th May
I went to see Mum. She presented me with a gift she had bought at the Yarnton garden centre antiques place. It was not however an antique. It was a money box in the shape of a mother and child pair of pink hippos with the child hippo being brushed among soap suds. When Mum buys me a thing, she always buys Val a thing of equivalent value. I look forward to seeing what is the thing Val gets.

Nicola rang, she's hoping to finish a cross stitch of a Ravenclaw badge (from Harry Potter) this weekend. When we got off the phone I wrote cross stitch for Nicola on a little bit of paper and put it in my snowman tin of Christmas present ideas.

Saturday 26th May
Big news today is that Ireland has voted to make abortion available. I have no patience for people who try and make women's lives harder by denying them the choice about motherhood. Choice is key, babies are some women's dream and other women's nightmare. Let us decide for ourselves. I thought of Tamsin next door and hoped next month would be the one. I don't think I'll ever be a grandmother. David has had quite a few girlfriends but

always gets cold feet around the two-year mark. Nicola has plenty of male friends but hasn't had a steady boyfriend for three years. Writing this, I realise I've assumed that you need a stable relationship to have a child and that isn't true! Come on Pam, keep up, it's 2018!

I spent the afternoon making cinnamon star bread. It makes the house smell so Christmassy. Val and Henry came round for dinner. We ordered from the award-winning Indian place on Rose Hill that we all like. I showed Val and Henry the pink hippos money box Mum gave me. Val will tell me what equivalent value gift she gets. Henry thinks I should take it back to Yarnton Antique Centre and tell them I already have one and ask if I can swap it for something else. It is an unusual item. It reminds me very slightly of the NatWest pig money boxes you see at every antiques place.

Sunday 27th May

I was woken in the night by a thunderstorm. Malc slept through it. He's an admirably heavy sleeper. I got back to sleep by imagining I was doing a Christmas food shop in Harrods. When I got up I went to the Co-op for milk and also got olive bread and paprika flavour crisps. Malc and I always get olive bread if they have it, because quite often they don't have it. Paprika is an excellent crisp flavour that you don't see often enough. Paprika makes me think of Christmas markets, I once had sliced potatoes with paprika, bacon and onion at Hyde Park's Winter Wonderland and they were delicious.

We went to Halfords and Malc bought a new satnav. He researched it thoroughly online first, and told the man in the shop he had done so to cut short his spiel. We're going to visit Viv and Eric (Malc's older sister and her husband) next month. They live in Norwich and we go to them once a year. It's the longest car journey we do.

Next we went to Notcutts garden centre to look at their garden furniture. We didn't come to a conclusion about what we want. I like what we saw last weekend at Bicester Avenue garden centre. We decided to think about it for a bit longer.

Malc has had his eye on the Acers (known to less botanically minded people like me as Japanese maples) for ages. Today was the day he took the plunge, with my encouragement. We chose an Acer each and we got a bag of John Innes number 2 compost and some aniseed balls for Mum. My Acer is called Orange Dream. The man serving us said it was his favourite. I held them all the way home and then we re-potted them. Nicola once said to me that retirement should be a time for realising your dreams, one of the borrowers told her this. She often chats to borrowers browsing the self-help section of the library and does a little joke about could they find what they were looking for, because the first step to self-help is helping yourself to the right book. Nicola says the self-help browsers are often full of wisdom.

We had fish finger sandwich for dinner. I wondered what is the most Christmassy fish? Malc said it's probably smoked salmon. Prawns are Christmassy but they aren't a fish.

Monday 28th May
The hunt for garden furniture continues. Malc has done some research online but he wants to see it in real life before we decide. We went to Burford garden centre today. We're starting to see the same garden furniture with different brand names attached to it on little metal plates at the back of the chairs. Burford garden centre is the Harrods of the garden centre world. It's expensive but lovely. We didn't buy anything, we drifted around imagining having lots of money rather than a just about adequate retirement income and some savings which probably won't go as far as we think. We went on to Burford itself and looked in the shops and had lunch in Huffkins. I had chicken and bacon sandwich and fruit scone (the Burford afternoon tea). Malc had the full English breakfast. I love the look of delight on Malc's face when a full English breakfast is put in front of him. He's like a little boy on Christmas morning. His face goes all glossy like the baked beans.

We went in a shop with loads of classic British clothing, they had Liberty fabrics and Arran jumpers, that type of thing. A shop assistant chatted to us and told us her recently retired husband (seventy-two) is getting under her feet so she has got a part time job in the shop. I said I had retired earlier this year but she ignored me and continued telling us how her husband never puts anything back where he found it. I couldn't help noticing, as she delivered quite a long list of marital grievances, that she had put her red lipstick on in the style of the Joker from Batman. David used to have a poster of the Joker on his wall. At the back of the shop there were some reduced-price Christmas jumpers and sweatshirts. There were a lot of green sweatshirts with kittens in Santa hats in size small. I saw a white, red and green fair isle jumper with Christmas trees, reindeer and snowflakes in size medium. The shop assistant goaded me into trying it on. It was a nice fit so I bought it! Malc said he bets they don't sell many Christmas jumpers in May.

When we were outside the shop Malc asked me if he ever gets under my feet. I said no, because he doesn't. I said it's lovely having all these days out together now I'm retired.

Tuesday 29th May

I popped round to Mum's and gave her the aniseed balls we got her at Notcutts. She was very pleased with them. She said it's getting harder and harder to find aniseed balls. I like the colour of them. Malc has some dahlias the same colour, a deep blood red. It occurred to me you can give someone a stocking filler gift at any time of year. Mum told me that today is National Biscuit Day. She opened a pack of chocolate Hobnobs. She told me about Mrs Matthews, a neighbour who eats mostly biscuits with the occasional tin of tomato soup. She said there's nothing wrong with her, she just can't be bothered to cook. Mum is having cod's roe on toast for her dinner today. When I got home I made a note in the snowman tin to get Mum some more aniseed balls at Christmas.

I finished reading Desmond Morris's *Christmas Watching*. It has facts about Christmas that I've never heard before, such as;

Almonds were believed to be protective against heavy drinking.

You can make a wish while eating your first spoonful of Christmas pudding.
Baubles are thought to protect against the evil eye.

Wednesday 30th May
Malc noticed that we can no longer see St Luke's Record Office from our back bedroom window. Every spring the leaves on trees grow to obscure it and then every autumn it reappears again when the trees lose their leaves.

Nicola rang. She has entered a competition to win dinner with Jamie Oliver! Malc really likes his food, I really like his passion for the sugar tax. I don't like the music he plays in his restaurants or his confusing description of salad as funky.

I started reading *The Country Diary Christmas Book* by Sarah Hollis. It has some very beautiful pictures.

Thursday 31st May
I met Val in town. She gave me a book called *Christmas Dodos* by Steve Stack. It's lovely to have a little collection of Christmas books to read, it's my rainy day fund of entertainment. I've discovered that while I was at work I wasn't missing much on daytime telly. Mum has given Val a gift of a Sooty money box which is in Mum's view the equivalent of a pink hippo money box. Mum told Val that *The Sooty Show* was her favourite show (Val doesn't remember this) and so she got the Sooty money box for her then had to find something nice for me too.

Val and I had lunch in The Alchemist. We had fish and chips. The batter was black! It was delicious. When I told Malc he said if anyone gave him black battered fish he'd send it back to the kitchen.

May reckoning, have I kept Christmas all May?
My Christmas reading is continuing, so far this year I've read thirteen Christmas books and I have a few waiting to be read. I've made marzipan fruits, fudge and twice I've made cinnamon star bread. This may become a favourite recipe. I've had some real treats of days out with Malc, most notably the Christmas shop at Lechlade but also Burford and Witney (two Huffkins lunches in one month!). I encouraged Malc to get the Japanese maple he's always wanted. I got a Christmas jumper. Be your own Father Christmas! I've also put a few ideas for Christmas shopping in the snowman tin. I've taken some things to charity shops.

I've spent time with Mum, Val, Carol and Gail. Christmas is meaningless without people. I've been cheered by the candles on the horse chestnut trees. I've watched blossom fall off fruit trees as if it was snowing, and collect in drifts on the pavement. I've listened to Trans-Siberian Orchestra who would make even the Scroogiest ears melt with festive joy.

June

Friday 1st June

I've accidentally bought pollock fish fingers instead of cod ones. I got distracted in Iceland. They never state pollock on the front of the pack, they say Omega 3 fish fingers, probably because pollock quite frankly sounds like bollock and puts people off. It puts me right off.

Today is the start of half Christmas advent. I had a browse of advent calendars online. There are so many now, it's not just chocolate, you can get a calendar filled with pork scratchings, tea bags, marzipan, nail varnish, jam, scented tea light candles, Baileys' Irish Cream or Pringles!

Saturday 2nd June

We saw two goldfinches having breakfast on the bird feeder while we were having our breakfast. I love how slow Saturday mornings are now I've retired. We had a lazy day. We had fish and chips from the chippy for dinner then Malc watched *Casino Royale* while I read *The Country Diary Christmas Book.* I skipped over the knitting patterns for toy hedgehogs and jumpers. I am not now, nor do I ever expect to be, a knitter. There was also a bit about how to make pot pourri. I'm not a fan of pot pourri or scented candles. I like cooking smells but not artificial smells.

Sunday 3rd June

Malc and I went to Thame, to a guitar show at the Spread Eagle Hotel. He bought a resonator guitar for £200! At the care home they have a music room and occasionally in quiet moments Malc pops in and plays the guitar. He has two guitars in the spare room too, one acoustic and one electric. I sometimes think if the gardening bug hadn't got Malc maybe the music bug would have done. On wet days he retreats to the spare room and I hear a bit of Wings' 'Mull of Kintyre' or Rod Stewart's 'Maggie May'.

Thame is a sleepy market town, we do them very well in Oxfordshire. We had lunch in the Spread Eagle Hotel's dining room. The waitress was very welcoming even though we weren't staying at the hotel. I had the beef roast dinner, Malc had the chicken roast dinner. The Yorkshire pudding was perfect. I had to ask what Semi Freddo was (a dessert option). The waitress didn't know so she went and asked, it's a bit like ice cream she said. I had imagined it being half a Freddo chocolate frog.

When we got home we took the plunge and ordered a garden furniture set. We're getting the Ascot bistro set (a table and two chairs) from Bicester Avenue Wyevale for £599. This will complete Malc's dream of sitting and playing his guitar in the garden. I took a tax-free lump sum when I retired so we're having a bit of a spree!

Monday 4th June

I went to see Mum. She has nothing planned to do tomorrow so I tried to encourage her to do something, maybe go and get new shoes in town. Each day is an opportunity and an adventure for me at the moment but I suppose there comes a time in retirement when retirement is what you're used to.

This afternoon I ordered myself an advent calendar with fancy French jam, like Val buys! I should have been more organised and got it for the start of June and my countdown to half Christmas but it has only just really occurred to me that there is half Christmas to be celebrated and I can celebrate it. Your world is largely made up of the thoughts you think about it. Especially when you're retired and you sit about thinking quite a lot. I want to have a head full of good cheeriness, not doom and gloom.

Tuesday 5th June
I met Lauren for lunch. The new supervisor is still being slow to bring change (I mean actual coins to whoever is working on the till to give customers, not making things different). Tracy has been skiving again and Dylan has got a girlfriend with a big bosom. Lauren looks lovely but tired. I'm sure the pressure to make something of yourself when you're young is more pronounced for women now, compared to when I was in my twenties. The pressure then was to find a husband.

I went to Poundland for some Frusli. I like the name Frusli. When I was walking home I thought about Reggie Perrin and his idea that you should retire when you're young and healthy, then later in life you can work when you're old and knackered.

I read some of *The Country Diary Christmas Book* this evening. In an extract from *The Diary Of A Nobody* Christmas cards are posted early for Christmas on the 21st December, this is not what we mean nowadays by posting early. I wonder what I'd call this diary if it was a proper book? The Diary Of A Retired Woman Trying To Stay Cheerful? The Diary Of A Christmas Fan? The Diary Of An Average Retiree Who Likes Christmas? Pam's Ponderings? Thankfully this diary will stay up in the roof behind the Christmas tree box so I needn't come up with a snappy title.

Wednesday 6th June
Malc and I went to Wallingford today. We had lunch in The Dolphin which does an over fifties discount every Wednesday lunchtime. We had beef roast dinner followed by chocolate ice cream. It's lovely to be in the pub in the middle of the day, it feels very decadent.

After lunch we had a browse in the antiques place. We saw some Pifco Noma Victorian Christmas lights, just like the ones we had when Val and I were little. Malc said they'd probably be dangerous now. I said modern LEDs are better anyway, but after I'd said it, I realised this is a thing that Malc thinks. Malc said we could get them tested, he said he could ask his mate at work. I said it's nice to leave them in the shop so other people can see them.

Thursday 7th June
My jam advent calendar arrived today! We have a jam backlog! We'll open two doors for the next few days. Malc and I opened a window each. There was apricot and mango jam behind the one I opened and lemon and yuzu jam behind the door Malc opened. We had to Google yuzu. It's a citrus fruit which is a bit like a small grapefruit and it can take a plant ten years to bear fruit.

Friday 8th June
Malc and I opened two more jam advent calendar doors this morning, he found raspberry and lychee, I found seedless raspberry, which felt like an anti-climax but is actually my

favourite flavour jam because it's in the middle of jam doughnuts. We had toast with raspberry and lychee jam for breakfast.

Malc suggested we go out somewhere. I suggested Bourton on the Water. We set off at ten, when all the people who have to work from nine to five have arrived at work. There were lots of coaches in the car park. We had a look round the model village then a look round the actual full-size village. The model village is very accurate, although not accurate enough to represent the enormous number of tourists with fancy cameras. I can't blame them, we're lucky to have this close by. We had lunch at the Old Manse Hotel restaurant. I said to Malc that I'll forget how to cook at this rate! We've had some lovely meals out since I've retired. I had macaroni cheese and chips, Malc had black and blue burger and fries. We sat at table number eight and ordered our food at the bar. I always have a pen and paper in my handbag for this sort of thing. We took our time over lunch. Slowly the tables round us filled up. There was a well-behaved child at the table next to us when we left.

After lunch we looked at the shops behind what Malc calls the main strip of Bourton on the Water. In the antiques place there was a Swarovski crystal Christmas tree, like I've seen on eBay. We left at four to get home before rush hour. Oxford has a lot of traffic.

Some days you go out somewhere and you're going through the motions and not really enjoying it, and some days, like today, you're really in it, absorbed and relaxed. I had the sense of an opportunity to have a good time realised. This is what I want retirement to be.

I had a cheque for £25 from ERNIE waiting for me when I got home!

Saturday 9th June

Day three of the jam advent calendar backlog. Malc got apricot and lavender, I got rhubarb and strawberry. We sniffed both then had the rhubarb and strawberry on our toast. Malc thinks lavender may be a step too far. Malc said one of the best jams he'd ever had was rhubarb and ginger. I made a note for the snowman tin. Two blue tits on the bird feeder were having their breakfast at the same time as us.

Nicola messaged me to say it is 199 days until Christmas! She has entered a competition to win a year's supply of wine, even though she doesn't like wine. She said she'll take it to parties. Val rang, she knows what a yuzu is. They've had yuzu in Summertown for ages she said. She wanted to know if Malc and I want to go to Duxford on Sunday 15th July to an air show. We said yes please so she'll sort out the tickets.

I read the chapter called Christmas Fare in *The Country Diary Christmas Book*. I'm glad we don't eat brawn and tongue nowadays.

Sunday 10th June

Day four of the jam advent calendar backlog, we've got up to window eight open. I found orange and cinnamon this morning, Malc got grapefruit and dragon fruit. We had the orange and cinnamon on our toast. We are broadening our jam horizons lately!

We nipped to Homebase on the rubbish retail park. Malc got a 17-inch saucer for a plant pot. It cost £5.34! Then we went to Aldi for bananas and diet lemonade. We found some whiskey that had won an award for Eric's birthday gift and some Irish whiskey cake. Then we came home and Malc trimmed the holly bushes.

We went to The Tandem Hungry Horse for dinner. It has been refurbished but isn't that different. It has different pictures and a wooden floor and new furniture. We both had roast dinner. The big Yorkshire pudding and roast potatoes were good. I thought about how each extra item you add to a roast dinner increases the complexity for the cook, but not the pleasure for the eater by the same amount.

I finished reading *The Country Diary Christmas Book*. The pictures were lovely and it had some interesting bits about Edwardian life. It wouldn't suit me though, I like central heating, online grocery shopping and I'm not very good at entertaining myself by doing embroidery or flower pressing. I like flowers in three dimensions.

Monday 11th June

Day five of the advent calendar jam backlog and we've got up to window ten open. Today's jams were apricot and bergamot, then sweet orange and passion fruit. We had sweet orange and passion fruit on our toast.

I went to the bank to put my £25 Premium Bond cheque in. The immediate deposit points were both not working so I had to queue for over ten minutes. There was only one cashier working but three other staff were there too. The man in front of me was wearing a pink shirt and was impatient. He kept jiggling. He let wind just before it was his go to be served. I'm sure people never used to let off in the bank. When I got home I logged in to my National Savings and Investments account and changed how I get prizes. It's nice to have a cheque but it's easier for the money to go straight into my bank account so I don't have to go to the bank again. Since January 2015 I've won ten prizes of £25! Thank you ERNIE! And I'll always be very grateful for the 1981 win that got us our loft conversion. The roof room is starting to feel like a Christmas grotto, I have Woolly Willy on the bed, my cardboard Santa and Reindeer I got just before I left work, a white honeycomb paper angel, plus we store the Christmas tree and decorations up here.

I started reading a new Christmas book, *Christmas Dodos*, which is about Christmas things that are dying out, for instance liquorice pipes. Although, Malc got one in Bognor and you can get them from Amazon.

Tuesday 12th June

Last day of the jam advent calendar backlog. I opened window eleven which was cherry and blackberry. Malc opened window twelve which was white nectarine and peach. Next year I'll make sure I've got my half Christmas advent calendar ready on the first of June. I'll also buy some half Christmas advent calendars for other people. Malc and I are really enjoying the little luxury of fancy jam in the morning.

I popped round to Mum's. She wants to go on holiday to Cornwall. I asked why Cornwall? It's because she likes *Poldark*, a BBC TV programme which is currently very popular. Bridget is getting brochures. They are off to Eastbourne this month, at the same time as Malc and I are off to Norwich.

David came for dinner. I considered making a Black Forest gateau then decided to buy a frozen one instead. There's no point in retiring and then creating work for yourself. David has to work weekends so gets days off in the week. Despite living closer David visits less than Nicola. It is always lovely to see him. We ordered Chinese from House of Tim. David saw the jam advent calendar and I explained half Christmas. He said it's the sort of concept which he's amazed hasn't permeated to retail. One of David's school reports read 'David is a smart boy but doesn't apply himself well'.

Wednesday 13th June

Malc got up in a very good mood this morning. He created a little song while I was opening the jam advent calendar, to the tune of 'I Saw Three Ships'. Malc sang 'I saw some jam come sailing in, come sailing in, come sailing in, I saw some jam come sailing in on half Christmas advent in the morning.' We had cherry and elderflower jam on our toast today. Then we stood and watched a blackbird in the cherry tree preening himself. Mornings which can start slowly are so much better than mornings when you have to rush out of the door for work.

Malc phoned his sister Viv late morning, to confirm we'll visit her and Eric from Sunday to Tuesday. He went to the allotment after lunch. Malc doesn't like to be away from the allotment for too long and likes to leave things ship shape before he goes. He says if you don't leave it ship shaped, it can soon turn shit shaped! Malc never usually swears.

Having so much jam about the place has made me think of scones. I popped to the Co-op for glacé cherries and whipping cream. This afternoon I made cherry scones, with big glossy cherries shining like rubies.

This evening I finished reading *Christmas Dodos*. It made me nostalgic for Woolworths. How Woolworths went but WH Smith keeps going I'll never know.

Thursday 14th June

I think I might be a bit addicted to Topics. I've had five recently. Prior to the last couple of weeks, I think I last ate one when I got it in a selection box at Christmas many years ago.

I met Val in town today. She has bought me a Fulton umbrella, as used by The Queen! She was getting herself one, ready for when we go to London in July, and thought she'd treat me too. I'm lucky to have such a thoughtful sister. In July we're seeing *Austentatious* at the Savoy Theatre. It's an improvised Jane Austen play that is made up on the night! Val said there will be so much football on (because of the World Cup) that we need to find some good stuff to do this summer. Val said she's delighted I've caught up with her and retired.

We had lunch in Gourmet Burger Kitchen. Val had the Hey Pesto chicken burger, I had The Chickdriver and we both had chunky skin-on fries which are Val's favourite chips. We overheard a very crude conversation. A couple who I'd judge to be in their mid-fifties were bickering about the frequency with which housework was done and with which marital relations were had. I heard her say 'Yours hang so low now you could take your pyjama bottoms off downstairs and dust the stairs on the way up with your swinging nut sack.'

Malc has drawn Morocco in the world cup sweepstake Carol's daughter Donna is organising at the care home. I tried to be interested but have no idea if Morocco are good at football or not.

Friday 15th June

Malc went off to the allotment this morning singing a made-up song about soft fruit, to the tune of Tom Jones' 'Sex Bomb'. I have rarely in my life been a sex bomb, but once or twice might have managed to be a sex sparkler.

I popped round to see Mum. She has dyed her hair with a hazel colour dye. It's come out different colours and looks like she's had highlights, it's a bit more exciting than her usual hair. She's pleased with it. Her and Bridget are off to Eastbourne with Shearings' coach holidays tomorrow. I won't get Mum a thimble from Norwich, she already has one.

When I got home I browsed Christmas thimbles on eBay. There are some that look like little shops. I checked the weather for Norwich, it'll be similar to here.

Nicola rang. She has entered a cake design competition run by Tesco and Mr Kipling. You can win £500 and a tour of the factory!

Saturday 16th June

Malc went to the allotment this morning, he'll not be able to go for a few days due to Norwich. I popped round to

Gail's for coffee. Len's family are very hard work according to Gail. She says they've never really accepted her. She said I wouldn't know, being a stranger to marital strife, (I did want to contradict her here, Malc and I have had our moments, as have any long-term couple, married or not), but once you've had a really big barney with your sister-in-law about her brother's infidelities it's very hard to come back from that and feel like a happy family. Gail said she's loved Len as well as she could but it wasn't enough. I said that maybe Len was going to be like this no matter which woman he was with. Gail changed the subject.

On my way home I popped to B&M to get sweets for the journey. I got a big box of wine gums, like you'd get at Christmas. A woman was trying to avoid going back to the front of the shop for a basket but she dropped her biscuits. She said 'Oh my days! Today is not my day!' and sighed. Then she dropped her Pringles. I picked up her biscuits. I always get a basket in B&M, the variety and pricing in the sweets/chocolate/biscuits/crisps aisle makes it impossible to buy only a couple of things. I got a carton of Cadbury's Roses. Whenever we leave Viv and Eric's I pop some chocolates and a thank you card on the bed for them to find when we've gone.

I packed to go to Norwich. For dinner we had chicken kebab and chips from Olivia's Greek. We're getting in a holiday mood!

Sunday 17th June

We set off for Viv and Eric's at a quarter to eight. I collected motorhome names to help pass the time. These are some of the daftest ones:

Swift Challenger
Elddis Autoquest
Swift Kon-Tiki
Ace Equerry Jubilee
Ace Diplomat
Autotrail Cheyenne
McLouis Ducato

We saw lots of Royal Mail vans claiming they safely deliver 16 billion items a year. Malc wondered how many get thrown behind a hedge by a disgruntled postie? They don't put that on a van. Or how many times they deliver a little red card instead of your item.

We stopped at South Mimms services for an early lunch. I had a tuna Subway sandwich, Malc had a Whopper from Burger King. We had two wees each. I like service stations, all those people on their way somewhere, it does you good to break your journey (and break your routine).

Viv and Eric were looking out of the window for us when we got to number 10 Hazelnut Avenue. Malc and Eric shook hands. Viv kissed us both and Eric kissed me. By the time you get to our age you have lots of people you don't see often, but it's very nice when you do. We had two cups of tea in the garden. Viv and Eric are the kind of people you can pick up with just where you left off. Before long you're all talking about the big stuff, like health scares and money, and all the small stuff like books you've read and what's on telly. We're never short of conversation. Today we wondered when did barley sugar stop being readily available?

Eric pointed out new acquisitions in the garden since we visited last year. He's got a third cold frame! His alstroemerias are an absolute picture and his bird boxes are well used. For dinner Viv did a roast turkey, chipolatas, roast potatoes and parsnips, Brussels sprouts and stuffing balls. It was basically a Christmas dinner. At Christmas they always go to Eric's family. He has two sons who both have children, so they like to see the grandkids open their presents. For pudding we had a Christmas pudding and cream! Viv had been saving it specially.

I helped Viv do the washing up. We always have a giggle when we get together. She tells me stories about Malc as a boy. Malc was asleep before I was. It was a long drive. I wrote this diary in bed, I've bought it with me, it's become such a habit. Unlike Malc's allotment it is portable. I think everyone who's retired needs a source of optimism.

Monday 18th June

We had a really lovely day out in Great Yarmouth with Viv and Eric. We saw the sea. We walked on the pier. We heard a small boy say 'Bollocks!' to a claw machine then get told off. We went to Harry Ramsden's for lunch. I had an excellent cod and chips. I hope Mum and Bridget are having a whale of a time in Eastbourne. We certainly are in Norwich. When Eric is being catty Viv says 'don't be ericaceous', meaning acidic. She told a very funny story about when he bought a faulty umbrella in TK Maxx and took it back. It wouldn't automatically open and the assistant was umming and aahing about giving him a refund. He said he'd been sold a stick rather than an umbrella and he needed his money back to save for a rainy day.

In the evening Viv did us a snacky buffet. I've rarely had so many quiche choices. Malc and Eric watched England v Tunisia in the World Cup (2-1 to England). Viv and I sat in the garden and chatted while flicking through a big pile of magazines from Beryl next door.

Viv is very fond of an Ulster Weavers tea towel she has which is getting a bit worn, I'm making a note here and when I get home I will put a note in the snowman tin. In less than six months I'll do my Christmas shopping!

Tuesday 19th June

Beryl and Bernard from next door came in for morning coffee, they do this every Tuesday. I like it when you visit people and see a little snapshot of their lives, while getting to be a part of it briefly. Beryl brought a homemade lemon drizzle cake and a box of M&S peach and passion fruit Jaffa cakes. They have lived next door to Viv and Eric for four decades, we've met them many times. They have a sign by their front door which reads 'Never mind the dog, beware of the owner'. Bernard and Eric play golf together. Bernard took a photo of us all in the garden and I wondered how many more Norwich trips Malc and I will make. When we first met Beryl and Bernard, I was pregnant with David and Nicola was a toddler.

We left Norwich after lunch. We stopped at a big Tesco in Bishops Stortford and had coffee, used the loo and got some milk. Malc had a look at the gardening things. I looked at the clothes. We don't usually go to a big Tesco. When we got back in the car I felt slightly sad in an end of holiday way, then remembered this is not a holiday where I have to go back to work the next day.

When we got home we both had a jam advent calendar window to open. I got pear and Mirabelle plum, Malc got pineapple and passion fruit. Malc said he likes to imagine they have two big spinning wheels in the jam factory, with all the available fruits and spices listed, then they give them both a spin, see where the pointers land, and that's how they choose their jam flavours.

I thought about doing the washing then decided to leave it until tomorrow. I browsed Christmas thimbles on eBay again. I think Mum would like one with an angel or a floral spray. I want to buy one soon and not leave it until December because Malc says the prices will go up. He said no-one will be buying Christmas thimbles in June, but once December hits they'll be looking. I saw some lovely non-traditional shaped thimbles, a set of three tiny Christmas shops, made by Birchcroft who are quite a big name in the thimble world. These are probably a bit too modern for Mum but I like them.

Wednesday 20th June

Today is our 44th wedding anniversary. We had a lazy morning then Malc went to the allotment for the afternoon and I did the washing. Malc came back from the allotment with a superb bunch of flowers for me; blood red, marshmallow pink and neon yellow dahlias, with gypsophila. I don't usually like cut flowers but these are stunning. We ordered Chinese from House Of Tim tonight to celebrate our anniversary. Nothing says togetherness like sweet and sour chicken balls. It was lovely being a June bride all those years ago.

Thursday 21st June
Malc is back at work today. He says one day a week isn't overdoing it. I went to Savers and got corn plasters for Malc. I browsed the nail varnish then decided to see what I've got already at home. Some days marriage is being given a bunch of flowers and some days it's buying corn plasters.

Friday 22nd June
Mum was back from Eastbourne at lunch time so I popped in. She and Bridget had a lovely time in Eastbourne with the exception of one night when they didn't like the entertainment in the hotel (Mum said it was like a very low budget Jane McDonald who couldn't carry a tune in a bucket) so they retreated to Bridget's room and watched the telly.

Mum said if Donald Trump came over here she'd tell him to bugger off, back where he came from (in the news today it is reported that Trump may visit us, by which I mean the UK, not me and Mum). Paradoxically, what Mum is saying is what Trump is saying to illegal immigrants. He has been separating children from their parents at detention centres and has had to repeal this awful policy today. I have no words for how inhumane this is. The bond between parents and children is sacred. It is evil and inexcusable to separate a family.

I'm reading *Christmas A Biography* at the moment. It's a bit more highbrow than most of the Christmas books I've read. The word Christmas used to mean the holly, ivy and other greenery that people decorated their houses with.

Saturday 23rd June

I got up early because we are having our garden furniture delivered between 7 a.m. and 9 a.m. They called at 7:50 a.m. to say it would actually be between 10 a.m. and midday so I got up early for no reason. We took delivery of the Ascot bistro set just before midday. Malc assembled the table then we sat outside and had bacon sandwiches. I had hay fever and shook my fist at a honeysuckle. This is why Malc does all the gardening by the way, I'm not lazy, it just sets off my hay fever. Malc is very excited about eating in the garden and playing his guitar in the garden.

I ordered some chocolate coins from A Quarter Of, which is an online sweet shop that Eric told me about when we were in Norwich. He likes Floral Gums and can only get them from this online shop. I made a note in the snowman tin to get Eric Floral Gums for Christmas.

Sunday 24th June

Today is half Christmas Eve! I opened the final door of the jam advent calendar (apricot and orange). It's been lovely having a tiny jam or marmalade every morning, it's like a bit of holiday hotel luxury.

I decided to make some mince pies. I left Malc doing the crossword and I went to the shop I used to work in to get ready rolled pastry. Someone new was on the till who I don't know. The new supervisor was in there but didn't recognise me. This place was such a huge part of my life and now isn't but I don't feel sad, I feel released. Next I went to the local Co-op, they stock mincemeat all year round.

I love the look of homemade mince pies. I like the little places where the mincemeat has escaped, creating a shiny patch, sometimes with an escaped raisin or bit of peel. I'm using my Gran's (Mum's Mum's) pastry cutters; pale blue, two crinkled edge circles, with the smaller one fitting inside the larger one. It makes me think of marriage, how as a woman you're meant to be the smaller one and fit inside the larger one. People expect retired men to have hobbies, but not retired women so much, and if they do they're expected to be focused on the family, things like knitting and cooking. I sprinkled the mince pies with icing sugar. There was a tiny sweet snowstorm in my kitchen.

Malc and I ate mince pies in the garden. A goldfinch watched us.

Monday 25th June

Today is half Christmas Day! In six months we'll be at Val's celebrating actual Christmas! It is very warm today and will reach twenty-eight degrees C. I had an urge to go for a walk so set out early and went to Florence Park. I get a feeling of calm in the park. I like to look at the huge fir trees. It got very warm so I decided to come home. I went in the corner shop on Campbell Road. I got an ice-cold Ribena. One of life's great pleasures is a very cold drink on a very hot day. The number 16 bus arrived just as I was coming out of the shop so I caught it home instead of walking. I feel very grateful for free bus travel. Tomasz Schafernaker says we're having a heatwave all week. I will walk early or late in the day. I have the freedom to do this now I'm retired. Malc was sat out in the garden when I got in. He had dozed off after doing the crossword.

Val and Henry came for dinner. We told them all about our Norwich trip. We had turkey burgers, crinkle cut chips and coleslaw. Later on we had Christmas pudding and coffee ice cream for dessert. Henry said the coffee ice cream was very invigorating.

At bedtime I finished reading *Christmas A Biography*. I feel like I could go on *Mastermind* with the specialist subject Christmas now!

Tuesday 26th June

Today is half Boxing Day! It is still a heatwave. I have had a lazy day, staying out of the heat. I've run out of Christmas books to read so I'm re-reading *A Christmas Carol*. The bit where Marley's ghost talks about the chains we forge in this life sticks out for me. I can make my life any shape I want now I'm retired. I need to forge the chains I want.

I wondered if I have managed to keep Christmas for half the year? I think I could do more to spread cheer to other people. I will try. The next half of the year I think of as the slope leading up to Christmas. We've gone past the longest day.

Lucy came round to see to Malc's corn. When she left he skipped about like Gene Kelly. Looking after your feet is a must at our age.

It is too hot for cooking so we had ham and cheese on crackers, crisps and pickled onions for dinner, a bit like a Boxing Day meal. We went for a walk round our Crescent at half past nine when it was cooler. Everyone has upstairs windows open.

Wednesday 27th June

It is still a heatwave. Malc tried to think of somewhere for us to go which has good air conditioning. He is wearing his summer pants, which are briefs. He usually wears a cotton boxer short. We went to Lidl. We got tomato, pesto and goat's cheese focaccia for our lunch and a pipe of what Henry calls their ersatz Pringles. It's lovely going to Lidl during the day when they have a well-stocked bakery rather than in the evening when they've run out of things.

We'd just got home when Tamsin knocked. We had a bit of a chat about how warm it was. She said she likes a bit of sun but Tom's not keen. She'd taken in a parcel for me, which was my chocolate coins. I'm glad these weren't left outside the back door, they would have melted. I put them in the cupboard under the stairs which is the coolest bit of the house (nineteen degrees Centigrade according to Malc's big thermometer).

Germany is out of the world cup. This is today's big news according to Malc. Val rang, they can't find their gazebo and she wondered if she'd lent it to us and forgotten. I said no, we just have the big parasol. She said they've only used it once.

We sat in the garden this evening. Malc was wearing his vest and I removed quite a few greenflies from his hairy shoulders. They were hanging about like aphid epaulettes. We had some chocolate coins. They made me feel Christmassy despite the heat.

Thursday 28th June

Today is still a heatwave! I told Malc to take it easy at work today. I have been retired for exactly four months. I love not being woken by an alarm clock. I love deciding what to do with my days. I painted my toe nails for the first time in decades (probably since I was a teenager). I'm seeing my bare feet a lot in this heatwave. Also, I have time now to be frivolous! I painted them bright red! They look both festive and summery.

Carol's daughter Donna was at work today at the care home. She brought Malc an ice cream on his afternoon break. Carol and Donna are good at making the best of things. Gail has a chest freezer upstairs in her box room, which is making the upstairs hot. Most people would have put it in the garage. This is Gail all over.

Friday 29th June

Nicola is coming to stay this weekend. She's going on a hen night tonight. Fiona, who she was in the Brownies with, is getting married to the oldest brother of Steven Knight who went to Cubs with David. I got some picnic type bits for today's dinner. Nicola only had a cheese and onion pasty and a Twirl before she went out.

After Nicola had gone Malc asked if I think Nicola and David are missing out by not being married. I said I didn't want to be one of those parents who thinks that their kids' lives are less valid if they do different things to what we chose to do.

I browsed jam on the internet this evening. I very much enjoyed the cherry and Christmas spices jam I got in the jam advent calendar. There is a Tiptree Christmas conserve and a Mrs Bridges Christmas preserve I'm considering. They are pricey. Once jam goes over £2 it starts calling itself preserve or conserve. I wonder what happens if you stir some cinnamon into some normal everyday jam?

Saturday 30th June

I heard Nicola come in just after two in the morning! It's like having a teenager in the house again! Nicola says she doesn't see the point of late nights. David says he does.

This morning I popped out to the Littlemore post office. I had to return a shirt bought for Malc online. Malc has quite long arms which David refers to as his monkey arms. Today is yet another day of heatwave and everything looks nicer in the sunshine. There are lots of bikes left on the streets, it's a new thing where you can use an app on your phone (if you have a fancy phone) to hire them. Usually all these randomly placed bikes make the streets look scruffy, but in the sunshine they look like two wheeled possibilities to take you somewhere fun, like Hinksey Outdoor Pool or Florence Park.

Nicola didn't get up until eleven. She said last night was mostly fun but she wouldn't want to do it all over again tonight and she doesn't like dirty Martinis. Nicola definitely has a need for alone time to recharge, she gets it from Malc. She saw my red toenails, 'Mother, why are your feet showing off?' she asked.

I did us all a bacon sandwich for lunch (while Malc and Nicola watched Nigella cook fluffy oat pancakes on BBC One). We ate in the garden. Nicola said the Ascot bistro set was exactly what she'd expect people our age and class to buy. I have no idea if this means she approves or disapproves and Malc and I like it so it doesn't matter.

Nicola and I went to see Mum/Nan in the afternoon and Malc went to the allotment. Mum/Nan said she's seen pictures of hen nights in the *Daily Mail*. Nicola said it wasn't that sort of hen night, Fiona works in IT. Her mother-in-law-to-be volunteers in a museum. I realised I have no job to define me now. I am a happy has been.

We ordered Domino's pizza for dinner. The website said it would be delivered by Mohammed the reliable. He lived up to his name, it only took twenty-five minutes and was kept upright. There was nothing much on telly so we watched DVDs of *Elf* and *Carry On At Your Convenience*. We all had a Cornetto. Nicola said Cornetto is Italian for little horn.

June reckoning, have I kept Christmas all June?
Most importantly, for Christmas would be hollow without family and friends, we've seen many of our most loved people; David and Nicola both visited, as did Val and Henry. We've been to see Viv and Eric. I've seen Mum and Gail and Lauren. I've not seen Carol this month, which I'll remedy soon. All these people are the links in my chain of happiness.

Malc and I have celebrated our 44th wedding anniversary and we've been our own Father Christmases with the Ascot bistro set, his resonator guitar, chocolate coins and a jam advent calendar to count up to half-Christmas. It's delightful having a tiny jam-based surprise in the morning. Raspberry and lychee is not a jam I'd expected but it was very tasty.

This month I've not had the time to be either bored or gloomy or at a loose end (pre-retirement people warned me that these would be my enemies), but if I had, I think

I'd find that having a pile of Christmas books is a sturdy fortress against this.

Sunday 1st July
We got up early and went to the car boot sale at Tetsworth. Nicola got some books. Malc got a plant pot and a box of screws. I got a silver container for putting After Eights in on the table. I used to think it was the height of sophistication when I saw it in the Argos catalogue. We all had a Mr Whippy ice cream.

A few stalls had Christmas decorations, but there was nothing unusual. I saw a single of Paul McCartney's 'Wonderful Christmastime'. I bought it when it came out. Nicola and David were small then and would dance round the room to it. It's a short cut to feeling festive for me. I'm fairly sure I still have it in a box in the spare bedroom.

Nicola left after lunch (cheese toasted sandwich dipped in salad cream, one of her all-time favourites) and the house felt quiet. It's been a lovely weekend.

Monday 2nd July
The heatwave continues. It was 29°C today! Val has booked us the Strand Palace Hotel for Sunday night in London, it's really near the theatre where we're seeing *Austentatious*.

Malc and I nipped to Tesco. We enjoyed their air conditioning. We got a strip of plasters (Malc is wearing in new shoes), some Coors Light and Aberdeen Angus burgers for dinner. We ate outside. Malc said we chose a good year to put the bistro set plan into action. I put dried cranberries in the coleslaw and called it Christmas coleslaw. It's a challenge to make summer Christmassy but there will be ways of doing it.

Tuesday 3rd July
Another day of hot weather. We had quiche for dinner with marrowfat peas. Malc said it was undoubtedly quiche weather. As I write this Malc is watching England v Colombia in the bedroom with all the windows open and only his vest on.

I've been in the spare room, trying to do some decluttering but actually just looking through the box of singles. I listened to Paul McCartney's 'Wonderful Christmastime' twice. I also found an old Index catalogue from autumn/winter 1996. They had some good value Christmas trees. Index was Argos's less successful cousin, it got swallowed up by Argos in 2005. Carol worked in the one inside Littlewoods for a while. They kept running out of things and sending people to Argos, but quite a lot of the time the people had come from Argos and been sent there! If Amazon.co.uk was a catalogue it would probably be as long as the Oxford English Dictionary!

Wednesday 4th July
England won on penalties last night so we're playing Sweden on Saturday in the quarter finals. This morning I successfully added cinnamon to jam. I put marge on our toast, then sprinkled on cinnamon, then put jam on top and spread it into the cinnamon with the knife. Malc is calling it Christmas toast.

Today is muggy. We need some rain. Malc has put some old plant pots with water in outside for birds and cats to drink out of. I did an Iceland delivery for tomorrow night so Malc has bread, milk, crisps and other things for the weekend. I'll be off to London on Sunday with Val! I do love a little getaway with Val. I have to remember not to feel guilty. The allotment is Malc's thing, mine is trips with Val. Any pleasure you can give yourself in retirement, you should give yourself in retirement.

Thursday 5th July

I have had a shopping spree this morning, buying Christmas books on eBay! ERNIE emailed me to say I have won £25 on the Premium Bonds. I decided to spend it on something frivolous and not be like Scrooge and Marley. I chose a second-hand bookshop with good feedback and searched for their Christmas books then put them in order from lowest price to highest. I have bought second hand copies of;

The Life and Adventures of Santa Claus by L. Frank Baum
Brandreth's Christmas Book by Gyles Brandreth
A Right Royal Christmas: An Anthology by Hugh Douglas
A Child's Christmas in Wales by Dylan Thomas
The Puffin Book of Christmas Stories edited by Sara and Stephen Corrin
Grumpy Old Christmas by Stuart Prebble
Calm Christmas and a Happy New Year by Beth Kempton
Christmas Fare by Alison Harding and Judith Holder
*The Christmas Pocket Bible: Every Christmas rule of thumb at your finger*tips by Guy and Steve Hobbs.

I have never bought nine books at once before! Some of them only cost two pounds. I'm usually careful with money, not because I'm a Scrooge, but because I like the idea of leaving money to Nicola and David. Nicola is buying a house with a uni friend, it's cheaper in Coventry. David has little hope of getting on the property ladder without help from us. Premium Bonds money is money that is unexpected, so it sort of doesn't count. I do love losing myself in a Christmas book.

Friday 6th July

Another day of heatwave. It is absolute luxury to not have to go out to work in the sweltering heat. Malc went early to the allotment. He's got an arrangement with Ken today. Malc has watered both their plots first thing and Ken will water them both again tonight.

I had a fabulous surprise in the post today, Val sent me a book! It's Maria Hubert's *Jane Austen's Christmas: The Festive Season in Georgian England* and I read it all afternoon. Val is re-reading *Northanger Abbey* at the moment.

Malc got very grumpy this evening about the heatwave (he was doing so well). He took his trousers off and watched the second half of Brazil v Belgium in his underpants on the telly in our bedroom (Belgium won). We had cheese and onion pasty and a strawberry split ice lolly for dinner.

Saturday 7th July

It's going to be 31°C today! Val rang, she's going to pick me up at ten tomorrow morning for our London jolly. She's had her Ocado delivery (no substitutions, delivered by Scott in the lemon van) so Henry will be well provided for while we're away.

I packed the least amount possible for London but I keep going back to my bag and adding extras. The first of the Christmas books I ordered on Thursday arrived, *Brandreth's Christmas Book*, so I started reading it. It reminded me that I love the carol 'Away in a Manger'.

England beat Sweden 2 – 0 this afternoon in the World Cup. Malc watched it downstairs in his underpants with the curtains closed.

Sunday 8th July

Val and I are going to London to see *Austentatious* at the Savoy Theatre!

This morning Val and I got off the Oxford Tube coach and walked up the Bayswater Road looking at the artists' exhibited paintings. I saw some lovely London snow scenes. We got a bus from Marble Arch to The Strand. We left our big bags with the concierge at the Strand Palace Hotel (our home for the night, but check in isn't until three) and we walked to Leicester Square, Piccadilly Circus, Regent Street and Carnaby Street. Every time I visit these locations with Val it feels like we add a layer to them, they are the places we go to have fun. Regent Street is shut off to traffic every Sunday in July this year.

We had lunch in Aubaine, a French restaurant. I had chicken burger in a brioche and fries. Val had fish and chips. It was very good or trés bien as Val said. After lunch we saw a Mariachi band on Regent Street.

We went back to the hotel at three to check in and for a shower before meeting at five for pre-theatre dinner. It's been so hot that the crooks of my elbows have been sweating! We had dinner in Leon. We both chose fish finger wrap. We went to Superdrug and browsed in its air-conditioned loveliness.

The theatre bar was hot. We had a strawberry Mr Darcy daiquiri which we enjoyed. *Austentatious* was very funny. They improvised a Jane Austen novel. There were two musicians playing the music and they played 'Football's Coming Home' on the violin and pianoforte. The play ended in a lesbian wedding. Val and I agreed we would go and see *Austentatious* again, it will always be different. They are such clever performers. Going to the theatre feels a bit Christmassy, even in a July heatwave. The first time Val and I went to the theatre was to see *Cinderella.*

We had a drink in the hotel bar before bed and some vanilla ice cream, served in a Martini glass! I had a text from Malc before I went to sleep. He said he's been watching *Prime Suspect* and he hopes Val and I are having fun.

Monday 9th July

It took me a while to get to sleep last night even though I was really tired. The absence of Malc at bed time is unsettling. I got up just after seven and met Val by the lifts at eight. We went to Dishoom for breakfast. I had egg naan, she had bacon naan and a sausage on the side. I still had my loyalty card with one stamp from last time so got it stamped. I need to eat two more breakfast naans to get a free one. This is a good retirement project.

After breakfast we walked round TK Maxx. I got a gingerbread house tin filled with jelly beans for a pound. We went to Covent Garden and sat and watched the world go by. We shared a chocolate orange Ben's Cookie. Ben's Cookies started in Oxford and have branched out. They are delicious.

We had lunch at the hotel. I had smoked salmon bagel and Val had chicken and pesto sandwich. Both were served on a wooden board rather than a proper plate. This is what Malc would disparagingly call a fancy London way.

We got the bus to Marble Arch and saw loads of landmarks. We got off and had a look in Selfridges (we ate free samples of seaweed crackers in the Food Hall) then got the Oxford Tube coach home. Time spent with Val always goes fast. We egg each other on to have a good time. We both think the other deserves it. It's refreshing to have some luxury and see some different things.

I was wondering what to cook for dinner when Malc came home, having been to collect a prescription from Superdrug and buy shorts and lighter pants from Peacocks. He'd accidentally bought size large pants (Malc is undeniably an extra-large). He insisted on trying to wear the too small pants (in spite of the fact he'd bought new pants to not be too hot). I watched as he grumpily tried to wriggle an extra-large bottom (and the bits round the front!) into a large pant. I suggested he go commando and he did! This heatwave is changing people's behaviour. I have missed my lovely husband. He said Ken's red-flowered runner beans have dropped their flowers due to it being too hot.

We watched the news. Boris Johnson has resigned as Foreign Secretary. Malc said he gets the feeling we haven't seen the last of him. David went through a phase of not brushing his hair.

Tuesday 10th July

While Malc was at work today I thought about our summer holiday which for reasons of economy we'll probably have in September. I sometimes feel a bit restless when I've been to London. Should we go to old reliable Bognor again? Or should we venture to a new seaside? Bognor has a comfortable charm and layers of memories. Are all seasides on the south coast of England basically the same and you should just pick one early in your marriage and stick with it? Or are we missing out by being creatures of habit?

Malc watched the Belgium v France football match. He said Belgium are playing very well. Malc is watching more football than usual because this World Cup has coincided with a heatwave. It's nice having him indoors more, it's usually a thing which happens in winter due to the cold and wet.

Wednesday 11th July

Tonight England play Croatia in the World Cup semi-final. Malc was up and off to the allotment early to water it before it gets too hot. He went on his bike and on the way back he cycled past a skip with some Christmas decorations in! They were in an old brown and orange WH Smith carrier bag. He spotted some gold balls peeking out of the top and brought the bag home! We emptied the bag on the bistro set table. There are six big gold balls, some smaller red and green balls and there was a partly used box of Woolworths luxury Christmas cards! I'm glad Malc was eagle eyed this morning. We have enough balls for our Christmas tree so Malc suggested we hang these ones outside! He got some string and hung the gold balls from the pergola. It looks like a festive Newton's cradle! The red and green balls I hung from a black obelisk which Malc is growing a star jasmine up. We sat and admired our handiwork and had a Mars ice cream.

This afternoon we went to M&S in Witney so Malc could look at their underwear. He has admitted defeat in trying to fit into the size large Peacocks pants he bought by mistake. I have permission to use them as dusters. Malc found some briefs which claim 'keeps you cool, dry and fresh all day' and I made sure he picked up the size XL. The man who served us asked if we were going to watch the football. We said yes. I do not have football fever but I think I've caught football sniffles!

Malc wanted to stop for an early dinner to avoid traffic. He doesn't like being caught on the A420 when people have just finished work, it gets snarled up around Eynsham. Kick off tonight is at seven. We went to Frankie and Benny's. The one in Witney is nice (Nicola once got bacon on a veggie breakfast in the one in Greater Leys). I had chicken parmigiana. Malc had meatballs. The waitress was lovely and told us about a special early bird offer so we had chocolate brownie and ice cream for pudding. Today has been a lovely day. Let's hope the football makes it even better!

Thursday 12th July

England lost to Croatia and will not be playing in the World Cup final. The best we can do now is come third. Football is like Christmas, everyone who wants to can take part and get excited about it. Then when it's over you feel a bit flat.

I need to make something for the cake stall at the care home summer fete on Saturday. I gave Carol a ring because her daughter Donna does a lot of the organising. She said to make something which won't melt. I'm not going to muck about with chocolate in this heat. I went for a walk to think. I went to The Goldfish Bowl and browsed their fascinating fish. I went in Silvesters, which is my favourite hardware store in Oxford. I saw some reasonably priced crystal trinket boxes in the shape of an apple. I decided to make Dorset apple cake for the fete. When Malc came home he said that Stacey who is new has been practising cheese straws for the fete. I never thought of a savoury but it's a good idea.

We watched the local news. Donald Trump is at Blenheim Palace for dinner and people are protesting about it. Malc is binge watching *Prime Suspect.* I think everyone I know is hiding something well.

Friday 13th July

It's a Friday and I'm not tired. I have not had the energy sucked out of me by a working week (although the heat has been a bit of a bugger at times). I made two Dorset apple cakes, one for the fete and one for Malc and I.

I finished reading *Brandreth's Christmas Book.* It suggested playing hunt the thimble, something I haven't done for many years. Thimble is the sort of word that sounds weirder the more you say it. I bought a Christmas thimble for Mum from eBay, it is made by Birchcroft and has a wonderful retro Father Christmas and gift laden sleigh design.

Saturday 14th July

Val phoned this morning about the picnic she's doing for when we go to the air show at Duxford tomorrow. She'd just had her Ocado delivery (Louis in the lemon van, free Ocado Life magazine not available, which she said was okay, it would only have been about risotto anyway and she got a free Coca-Cola World Cup football). Val wanted to know if Malc likes pastrami. It was a substitute for corned beef. I said I'm sure he will.

Early afternoon we went to the summer fete at the care home. I asked Malc if he minded going to his work place on a weekend. He said no, he knows he can pack in this job whenever he wants and he likes how the events they run pay for extras like seaside trips for the residents. Carol was running a tombola. I won a tin of corned beef! Val will laugh when I tell her tomorrow! I also won a box of sugared almonds. Malc won some Radox bubble bath.

I bought some cheese straws from the cake stall. I'll take them to Duxford tomorrow. My Dorset apple cake had been sold. The book stall was quite big, Malc pointed out *This Morning's Countdown to Christmas* by Richard Madeley and Judy Finnegan so I got that. Before we went I arranged with Carol to meet up on Tuesday.

It was only two o'clock when we got home from the fete. Time seems to go slow in the care home. Malc went to the allotment. I went to TK Maxx to look for a hat to wear tomorrow (it's going to be warm). I tried on a lot of broad brimmed hats and overheard two women talking about the boyfriend of one of them. He's got a bit obsessed with the football and he shouted 'It's coming home!' on the completion of intercourse! I got a straw hat from George at Asda, it's got gold sparkly thread and a gold hat band.

England came fourth in the world cup. We ordered a Chinese takeaway for dinner. Malc had beef and tomato, I had sweet and sour chicken balls. Malc watched *Immortals*. It's a good film. I started reading L. Frank Baum's *The Life and Adventures of Santa Claus*.

Sunday 15th July
Duxford flying legends air show with Val and Henry.
Val and Henry picked us up at nine to go to the Duxford Imperial War Museum for the flying legends show. There were eleven Spitfires! There was little traffic on the way to Duxford. Henry's car has good air conditioning. It was well organised getting in to the air show. There were lots of hangers to look in, which was good because you needed a break from the sun. There was mainly WWII stuff (some good tanks) but also a hanger with non-war stuff which included Concorde. My highlight of the day was Concorde. They have Concorde 101, the test plane and for £2 you can get on board and walk through it. It's smaller than I imagined. I always wanted to go on Concorde but never did. Now I have, sort of. Val and I talked about doing a New York Christmas shopping trip. She said Henry wouldn't like New York (too busy) and she could get us the flights with her air miles so we'd just have the cost of the hotel. This sounds wonderful. I like how being on a day out and relaxing makes you think of other excursions.

For lunch we had a lovely picnic organised by Val. She got the ratio of pickle to cheese just right in the sandwiches. Henry brought four chairs in his big boot so we were very comfortable. We had proper cutlery. All the cheese straws got eaten. Malc said he'd tell Stacey on Tuesday. The fly pasts began while we were eating.

It was about 29°C and we all got hot. We looked at the stalls selling aeroplane tat, sunglasses etc. We had some more picnic before the drive home and we let some of the traffic dissipate. We talked about family and holidays and all sorts of things. I'm glad Malc and I get on with Henry and Val, it doesn't always work like that. We got home at 9:20 p.m. Malc had a text from Ken saying he'd watered the allotment and all was well. I don't have work in the morning to get up for. Malc doesn't have to go to work until Tuesday. We have the time to have the time of our lives.

Monday 16th July

I've been reading *The Life and Adventures of Santa Claus* this morning. It's very detailed and original. It's written by the man who wrote *The Wizard Of Oz*, which is a beautiful film. The bit where it changes to colour from black and white is magical. You get bits of your life that feel like that sometimes, like when you walk up the steps of a Concorde, or you walk down the aisle on your wedding day, or you watch your son and daughter splash about in the paddling pool in the summer holidays against a perfectly blue sky.

I went to see Mum this afternoon. She and Bridget have been to Henley. They like the charity shops. Mum bought me a Wedgwood Christmas ornament which

Bridget spotted, it is blue and white jasperware and is a white Christmas tree on a blue background. It's very delicate and lovely. As well as going to the shops Mum and Bridget went on a boat trip. Mum said she didn't think much of it, they only saw the river and the town, but Bridget seemed to enjoy it.

Tuesday 17th July

Today is a nice temperature, around 23°C. I met Carol outside WH Smith at Templars Square at ten. We went in Poundland. I got some hazelnut and raisin Frusli. I used to buy the apple and cinnamon ones for my break at work but I've switched to hazelnut and raisin now I've retired. Carol gets her cereal bars in bulk from Approved Food when they have a flash deal and thinks buying Frusli from Poundland is extravagant! People's shopping habits fascinate me. Many, many years ago Malc and I had an argument because I bought an onion and he had plenty on the allotment. He said I only had to ask and he'd provide all the onions I needed. He has been true to his word ever since and I've never purchased another onion.

Carol and I went to Wetherspoons for coffee. She said the care home fete raised £263 and Donna was pleased. The activities co-ordinator will hire a minibus and take the residents that are fit enough to Bournemouth. I asked Carol which she thinks is the best seaside. She said Bream Sands and Weymouth. I've been to Weymouth but not Bream Sands. We stayed in the Wetherspoons for lunch. We both had ham and cheese panini and chips. I said it could do with a bit of Branston pickle and Carol agreed but they don't have any in Wetherspoons so she nipped out and got some from B&M! She gave us both a big dollop. We agreed that Branston pickle is a thing you have to have at Christmas. Carol said Christmas is good for you, especially when you remember lovely little slices of it at times of the year other than December.

Wednesday 18th July

Malc and I went to Lidl this morning. We bought goat's cheese and pesto focaccia which we had for lunch. We spent thirty pounds on things we don't usually buy and don't really need. This makes going to Lidl like doing a Christmas shop! I bought some Turkish delight for Mum.

I went for a walk this afternoon. The delicate lilac of the blackberry blossom reminded me of a dress Nicola had when she was at primary school. It was lilac Broderie anglaise and she loved it. She didn't want to wear anything else. I tried to find her another one when she grew out of it but couldn't. We didn't have internet shopping in those days. When I got home I made a note in the snowman tin to look for a similar dress.

Thursday 19th July

I went out early and bought a five pack of trainer socks from Peacocks today. The heatwave is continuing. My trainers are from the Pavers catalogue and I think they're snazzy because they are gold but David says they are old people trainers. The Pavers catalogue has an enormous load of shoes for women and then just four pages of black, brown, blue, green and beige shoes for men. Next I walked to the Helen and Douglas House charity shop on Rose Hill. I bought a book, *Christmas Angels* by Rowan Dobson. I spent the afternoon reading it (sat in the garden, admiring our decorated pergola and obelisk). It has photos of angel decorations and a little bit about each one. Then I came up to the roof before Malc got in from work and wrote this diary. Walking, reading and writing are the anchors of my life now and I like to do them every day.

Nicola rang, she has entered a competition to win a year's supply of ice cream. I hope she wins, she really likes ice cream.

Friday 20th July

I went to see Mum. She has got a new jumper with blue hummingbirds on. She was delighted with the Turkish delight I got her from Lidl. She opened it while I was there and we both had a piece of rose and a piece of lemon. The first time I ever had Turkish delight was at Christmas from a wooden box that Mum had won in a raffle at the Conservative Club. Neither Mum or Dad ever voted that way but they would go to the club once a year for a Christmas drink with Dad's friend Jasper and his wife Marjorie. She was always known as Marjorie and never Marge. Val and I only met her a dozen times but she made quite an impression because she was always dressed to the nines. At Christmas Jasper and Marjorie would come in and say hello before we were left with the babysitter (Yvonne Cox from over the road, I only remember her babysitting at Christmas, Mum and Dad rarely went out in the evening). In the summer we would go on a picnic with Jasper and Marjorie who didn't have children. One Christmas Marjorie was wearing a necklace which Val and I thought was diamonds but Yvonne said it was just paste and this made no sense to us because the only paste we could think of was wallpaper paste or fish paste.

We had some rain this evening after weeks of none at all. Malc was delighted to not have to go and water the allotment. I'm going to lie in bed reading with the sound of the rain outside. I love doing this.

Saturday 21st July

I finished reading *The Life and Adventures of Santa Claus*. His immortality was well established and he made parents his deputies, which is tidy. Speaking of tidy, we went to the tip this morning and disposed of three old chairs and two old rugs. We were not allowed to dispose of our four old paint tins. We have to take them home and fill them with soil. The tip will no longer take liquid paint. The man telling us explained this at great length implying we were daft not to have known already. I could see Malc getting impatient.

Tom and Tamsin next door have got a hot tub. A hot tub is just a glorified paddling pool if you ask me but Malc and I are discovering this summer that everyone except us thinks they're the bee's knees. This afternoon we went to Peacocks and got Malc a pack of trainer socks. We ordered pizza from Pizza Hut for dinner. Malc watched *300*.

Sunday 22nd July

We went to Heyford Hill Sainsbury's and Malc got olive green shorts. Then we went to Next on the retail park and he got a short-sleeved pale blue shirt and then M&S where we got a melon because the woman in the queue behind us in Heyford Hill Sainsbury's mentioned melon so Malc decided he wanted some. Malc can be very suggestible when it comes to food shopping. I got some jam doughnuts. When we got home Malc decided he'd rather have a doughnut than some melon. He does eat well usually, he's brought potatoes, onion, beetroot and peas home from the allotment recently. He did the crossword and I browsed Wedgwood Christmas jasperware on eBay. It is wonderful to have a lazy Sunday with no work on Monday to play on your mind and spoil your peace.

Monday 23rd July

Today is another heatwave day, about 29°C. I lay on the sofa reading *Christmas Fare* by Alison Harding and Judith Holder. It's a book which combines pictures of Victorian and Edwardian Christmas cards with writing about Christmas food from the past and recipes for it. I made myself hungry reading about mince pies and tarts.

Tuesday 24th July

The heatwave is continuing, it's 28°C today. I lay on the sofa reading *Christmas Fare* and made myself hungry reading about shortbread. I have not had a long summer break from work since nineteen-eighty-three! I have spent the past thirty-five summers in full time work. It is so lovely to have a summer of freedom.

This afternoon I browsed cotton nighties on the M&S website. I made chili non carne for dinner. Malc said it doesn't feel like chili con carne weather. He's right but I really fancied it.

Wednesday 25th July

Today is Christmas in July. This isn't really a thing in England. I bought myself a pink broderie anglaise nightie from M&S which will be ideal for heatwaves.

I read in *Christmas Fare* that a turkey surrounded by sausage links used to be called alderman in chains, because the turkey was plump like an alderman and the sausages were like his chain of office.

Thursday 26th July

It's the hottest day of the year, about 30°C. I had a shower and enjoyed being briefly cold. I certainly didn't bother pretending to be Wim Hof. Nicola rang, the library is air conditioned so she's cool during the day but her house is very warm. She is reading *Moominland Midwinter*. She asked what I'm doing to celebrate Christmas in July Boxing Day? I said I'd rather let Christmas in July sneak up on me. Like very cold weather, very hot weather seems to excuse you from feeling you should be doing something productive.

Friday 27th July

It rained a bit today but not enough to clear the air. Both Malc and I have got into the habit of shouting out the temperature when we walk past the thermostat. I went for an early morning walk. There is a massive patch of St John's Wort I walk past and just seeing its yellow cheerfulness lifts my spirits. It is used to treat mild depression. I try to watch all the people I love for signs of depression developing, and myself too.

Malc and I went to Homebase this afternoon. They have a cardboard cut-out of a policeman which is probably an attempt to deter shoplifting. We got a red and white dahlia which made me think of raspberry ripple ice cream and also of candy canes. Malc thinks the ice cream van is getting quieter. I'm not sure it is, I think his hearing is getting less good. Neither of us can hear the other speak now if the kettle is boiling.

Saturday 28th July

I counted my unread Christmas books, I have seven! I see this pile of books as insurance against boredom and something to do if I'm stuck for an activity now I'm retired. Wikipedia has this quote from A. Edward Newton; 'Even when reading is impossible, the presence of books acquired produces such an ecstasy that the buying of more books than one can read is nothing less than the soul reaching towards infinity ... we cherish books even if unread, their mere presence exudes comfort, their ready access reassurance'.

I agree with Mr Newton and I know Nicola does too. Wikipedia is amazing. Looking things up used to require a trip to the library unless you were lucky enough to have a set of *Encyclopaedia Britannica* in the house. When Nicola was small we bought a second-hand set of the eight volume *Book of Knowledge* from an advert in the *Oxford Times*. We couldn't afford the thirty-two volume *Encyclopaedia Britannica* and we didn't know Google and Wikipedia were going to happen later. You want to give your children advantages.

Malc watched *Skyfall* this evening. He likes Daniel Craig being James Bond. I think he has cold eyes.

Sunday 29th July
This morning I caught Malc entering the kitchen stealthily making a gun with his hand. He checked for threats then went straight for the ginger nuts tin. I was out in the garden and I could see him through the kitchen window. Sometimes I think Malc has a rich inner life that I know nothing about, and sometimes when I ask him what he's thinking about it's if he should plant more or less runner beans next year.

We picked Mum up in the car and went to Yarnton garden centre for lunch. Malc and I had beef roast dinner and Mum had chicken roast dinner. It was a generous portion. Mum insisted on paying so we let her and said thank you. Mum mentioned over dinner that if you put your pants on inside out you have to leave them like it all day or it's bad luck. Mum is in a good mood because they're making more *Poldark*.

I finished reading *Christmas Fare*. I enjoyed reading about what Queen Victoria ate at Balmoral. I'm sure I'll re-read this book, it has beautiful pictures.

Monday 30th July
Val phoned up this morning to invite us to a little party tomorrow evening. Henry's cousin Quentin will be in Oxford for one night. When I worked my heart would sink at being invited to a last-minute thing because the thought of having to get up early and go to work without my usual amount of sleep was depressing. Now I can have a late

night on a Tuesday and get up when I want on Wednesday (and Malc can too because he doesn't work Wednesdays). I asked Val if she wanted me to bring anything but she said no, she'll pop along to M&S today and get a lot of party bits. Quentin hasn't said exactly what time he's arriving. This is the sort of behaviour of someone who isn't used to preparing a meal for other people.

David has a day off today so Malc and I went over to Bicester at lunch time and we all went for lunch at Wimpy. We love Wimpy. I had coronation chicken jacket potato, Malc and David had burger and fries. David said the women who shop in his shop at Bicester Village would turn their nose up at Wimpy. Malc said anyone who doesn't want a Wimpy needs their head examined. David's idea of a good day off is playing on his computer. He seems happy. He seems (and looks) young for someone who's almost forty. People don't age like they used to, you see women of my age still dressed like teenagers and people opting out of the traditional marriage, mortgage and two offspring sort of life that was thought to be the be-all and end-all when Malc and I were young.

We dropped David off at his house then Malc and I called in at Bicester Avenue garden centre. There was a man in a polo shirt which read 'visual merchandising manager' talking to another member of staff and saying it won't be long until he has to think about the Christmas displays!

Tuesday 31st July

Quentin hasn't visited Val and Henry for a decade. He has just semi-retired from work. This seems to be a thing people do nowadays, especially people who've had what I think of as proper careers rather than just jobs. Malc and I arrived before Quentin so we formed part of the welcoming committee. Val put out a lovely buffet on the dining table; smoked salmon and cream cheese sandwiches, chicken satay, goat's cheese tart, lamb samosas, mini pork pies (especially for Malc), arancini balls (first time we've had these, quite nice), halloumi, olives, potato salad containing purple heritage potatoes as well as normal white ones, couscous salad, physalis and cherry tomatoes still on the vine.

We ate in the garden. Quentin is flying to Edinburgh tomorrow to see an old school friend. He and Henry went on lots of boyhood family holidays together. They fondly remembered a summer in Cornwall that seemed to last forever but was actually one month. They have a wonderful Christmas memory of visiting a friend of Quentin's mother in a big house in Bath. She gave them both a wooden pop gun and a bag of mint humbugs and let them run around her big garden pretending to shoot each other. It's lovely when you glimpse the shadow of remembered excitement in the faces of men in their early seventies.

For dessert we had what Val calls a dessert medley where you get three small puddings. We had Eton mess, lemon tart and chocolate mousse. Quentin said it was heavenly. Malc and I left at eleven, promising to visit Quentin if we're ever in Bern, Switzerland where he lives. I put a note in the snowman tin to buy Henry some mint humbugs. I know humbug is usually a thing people say to be anti-Christmas but they will remind Henry of being a boy in Bath (the city, obviously, not a bath).

July reckoning, have I kept Christmas all July? I've discovered you can train yourself to feel Christmassy in the summer, even during a heatwave. I'll make my Christmas coleslaw with cranberries again. I love looking out of the kitchen window and seeing balls swinging on the pergola and hanging from the obelisk. I've had a London theatre treat with Val and a lovely day at Duxford. In idle moments I imagine nipping to New York on Concorde for a spot of shopping. In my fantasy I'm sat next to Joan Collins and she admires my gold trainers and asks where I got them from. I've listened to Macca's 'Wonderful Christmastime'. Val and I used to say Macca instead of Paul McCartney because we mentioned him so much.

I've learnt that reading about Christmas is enormously helpful in feeling Christmassy. Of course I'm probably not the first Dickens to think this. I enjoyed a book buying spree with money from ERNIE. So far this year I have read twenty Christmas books! Having time to read is an underrated luxury.

I've seen my nearest and dearest; Malc has brought home the Christmas bacon in the form of balls from a skip, Nicola stayed over and with David we went to Wimpy. Mum very kindly bought me some festive Wedgwood. We've eaten some fab food with Val and Henry. I've had a very jolly lunch with Carol who made it perfect with pickle and her company.

I could sum up my July with four f's; family, friends, food and festive fiction (and non-fiction). This reminds me that when Nicola was small and tired and needed a wash before bed on holiday we used to do what we called the three f's (face, feet and fanny!).

August

Wednesday 1st August

This is my sixth month of retirement! I am slowly starting to believe that I am really retired. I have been paid my pension every month. I have not been to work. There is no trick. This is my life now. I need to stop feeling a flicker of guilt when Malc goes to work on Tuesdays and Thursdays, he's choosing to do it, he doesn't have to.

I popped round to see Mum this morning. I took her some fig rolls and we had a couple with a coffee but they seemed to have less fig and more roll than when I last bought some. I got them in Poundland so maybe the ratio of fig to roll has been altered to favour the cheaper ingredients. Perhaps I'll get Val to get me some Waitrose ones and I'll compare. When I was working in the shop I noticed that the fig roll and the Garibaldi generally have quite loyal purchasers. People buy a pack of them every week or not at all, except for me who buys them on occasion because Mum likes them.

This afternoon I read some of *A Right Royal Christmas*. On the whole, I'd rather not be royalty. Although they get big Christmas parties it would be exhausting after a while. I don't think Malc or Nicola would take to being royal. David might, he once spent £95 on a Vivienne Westwood tie which he then lost. I am going to add Vivienne Westwood tie to the snowman ideas tin and think about it again nearer Christmas. Would David take better care of it if he got another one?

Thursday 2nd August

I did an online shop this morning for delivery tomorrow evening! How convenient is that? Online grocery shopping is a real boon and I have plenty of time to browse now. I popped round to see Gail after lunch (jacket potato and cheese, one of my favourites, and I added a dollop of pickle which made me think of my lunch with Carol when she ran off to get some). Gail asked if all my extra time was a burden and if Malc was getting on my wick but I don't find this with being retired at all. I suppose it's early days though. Gail does shifts in the betting shop and sometimes works until ten at night. I left when she had to get ready to go to work.

Gail thinks the John Allen Centre Poundland is the best Poundland in Cowley but I think the best one is the Templars Square one. We're lucky to have two Poundlands. I'm not sure we're lucky to have so many betting shops. Gail asked if I was still Christmas mad. I said I'm still a Christmas enthusiast.

I looked round the charity shops after I'd been to see Gail. I got some summer trousers for Malc, they're a pale orange and made by Samuel Windsor. He's always saying he wants some more exciting coloured trousers. I showed him them as soon as he got home from work.

Val sent me an email showing me a picture of this year's Harrod's Christmas bear. He is called Oliver and is wearing a Santa style anorak. I had a look on eBay for previous years' bears. They always have quite posh names. There's a Giles, James, Jasper, Maxwell, Bertie, Eddie, Benjamin, Sebastian, Alexander, Benedict, Freddie,

Andrew, Rufus, William and Henry. In 1993 they went a bit rogue and came out with Carol the panda.

Friday 3rd August

Nicola is coming to stay this weekend because she's going to Fiona and Darren's wedding tomorrow at Hawkwell House in Iffley. Nicola arrived at the same time as the grocery delivery. I'd got lots of things she likes. We didn't get the Wispa Golds I ordered but instead they sent us six normal Wispas for the same price as three Wispa Golds. I can't decide if this is a good result or not, I like Wispa Golds quite a lot more than normal Wispas. We got the triple chocolate cookies I'd ordered for Nicola and the chocolate trifle and the chocolate cheesecake. Malc was cross because the bananas were bruised. He said he'd grow them himself if he could. He said they've made it safely all the way from Cameroon, Colombia, Dominican Republic, Ghana, Panama or Saint Lucia, only to be damaged at the last moment. I promised to get bananas from the local Co-op in future, he was going on a bit.

We had macaroni cheese for dinner followed by chocolate trifle. We watched *Gardeners' World.* We offered to watch something different because Nicola was there but she said she didn't mind.

Saturday 4th August

Nicola wore a lovely purple and gold dress from Monsoon to the wedding. She had gold ballerina flat shoes and a purple bracelet. She has a special bag for attending weddings which has two rabbits kissing on it. The house seemed quiet when Nicola went out and Malc went off to the allotment. It's a long time since I've been to a wedding or an allotment. There are many things people can do on a Saturday. Malc keeps making noises about us going to an allotment open day but I'm leaving it up to him. He likes to grow his veg and not get bogged down in allotment politics, networking or red tape he says. He says there are two types of allotmenteers. I wouldn't know about this, it's not my world. He says Ken could tell you some tales about his days on the committee.

I read some of *A Right Royal Christmas*, about Henry VIII's first banquet. I think Christmas is definitely my hobby now. Malc and I had a banquet of Domino's pizza for dinner and saved plenty of pepperoni pizza for Nicola. We watched *Crossroads* (the blues film with Ralph Macchio, not the 1980s soap opera about a motel).

Nicola got in at almost midnight. Malc had offered to pick her up but she walked (it's only twenty-five minutes). We were still up watching *Iron Man 3*. She told us all about the wedding. I asked if she danced with anyone. She said people don't do that nowadays. She saw Steven who went to Cubs with David and said he's swapped his runny nose for a beer belly. She took some pizza to bed with her.

Sunday 5th August

We all went to the Tetsworth car boot sale this morning. Malc sang Rod Stewart's 'We Are Sailing' but changed the words to 'We are car boot sailing.' It's lovely seeing him trying to amuse Nicola. I got an old shoebox of Christmas decorations for fifty pee. Nicola got some books. Malc got a bright pink astilbe (also known as false goat's beard) from the plant stall. We had an ice cream before we got back in the car.

For lunch we went to the Oxy Oriental buffet restaurant and then we went to see *The Producers* at the Vue cinema. It's one of Malc's favourite films. It was quite good on the big screen. The Oxy was nice. All their desserts were a bit melty due to the heat. The cheesecake had a soggy bottom but I actually prefer it like that. Nicola refers to the Oxy as the cathedral of overeating.

Nicola left at six. It's been lovely having her home. I'm going to visit her in Coventry on the 15th and we'll go shopping. Malc found a shady spot for his astilbe. It occurred to me that people, like plants, need to be in the right places, with the right conditions, to do well.

I looked through my shoebox of decorations. It was fifty pee well spent. I've got a couple of angels, a reindeer, two snowmen, four lanterns, some bells and a lot of balls, some with wintry scenes on them that I'm sure were originally from Woolworths.

Monday 6th August

Malc hasn't tried on the pale orange summer trousers I bought him yet. I pointed them out to him today but he said he had a day's wear left in his current trousers which are navy blue. Mum phoned to say *Homes Under The Hammer* has got Leamington Spa on it.

I went for a very warm walk this morning, it was already 30°C at ten. I went into the newsagents on Phipps Road to get a cold drink. I remembered that they have some old Christmas stuff down the back of the shop so I looked at it again. They have foil garlands, very old-fashioned thin paper gift wrap and those fold out foil things in a sunburst shape and a star shape. I bought a multicoloured sunburst and a multicoloured star and a bottle of Sprite Zero.

There was a moving van next door but one today. Malc was talking to Tom over the fence and Tom said the couple who lived there have split up. She was having an affair while he worked nights. Malc and I had cheese on toast for lunch and a conversation about fidelity. We're for it.

Tuesday 7th August
I broke the shredder. I was shredding old bank statements from 2010 and previous. The shredder stopped working properly and then smelt of burning plastic so I've ordered a new one from Amazon. What did we do twenty years ago when we didn't have Amazon? I suppose we had the Argos catalogue and Cowley Centre shops. Some of my retirement will be spent on life admin. Everything feels like a chore when it's been 30°C for over a week so I thought I may as well do something dull this morning. The care home residents are being given ice lollies at regular intervals. Carol's daughter Donna is also making sure Malc gets ice lollies at regular intervals.

I was looking in the fridge and cupboards for the third time, trying to decide what I fancied for lunch when the ice cream man pulled up outside so I got my purse and chose an Oreo sundae. It's a big splodge of Mr Whippy ice cream in a see-through cup, with biscuit pieces, chocolate sauce and a chocolate Flake with a tiny fluorescent pink shovel to eat it with. Delicious! And very much the lunch of a lady of leisure.

I watched the 2016 Christmas special of *Inside the Factory* this afternoon. It featured tinsel, wrapping paper, mince pies and Yule log. I love watching Christmas being manufactured. I wonder when I will see the first box of mince pies in a shop? I think we got them at the end of August last year when I was at work. I will have no shelves to stack this Christmas!

Wednesday 8th August

The heatwave has finally broken. I'm going to enjoy being a sensible temperature today. Malc has changed trousers but still not tried on the new pale orange ones. He went off to the allotment early. I did some ironing, it's been too hot to do it for the last week and a half. I had rice pudding for lunch with a big swirl of golden syrup.

This afternoon I finished reading *A Right Royal Christmas*. I like watching the Queen's speech at Christmas. You know you're slap bang in the middle of the throes of a Christmas when the Queen appears on telly. I like it when she wears pale blue, it really suits her.

Malc came home and did a post on Freegle offering some plant pots. He has way more than he needs. Henry says Freegle works well in Oxford because we have lots of visiting academics and lots of people who care about the planet. He says even people who can afford it don't like the ethics of wasting the world's resources. Malc says one man's trash is another man's treasure.

Thursday 9th August

My walk today smelt of freshly cut grass and lavender. When you retire you have time to walk slowly round your local area and you can see the detail of it, you can stop and read the noticeboards, or admire a rose bush, or browse a newsagents you haven't been in for years. Other people of a similar age smile at you, you are a member of the unhurried now. I had a little chat with a woman with the same hairdo as Prue Leith who was posting a letter on Addison Drive. She used to come in the shop. I recognise a lot of local faces from having sold them groceries. She was a muesli buyer. She probably still is, it's just not a thing I see happen now.

Malc came home gloomy, one of his favourite residents, Bert Brookfield, has died. Bert was jolly and told Malc he did a lovely job of the garden. Carol's daughter Donna says there's a lot of heartbreak in a care home, but it's parcelled out in little daily portions, so you almost don't notice it until the big final heartbreak.

Malc's spare plant pots have been snapped up. The Freegler who wanted them is moving house and is getting a greenhouse. She was delighted to have them at this expensive time in her life. She asked about my gardening and I told her Malc does it all and I explained that when we first got our own garden I thought I was Barbara but turned out to be Margot. She asked me how I satisfy my creative urge without gardening. I told her my main hobby is reading about Christmas, writing little thoughts about it and cooking. She nodded encouragingly while I was speaking.

Friday 10th August
I read *A Child's Christmas in Wales* today. I liked this bit about sweets and games; 'Hardboileds, toffee, fudge and allsorts, crunches, cracknels, humbugs, glaciers, marzipan

and butterwelsh for the Welsh...And Snakes-and Families and Happy Ladders'.
I had to Google butterwelsh, it's toffee, often with nuts in it.

Today is Henry's 70th birthday. We got him a special card and a 70th birthday pint glass from Card Factory. I put up some balloons. Val and Henry came for dinner and we got an Indian takeaway from a place at Rose Hill. Henry had a chef's special, honey chicken and lemon rice. He said it was wonderful and that after ordering he worried that he might have made a mistake and that the honey and lemon combination would be redolent of Strepsils, but it was a perfect balance of flavours. We had fresh cream Victoria sponge for afters. Tomorrow Val and Henry are flying to Rome for a week.

Henry has no plans to retire yet. Men get a bit more choice career wise than women do, especially men with some education.

Saturday 11th August

Malc and I went to an open day at one of the biggest allotment sites in Oxford this morning. We saw Ken who asked after Nicola and David then spoke about his leeks as if they were his offspring. Ken pointed out some of the movers and shakers of the allotment world to us. One of the men had the most creased grey trousers I've ever seen, it looked like he was wearing two elephant trunks. I bought a jar of greengage jam. I love getting a new jam flavour.

On our way home we bumped into Gail, on her way to start her shift at the bookies at midday. I showed her my new jam. She said she never bothers with jam because it's full of sugar. When she'd gone Malc said that he'd seen Len in the petrol station but Len hadn't bothered saying hello. I'm glad Malc always says what time he'll be back from the allotment. Gail has trouble with Len going off for hours. Actually, I don't think I'd stand for it.

Malc said his bacon and tomato ketchup sandwich was a perfect balance of flavours when we sat in the garden eating lunch. It made me think that our marriage seems to be a perfect balance of time spent together and time spent apart with our own interests.

I started reading *Grumpy Old Christmas* this afternoon. It must be annoying if you genuinely don't like Christmas to have people trying to bring you round to it. I don't like hot tubs or coriander and I can't see that changing. I'd be annoyed if people kept trying to change my mind.

Sunday 12th August

Malc took the notion that we should go to Ducklington car boot sale this morning. Someone at the allotment open day yesterday told him that there is a stall holder there who makes his own frost proof garden ornaments and they are better than what's available in most garden centres. We set off just after ten. Malc caused me a moment of panic just before the Evenlode roadside restaurant when he said he had to stop the car as soon as possible. My brain assumed Malc was feeling ill with his heart. He pulled into the Evenlode car park. He got out and shooed a wasp from the back window.

It cost two pounds each to get into the boot sale! Tetsworth car boot sale is free for buyers. We didn't see any garden ornaments. There was a field of sheep nearby. There were three Portaloos which in part justifies the cost, however Tetsworth has two Portaloos. I saw a jigsaw of two Golden Retrievers in a wheelbarrow which I was oddly drawn to. They looked very relaxed. We didn't buy anything which is unusual. I saw some ice cream sundae glasses which reminded me that we have sundae glasses in the back of the cupboard. Malc had a hot dog and I had some chips. It's nice to eat chips outside, it reminded me of being on holiday and I had a sudden longing for Bognor.

There were no wasps in the car on the way home. Malc dropped me off at Cowley Centre shops and went on to the allotment. I got some Oreo biscuits, vanilla ice cream, crispy wafers and chocolate ice cream sauce. I found the sundae dishes from the back of the cupboard and when Malc came home we had sundaes with crushed Oreos. At this part of August I feel I should enjoy summer because soon it will be autumn.

Malc is watching the Benedict Cumberbatch *Sherlock* at the moment. Una Stubbs is in it. She was very good in *Summer Holiday* with Cliff Richard and in *Til Death Do Us Part*. Gail's Len reminds me of Alf Garnett a bit.

Monday 13th August

Blessings counted when I got up this morning; I feel well, the people I love are well, it isn't raining, I have the ingredients for ice cream sundaes.

Malc left for the allotment then came back moments later saying there was an emergency. It was that he had run out of chocolate eclairs in the car. Phew! We've been through a few emergencies together. There were chocolate eclairs in the cupboard.

I watched a video of how to crochet a robin on YouTube and then a video of how to crochet a pine cone. Before I retired I thought I'd knit and crochet when I had more time but actually just time is not enough, you need the motivation. I do not have the motivation so I'm going to do other things instead. Where Christmas goes wrong for some people is when they think they have to do things and they put too much pressure on themselves.

Malc came home at lunch time with a lot of tomatoes. We had ice cream sundaes for lunch. We went to B&M where we got a big box of chocolate eclairs at a very reasonable price. They are probably Christmas stock from last year. It is the time of year when there is still a little bit of Christmas stock hanging about from last year but if you wait a month some of this year's stuff will be available.

This evening we booked Bognor for September! Just two nights, but that'll be enough. The pale orange trousers I bought Malc would be an ideal holiday trouser.

Tuesday 14th August

Freed from the obligations of paid employment you have to make your own agenda. You have to quiet the voice in your head telling yourself that things you fancy doing are a waste of time or self-indulgent. What with that and ignoring the voice that tells women of my age to be unselfish and focus on others it can be quite busy up in brain junction. I usually get these voices on a Tuesday and Thursday just after Malc has left for work. I sit quietly until they give up. Sometimes I walk slowly round the kitchen, seeing if anything needs adding to the shopping list. Lists are a good way of soothing a busy brain. Bananas have a lot to teach us by becoming more strongly tasting of themselves with age.

I will be having a busy day tomorrow visiting Nicola in Coventry so this morning I settled down on the sofa with *The Puffin Book of Christmas Stories* and this afternoon I popped to the shops. The first story in *The Puffin Book of Christmas Stories* was 'Christmas with the Chrystals' by Noel Streatfeild, an author whose surname looks like a misspelling. It was one of those difficult frosty person is improved by Christmas kindness stories.

I bought quiche Lorraine for dinner. We had it with Christmas coleslaw which is coleslaw with added cranberries, chopped apple and a touch of cinnamon.

I gave Carol a ring this evening. Malc came home and said Carol's daughter Donna has been promoted to activities co-ordinator at the care home. Malc says she has big ideas. Carol is very pleased that Donna is getting on with her life. She had a spell of depression a few years ago but has come through it. Carol and I are going to have lunch a week today.

Our ice cream man who only appears intermittently appeared this evening. We had a Mr Whippy each. Malc thinks that the Flakes in ice cream taste different than normal Flakes not in ice cream because they've been left open in a box in an ice cream van for too long. I think they taste different because the ice cream makes them a bit cold.

Wednesday 15th August

Today I got the train to visit Nicola in Coventry, the city of peace and reconciliation. I remember her graduation day in the cathedral. Me and Malc were proud enough to burst. Neither of us went to university. It sounds daunting but I never said that to Nicola at the time because we could tell she was bright.

We went round the shops. I bought books in the Oxfam bookshop; *Remembering Christmas An Anthology Of Childhood Christmases* compiled by Anne Harvey and *Miracle On 34th Street* by Valentine Davies. We spent ages in TJ Hughes. It's good, it's a bit like Boswells in Oxford. There was some reduced Christmas stuff and I got some little red glitter birds that clip on to things. Nicola has flown the nest but we're still close.

We had lunch in Las Iguanas. We both had burritos. Nicola's favourite telly programme at the moment is *This Country*. Her favourite chocolate bar is still the Twirl. My train home was late. Malc made us beans on toast for dinner. I've had a lot of beans today.

Thursday 16th August

I went to the Emmaus charity shop to look at books (three for a pound) this morning. I didn't get any books but I did get a slightly bent tree top star which is ideal for the top of the obelisk in the garden. I unbent it with some pliers and put it up and decided to wait and see how long it takes Malc to notice. Malc had a staring contest with a black and white cat in the back garden this evening and lost. He suspects it of pooing near his buddleia.

Friday 17th August

I had a big browse of Approved Food's website. The expensive Cottage Delight brand jams and chutneys that most garden centres have always end up on the Approved Food website. No-one I know would pay a fiver for a jar of jam, it's just too steep.

Malc made us a ploughman's lunch and we ate it in the garden. As well as a pickled onion we had olives. Our ploughman is a fancy one. Malc watched a blue tit on a branch. He said he sits on the same branch every day. The blue tit probably says the same about Malc sitting in his chair. I had to point out the star on the obelisk. Malc said we might get wise men in the garden now.

Malc making us lunch is a turn up for the books.

Saturday 18th August

I did the lying down bit of my yoga DVD. It's in three sections, lying down, standing up and kneeling. Each takes ten minutes. Before I retired I thought I'd become a woman who does yoga. I have started. You have to slot things into your newly free time when you feel inclined to do them.

Malc found Nicola's old glass paints in the shed. There is blue, purple, green and red. He thought I might want to do something Christmassy with the green and red. I Googled glass painting Christmas projects then felt a bit overwhelmed with choice. I'll come back to this, I've already done yoga today.

We watched the *Blues Brothers*. Aretha Franklin died this week and she gives a great performance in it. Respect is very important in a marriage.

Sunday 19th August
Malc was restless this afternoon which is unusual. He can get fidgety when autumn approaches and the amount of time he needs to spend outside begins to decrease. I suggested we went to The George pub in Littlemore, so we did. I often walk past it. I liked it a lot. It's how I remember pubs being and they still have a meat raffle. I had a Malibu and Diet Coke, Malc had a Strongbow Dark Fruits. It came to £7.35. There was still a Christmas decoration left up from last year. It was quiet, as you'd expect on a Sunday afternoon around three p.m. Pubs used to shut on Sunday afternoons. Now on Sundays we have more choice of when to go to the pub and when to shop.

The world opens up when you don't have to work. It used to really take it out of me, doing a full weeks work when I hit my sixties. I would get Sunday afternoon work dread, knowing the weekly cycle was about to repeat. Life is simpler now I'm retired. I'm untired, I don't say no to things because of not having the energy and I have the get-up-and-go to think of new things to do.

Malc finally tried on the pale orange trousers and they are a good fit but he made a doubtful face when he was wearing them. The pockets are adequately deep. They are a zip fly. Malc does not get on with a button fly.

Monday 20th August
Malc and I went to Notcutts garden centre today. We had ham, egg and chips for lunch. It was perfectly cooked, the golden chip broke the gooey but not too runny yolk with just the right amount of liquidity. It was like a sunrise of egg and potato. I looked around the restaurant and felt

blessed to be a retiree who can be there on a Monday lunch time. It still rankles that my Dad did his full quota of work but didn't even get a full year of retirement. After lunch we bought a spruce tree we've called Forsyth.

I finished reading *Grumpy Old Christmas*, I enjoyed it more than I thought I would. It's not that I think absolutely everything about Christmas is brilliant, some things about it aren't, it's just that Christmas, like life, needs moulding to be the thing you want it to be.

Tuesday 21st August

Today is Val and Henry's wedding anniversary. It's their 45th, which is sapphire. They're going to York for a city break. They've only just got back from Rome.

I had a lovely long lunch with Carol in Wetherspoons. We had fish and chips. Carol says she'd like to be remembered as the kind of woman who when she wanted chips, she had chips! She is delighted that Donna has been promoted to activities co-ordinator. You want your children to do well at work and not be exploited. I'd already been at work for a couple of years when the Equal Pay Act happened and women got the same money as men for the same work. There's still a lot of exploitation today with these zero hours contracts. I wish the Labour Party would pull their finger out and fight harder to protect workers like they used to.

Where we sit in the Wetherspoons is quite dark and you can forget what time of day it is or even what time of year it is. This makes it relaxing, a sort of time out of time. There was a toddler doing some colouring in and he brought his picture over to show us! We both admired it.

Carol told his mum she might have the next Picasso there. His mum smiled and said 'Every child is an artist. The problem is how to remain an artist once he grows up. Come on Jayden, let the nice ladies have a bit of peace.'

Carol was quite good at art at school. I was hopeless at it. Gail and I used to distract each other. Carol has a lot of hobbies. She knits blankets for the special care baby unit. She is crocheting pumpkins for the care home harvest festival fete in September. She told me she's going to crochet Christmas puddings for the Christmas fayre and she'll do an extra one as a gift for me!

Wednesday 22nd August

We had David over for dinner today. I find it harder to see David as a grown up than I do to see Nicola as a grown up, but then David is the youngest. We had sausages and potato waffles with feta and olives placed alternately in the gaps. You can do a lot with a potato waffle, they're tremendously adaptable. For dessert I made chocolate Angel Delight and cinnamon star bread. The bread was the neatest I've ever made it. Malc said it looked like a snowflake. David said his bit looked like a vagina! Malc said to David they should probably have a repeat of the little chat about the birds and the bees!

Thursday 23rd August

I had a declutter of the kitchen cupboards today. I've decided we no longer need a wok (we just use the frying pan), two spare cruets, lots of ramekins from those Gu puddings which Val says are a godsend when you don't have time to make a dessert and a set of six mugs which we don't use because they're just a bit too small. I've put it all in a bag ready to go to a charity shop. I dithered over putting the ramekins in the bag or in the recycling, do people actually want ramekins?

Malc came in from the garden this evening and gloomily said the nights are drawing in. I felt gleeful then sad that Malc and I like different bits of the year best. I love it when the nights draw in. I want the dark to wrap me up in cosy autumn. I made us a milky hot chocolate in our Christmas mugs to remind Malc of the nice bits of this time of year.

Friday 24th August
Sometimes on a Friday I want to do something and Malc doesn't but that's okay and I have to remember that he was at work on Thursday. I left him looking at the Thompson & Morgan catalogue with a cup of coffee and I went for a walk. I wandered to Florence Park. There were big flowerbeds filled with red dahlias.

This afternoon I read the fourth story in *The Puffin Book of Christmas Stories.* It was 'The Real True Father Christmas' by Roy Fuller. The little girl in it reminded me of Nicola. When Nicola rang tonight I asked if she wanted her glass paints. She said no. I said I might do something Christmassy with the red and green ones. She said you can get glass paint pens now. One of Nicola's favourite places is Hobbycraft. There is a big one in Coventry near the train station. I added Hobbycraft voucher to my list of Christmas present ideas in the snowman tin.

Malc and I watched *Gardeners' World.* There was a bit about giant gooseberries.

Saturday 25th August
I took the bag of kitchen stuff I'd sorted out to the Emmaus charity shop. I bought three Christmas craft books for a pound which I'll flick through for inspiration then see if Nicola wants to flick through. It's cheaper than buying a magazine and Emmaus get some money. I'm not a magazine buying woman. I went to the Co-op to get bread, Malc's favourite at the moment is farmhouse seeded, and I was pleased to see the appearance of tubs of Quality Street and Celebrations for £4. I'm sure Roses and Heroes will be joining them soon. These are a herald of the festive season. I can't remember when the metal tin became a plastic tub. I used to like it when customers went through my till with a tin/tub of chocolates, we'd often have a chat about which were our favourites and people buying early would make a joke about them probably not going to last until Christmas. I'd say they could always buy another, we've got plenty.

Sunday 26th August
We had a lovely Sunday lunch at the Prince of Wales in Iffley. Me, Malc, Val and Henry all had beef roast dinner and Mum had chicken roast dinner. For dessert Malc and Henry had mixed fruit crumble, I had sticky toffee pudding and Mum and Val had Iffley Mess. Val and Henry told us all about Rome and York. I quite fancy York. Val gave us some chocolate from York's Chocolate Story, a sort of museum which sounds wonderful. Val and Henry had to leave when they had finished pudding, Val was expecting Geoffrey from Ocado to deliver her shopping in the cabbage van. Val kindly gave us some tickets for a Foodies Festival at South Park this weekend, they were going to go

but can't now, they're visiting friends of Henry's in Henley. Malc and I took Mum home. I had to do her shoelace up for her. At the start of the year she could have done it herself. This makes me sad.

I lay on the sofa full of wonderful food eaten in good company and it felt like Boxing Day. I read a story in *The Puffin Book of Christmas Stories* called 'The Weathercock's Carol', it was a bit bleak but had a happy ending. Although *The Puffin Book of Christmas Stories* is a children's book it doesn't pull any punches or dumb down the language. Henry would approve. Despite having no offspring he has a lot of theoretical views on what's good for children. It's usually the things he had as a boy, which is nice, because he must have enjoyed his boyhood.

Monday 27th August

Summer Bank Holiday. Malc and I bickered first thing. He wants to go shopping and can't decide between driving into town and parking at the Westgate (a new option) or getting the bus as usual. Parking is always expensive so we got the bus. He got a shirt in Debenhams. It says it's easy iron but we'll see. I asked Malc if he's going to take his pale orange trousers to Bognor and he said he might. We had a look in Boswells. I used to love bringing Nicola and David to the toy department and giving them a two pence piece to put in the slot to make a toy train go round a track. I recognise a few of the staff in Boswells from Littlewoods which closed quite some time ago. I used to take Nicola and David to Littlewoods for school clothes at this time of year. David was always very fussy.

Malc decided he wanted a full English breakfast with scrambled eggs for lunch. We went to Café Coco at The Plain end of Cowley Road. He got a well-cooked fried egg because they don't do scrambled eggs the waitress said. Malc can be fussy about eggs. I had feta and bacon omelette. I've eaten more feta in the last week than I have in my previous sixty-five and three-quarter years (because I opened a pack of feta to make olive and feta stuffed potato waffles and now I need to finish the feta).

Since we were so close we walked to the Foodies Festival at South Park. There were lots of food stalls, I've never seen so much olive oil. There was also a music stage and some cookery demonstrations. I liked the look of some rainbow fudge but it had a great many wasps on it. I saw a lot of happy dogs eating bits of things which had fallen on the ground. There were lifestyle things there; Alfa Romeo cars, teeth whitening, Greenpeace, WWF, a massage stall and a psychic operating from in a taxi. Malc said the car boot sale is more his sort of thing.

Tuesday 28th August

I met Lauren for lunch. Her studies are going well. There are vacancies in the shop, Tracy handed her notice in after a massive row with the new supervisor after the new supervisor hinted that she thought Tracy was lying when she rang in sick. Lauren said there's an atmosphere but she just ignores it. Tracy is leaving on Friday. The new supervisor hasn't signed the leaving card yet.

I finished reading *The Puffin Book of Christmas Stories*. It contained O. Henry's 'The Gift of the Magi', a story which I think shows how important it is to communicate in a marriage. It's about a young couple at Christmas. She sells her hair and buys him a watch chain, but he has sold his watch to buy her fancy hair combs for her long hair. If they'd spoken to each other they could have had more suitable, less extravagant presents. Malc bought me an egg slicer early in our marriage.

Great British Bake Off starts tonight. I will watch it, I like seeing what Noel Fielding is wearing and I like all the variety you get when they do the signature challenge and the showstopper challenge.

Wednesday 29th August

Malc and I got the number 10 bus to Headington for a change. We went to Waitrose and got iced Belgian buns. We looked at books in the many charity shops. I bought some Christmas cards in the British Heart Foundation shop, they have a lovely colourful town scene with a big Christmas tree and Father Christmas flying overhead.

We went to the Butcher's Arms for lunch. Malc admired their hanging baskets. He said he doesn't have the patience for hanging baskets because of all the watering. A cat gave us a dirty look while we waited for our food. We both had fish and chips.

The bus home took ages but it didn't matter, Malc and I were quite content watching the world go by. I thought about who would like the Christmas cards I bought today. I try to match the style of the card to the recipient. For dinner we had Belgian bun. I thought about baking some biscuits, it was biscuit week on *Bake Off* yesterday. What is the most Christmassy biscuit?

Thursday 30th August
I went in the shop today, the shop I used to work in. I saw shelves that weren't stacked by me. I saw the door that goes out the back to the stock room and break room but I'm not allowed through that door now. There were lots of cages of stock waiting to be put out. The new supervisor didn't even say hello, I don't think she recognised me. I went through Lauren's till. I got a chicken and avocado sandwich for my lunch, I just fancied it. You have to be in the mood for avocado. I sat and ate it in the park between Gaisford Road and Bartholomew Road. There is a tree in this park which grows along the ground rather than upwards. It has survived and I like to see it.

This afternoon I started reading *The Christmas Pocket Bible* by Guy and Steve Hobbs. On the back cover it has a quote from Alexander Smith 'Christmas is the day that holds all time together'. I looked up who Alexander Smith is, he's a Scottish poet.

Friday 31st August
Thinking about the Alexander Smith quote, we use Christmas to navigate in our lives, thinking of time since the previous one and time to the next one. It's a lighthouse. Often when people buy a house they want to move by Christmas. DFS promise to deliver new sofas by Christmas. It's a big solid rock of a day, looming in the calendar.

Today is the last day of summer. From tomorrow shops start to get gradually more Christmassy! Ken gave Malc a big bag of plums.

August reckoning, have I kept Christmas all August? Gail once told me about recording angels (she dabbles in religion sometimes), a recording angel makes a note of what you've done in your life, good and bad. This reminds me of the ghost of Christmas past and the ghost of Christmas present. Really, I think no-one but you is looking at what you've done in your life. Having a diary is a sort of ledger of what you've done but because you do it yourself it doesn't have the objectivity of a recording angel or Christmas ghost. Also, in a diary you can record your best bits and not the boring bits or bits you think show you in a bad light. Someone else recording your doings could be your judge, but you doing it could be your conscience. Anyway, this diary is for a very specific purpose, to help me keep Christmas, and by that I mean I want to keep cheerful and do some little bits of good in the world where I can, even if it's as small as buying charity Christmas cards.

In August you feel you should be having a last hurrah of summer, but you also know that autumn is waiting just behind the curtain. It's a tricky month to be keeping Christmas in. I've done some reading of Christmas books. I've seen people I love. I've added to the snowman tin of present ideas and bought some Christmas cards so I think I have kept Christmas in August but maybe not every single day.

September

Saturday 1st September
Today is the first day of meteorological autumn. Wouldn't it be good if conker trees grew Ferrero Rocher instead? I read in *The Christmas Pocket Bible* that in medieval times arguments were settled under holly trees because they thought this would help. Trees are a big part of autumn and Christmas.

Sunday 2nd September
Malc and I went to the Tetsworth boot sale this morning. I bought a Cath Kidston mug which says Merry Christmas and has decorated trees and a deer wearing a big red bow on it. The man on the stall insisted on giving me a free Christmas jigsaw. He said it was nearing the end of the booty season and it was better to not put things back in his conservatory for another year. It's a lovely jigsaw, the picture is a robin looking at a slice of Christmas cake which has a tiny plastic robin on it, with a background of winter foliage. I'm not a doer of jigsaws but I do have a tiny plastic robin to put on Christmas cakes.

Monday 3rd September
We went to Yarnton garden centre. Malc has got his eye on a tree fern but they're pricey. When we got home I added the tree fern idea to the snowman tin. How do you gift wrap a tree fern? Where would I hide it? We watched some *Plebs*. Malc thinks it's clever. He likes the Romans a lot, although doesn't seem very keen to go to Rome. I added

Roman things to the snowman tin. September is a good time for coming up with Christmas gift ideas.

Tuesday 4th September
I met Val in town today. We had lunch in Dirty Bones in the Westgate (salmon and egg on crumpets for me and chicken on waffles for Val). Val would like to eat in all the places in the Westgate, there must be twenty! We both left town in time to be home when Henry and Malc return from work. I am always delighted when Malc gets home from work. When he retires I should remember this feeling. For dinner we had crumpets with cheese. I wanted Malc to have crumpets because I've had crumpets and he really likes them.

I read in *The Christmas Pocket Bible* that the Roman statesman Cato thought that sprouts were the best thing to cure a hangover. Malc and I try to avoid hangovers but not sprouts. When you get to our age your body has enough to contend with so we go easy on the booze. Thankfully we've never been big drinkers.

Wednesday 5th September
David's 40th birthday. Malc and I went to Heyford Hill Sainsbury's this morning and got a lovely big chocolate cake. David is forty years old today! He, Nicola and Mum/Nan came for dinner. We invited Val and Henry but they couldn't make it and David is working at the weekend so we couldn't rearrange. We had Chinese from House of Tim. We talked about all the birthday meals we've had over the years. One year we went to KFC because that was what David wanted. Another year Nicola wanted ice cream

so we went to George and Davis. Mum/Nan said she liked both. She won't seek out new food experiences but she'll give things a go if the occasion arises.

Some people are good at birthdays, I'm always grateful for mine and those of the people I love, we don't know how many birthdays or Christmases we'll get.

We gave David some money because he has got all the Transformers he wants and he has moved on to buying Lego. Nicola got him a Lego set, it's a Hulkbuster: Ultron Edition and is basically Iron Man's fancy suit. Nicola asked if I'd seen the Lego Christmas tree or gingerbread house. She showed me some photos on her phone. Lego is ideal for making Christmas things because of the bright jolly colours.

Nicola gave Mum/Nan and David a lift home then went back to Coventry because she has work tomorrow. Nicola has got a better job than Malc and I had, but I'm not sure David has, shop work is not well paid and the hours are long.

Thursday 6th September

I went blackberry picking with Gail today. She said the best ones are always just out of reach. Both of us will make apple and blackberry crumble. Gail will use low fat margarine in hers and I'll use butter. She said Len has ruined his taste buds by smoking twenty fags a day since nineteen-sixty-six. Gail smokes, but she smokes less than Len.

It is one hundred and ten days until Christmas. I finished reading *The Christmas Pocket Bible.* It's a nice whirlwind tour of Christmas. My little library of Christmas books is steadily growing.

Friday 7th September

I made some butterfly cakes for the care home Harvest Festival Fete tomorrow and took them round to Carol's. Donna was there, she has a day off today. I congratulated her on being made activities co-ordinator and said me and Malc would pop in to the home tomorrow afternoon. Carol was busy getting her tombola in order.

I went in B&M and got ginger jam, Malc and I agree it's a very good jam. Then I went to the Co-op and got olive bread and Bolognese pasta bake. They had a shoplifter. I heard one cashier to tell another to call the police. I'm so glad I don't have to deal with this sort of thing any more. I used to turn a blind eye to shoplifters in the shop I worked in if they were nicking things like baby food and cheap pasta.

I was pleased to see that the tubs of Roses and Heroes have joined the Quality Street and Celebrations for £4 each. The Roses tub no longer contains the Brazilian darkness which is a shame. It was my favourite chocolate coated toffee. This position is now occupied by the toffee deluxe from the Quality Street assortment.

I seem to write a lot about shops and shopping. This is probably partly due to my long career in retail (when I first started as a shop girl no one ever said 'career in retail') and due to shopping being my responsibility. Malc will happily browse but gets in a panic if you ask him to find two items in even a small shop. He once telephoned me from Tesco when I had flu because he couldn't find the cheese.

I started reading *This Morning's Countdown to Christmas* by Richard Madeley and Judy Finnegan. It has some lovely recipes.

Saturday 8th September

My butterfly cakes went down well at the Harvest Festival Fete. It was quite a successful event. Donna will spend the money on Christmas craft supplies for the residents. Carol had crocheted pumpkins and bats. Donna had made owls out of felt. I bought one of each. I also bought a ginger cake and a book, *A Cotswold Christmas* compiled by John Hudson.

Malc won some biscuits on the tombola, they were salted caramel shortbread. Malc thinks too many things have salted caramel in now rather than just normal caramel. I'm inclined to agree with him.

We went to Val and Henry's for dinner. They were raving about some olive and sun-dried tomato tapenade they got from a farmer's market. It was a bit oily for my taste. For main course we had a lovely chicken and asparagus risotto. We told them about all the fun things we plan to do in Bognor.

Sunday 9th September

We have eaten all the things in the fridge we need to eat before going to Bognor. This is satisfying. I popped to Iceland to get some fruit pastilles for the journey. I saw a poster for their savings club. It's a bit like a goose club for Christmas. You get a pound back for every twenty pounds you save. I decided to save twenty pounds. I will spend it in December on Christmas food.

Monday 10th September

Bognor. We had a good journey to Bognor and arrived at half past three. There's a tricky bit round Portsmouth where you can get accidentally sucked off the main road and end up going the wrong way but we didn't. Malc likes the hotel car park because it's secluded so the car will be safe. The hotel is unchanged from our last visit which made me feel immediately relaxed.

We had a cup of tea in the room and sat by the window looking out at our sea view. Then we went for a walk on the beach and saw the sea up close. It's grey and relentless, like old age. It smells wonderful to our usually land locked noses.

We went to an Italian restaurant we like for dinner. I had a cheese risotto and Malc had a pizza with spicy nduja sausage. We took another walk on the beach before we went back to the hotel. There is entertainment in the evening but it's usually singing or bingo.

We sat in bed with our sea view window open. I read all about wines in *This Morning's Countdown to Christmas*. I'll be able to hold my own in a wine conversation with Val and Henry's neighbours now. They have a wine cellar and are unable to stop themselves mentioning it no matter how many times you meet them.

Tuesday 11th September

Bognor. We both slept well last night. No-one in this hotel seems to come home late, drunk and noisy like they do in the hotels Val and I stay at in Soho. I suppose Bognor is very much not Soho. Breakfast is a buffet and quite traditional. We both had the full English. Fried bread is available which you don't see much these days, certainly not in Oxford. I love a long slow holiday breakfast with plenty of coffee and a whole day ahead of us and the sea to the side of us.

We walked to Hotham Park and admired the trees. We were last here in spring, in March. I've become more relaxed since then due to retirement. We had lunch in a Turkish restaurant in the arcade where Wimpy used to be. We both had stuffed vine leaves followed by chicken kebab.

After lunch we looked in the shops. Malc got some banana eclairs in the sweet shop, I got some apple and cinnamon balls. We went to the bookshop. The man in there is very helpful. I bought *The Best Christmas Pageant Ever* by Barbara Robinson. We looked in the charity shops and from this I concluded that Bognor is similar to Cowley prosperity-wise. One shop had three different Christmas biscuit barrels! There was a Santa on his sleigh, a jolly snowman, and a Christmas woodland scene with deer, rabbits, foxes, an owl and a little moulded robin on the lid. Sadly the Santa biscuit barrel was chipped, but it could have been made less noticeable with a bit of red paint.

We went to the arcade and each blew a pound in the 2p machines. Then we went back to the hotel for a sit down and a think about what we wanted to eat for dinner. Malc had forty winks. We got fish and chips for dinner and ate it on a bench looking out to sea. When we went back to the hotel we could hear someone singing Tom Jones' 'It's Not

Unusual'. Malc said it's not unusual to hear 'It's Not Unusual' sung in seaside hotel lounges.

Wednesday 12th September
Bognor. It's the last day of the holiday, we check out at eleven, and Malc still hasn't worn his pale orange trousers. He moans that men don't get as much choice as women but then when he gets the opportunity for something a bit different he turns his nose up at it.

After breakfast we walked into town and I bought the Christmas woodland scene biscuit barrel I saw yesterday. Then we went to the Bognor Regis Museum. I'm so glad we did. It's fabulous! It has a display of vintage Christmas decorations, the old village stocks, details about who has stayed at our hotel, the same Spirograph Nicola loved as a child and very friendly volunteers.

We had a last look at the sea then checked out. Behind the woman we gave our key cards to was a man working on a computer humming Tom Jones' 'Delilah'.

We stopped at the Manor Nursery garden centre on the way home. Malc bought spring bulbs to do two pots, he's doing what is called a lasagne, where you have bulbs that flower at different times in the same pot. He's got cream crocuses with bright orange middles which will flower first, hopefully in February. Next to flower will be pink hyacinths, followed by some red tulips. Gardeners are always thinking six months ahead. His taste in bulbs is much brighter than his taste in trousers.

We also went to Chilton garden centre on the way home. They have just started putting their Christmas stuff out. They had done the pink display and the musical things that move (train, carousel, big wheel) and there were hundreds of brown cardboard boxes with made in China on. I'll be interested to go back in a week or so. A man jokingly wished us a Merry Christmas!

Thursday 13th September

I popped to the shops to get some milk and I bumped into Gail. I said I might have felt a bit flat coming back from Bognor but I don't because there is Christmas to look forward to. She said it's way too early to think about Christmas. I replied that different people like to start planning at different times. You can't tell other people where to put their focus. No-one moans at gardeners for planning what plants they'll put in next spring. I think Christmas, like seeds, takes time to grow in people's minds so we need to start thinking about it before the event. Also, it's not just one day, it's a season.

I said we'd enjoyed Bognor and Gail said 'It's all right for some!' and she asked me if I'd put on weight in Bognor (I don't think so, I don't weigh myself very often) then she said she was having trouble with Len not putting things away in the fridge properly. He'll make a sandwich late at night, then leave things on the kitchen counter. He thinks it's women's work to put it away and then the ham goes off.

I finished reading *This Morning's Countdown to Christmas*. I'd forgotten how much we used puff pastry in the 1990s. If we weren't making a puff pastry parcel we were stencilling a chest of drawers. The book ends with a Rosemary Conley workout. Her mouth is smiling but her eyes aren't. She wants you to undo your Christmas overindulgence. I'm going to start mine early and spread it out so there's not so much to undo. Also, as a woman in her sixties I am rather resigned to being chubby.

The new Body Shop festive smells for this year are peppermint, vanilla and berry.

Friday 14th September

Malc and I got fish and chips from the Littlemore chip shop for dinner. It was busy. A man asked the owner if he'd had a nice holiday and spent all his profits. The owner said yes and he'd have to put the prices up. There was a collective gasp from the queue.

Malc told me Homebase have got some Christmas things on their website. He left the computer on so I could have a look. We've never had outside decorations. I love walking past other people's, maybe we should get something?

I started reading *A Cotswold Christmas*. One of my favourite places in the Cotswolds is Bourton on the Water. It has the best model village I've ever seen and is so pretty. Malc and I always say we'll go to Beaconsfield model village one day but so far we never have.

Saturday 15th September

I have started a Christmas craft project today. I am making a felt owl. I have a completed one made by Donna and bought by me at the Harvest Festival Fete. The one Donna made is brown and orange, with gold thread chevrons on the tummy. I have a pattern and instructions from Donna and she said to let her know if I want to use her glue gun to stick any bits that can't be sewn. Some of the felt owls she makes have button eyes, some have googly eyes. Googly eyes have to be stuck. Donna said 'A glue gun, like any other gun, can have terrible consequences and lead to bad craft items. The trick is to plan your project and keep it simple.'

While I was cutting out my owl and choosing some button eyes from the button tin Malc got the printer working. He always tests printers by making them print a sheet that reads 'I'm an ink hungry bastard'. He's very good with most things but printers really wind him up. We've had many over the years and they are always awkward and expensive to buy ink for.

For dinner we had Domino's pizza. I chose pepperoni for my half. We watched the *Lego Batman Movie*. I liked it. Before we went to bed Malc asked if I fancied a day trip to the seaside tomorrow. He said Ken goes to Southsea and back in a day so as not to leave his veg unattended for long.

Sunday 16th September

I weighed myself this morning. I weigh eleven stones and one pound. Does this sound better if I write one hundred and fifty-five pounds? I'm not sure. Anyway I am a pleasingly average shape if you look round an M&S changing room so I'm not going to worry.

Today is one hundred days until Christmas! Malc got up, put on the pale orange trousers I bought him and said let's go to Southsea!

On the way I noted down caravan names;

Swift Celeste

Pastiche

Sightseer
Pilote Sensation
Sprite Musketeer
Buccaneer Schooner
Avondale Chiltern
Swift Freestyle
Senator Carolina
Ranger 460/2
Quasar 462
McLouis Tandy
Coachman VIP.
I liked noting these names because they are mostly nonsense. McLouis Tandy is especially odd, it could equally be McNulty Rumbelows or Findlay Dixons (a Scottish surname and a defunct electrical retailer).

We parked near the South Parade Pier and explored that then walked along to the Clarence Pier. We also walked into the Southsea shopping centre. We did ten miles of walking today!

The South Parade Pier had some stalls at the end. We got posh cheese toasties for lunch; smokey bacon and cheddar, and brie and walnut and we had half each. The bacon and cheddar was best. I like brie cold better than warm. There was a Wimpy at Clarence Pier but sadly it didn't do the Knickerbocker Glory. It did the Brown Derby though.

We had a wee in the library loos. I did not know libraries opened on Sundays. There is a small John Lewis and a Debenhams in Southsea and we went in both. Malc kept catching sight of himself in mirrors, probably because of the new trousers.

It was fab weather today. We stopped in a cake shop and had a cupcake and a drink. I had a strawberry ice cream cupcake, Malc had a chocolate orange one.

We walked back to the seafront and briefly went in the castle which was very, very full of squealing children and had a Henry VIII. We went in the arcade on South Parade Pier and Malc won two keyrings in the two pee machines. I paid Zoltar a pound to tell my fortune and he nicked my pound and I had to go and tell the woman on the change desk in the arcade who came out and made it work. She did it in a resigned way as if Zoltar is always doing this.

Malc had chips and a battered sausage and I had a Mr Whippy ice cream. Then we sat by the boating pond and Malc had a coffee then we came home. It took about an hour and a half to get home. We had a great day. Malc said trips to Southsea are additional to Bognor, not instead of. He said sometimes when he's at work at the care home he remembers that he needs to go places now while he can still drive. Malc will be sixty-nine years old in November. He says he will consider retiring when he's seventy.

Monday 17th September

I went to see Mum this morning. She said Tinker from Lovejoy has died (the actor, rather than the character). She said she enjoyed the sweet and sour chicken balls and rice she had on David's birthday. She said Bridget likes Thai food. I asked Mum what sort of things that is but she didn't know. The next family birthdays are Malc's then mine, both in November.

This afternoon I read all of *The Best Christmas Pageant Ever* by Barbara Robinson. It is truly a luxury to have time to read a whole book in one go. Malc came home from the allotment with three large courgettes. He announces his produce differently depending on the novelty and scarcity of it. If he's bringing home raspberries he'll show me the container and say something like 'Look at these little beauties!' and I'll say something like 'All grown by your fair hands and the sun!' but if he's bringing home something we get a lot of, like courgettes, he'll just put them on the kitchen counter and nod at them.
Malc and I had beans on toast and a Cadbury chocolate mousse snowman for dinner. Nicola sent me a message to tell me it's ninety-nine days until Christmas!

Tuesday 18th September
I met Carol outside Matalan this morning. She very kindly gave me a book, Jeanette Winterson's *Christmas Days* and some mini Lindt Lindor balls. We browsed Matalan but didn't buy anything. They have a lot of reduced-price boob tubes.

We had a coffee in Asda's café, then looked round Asda. I told Carol that I thought keeping this diary helps me be more me. She said who I am is lovely and not to ever change. She asked how I was getting on with my felt owl. I said I'd almost finished blanket stitching the two halves together, then I'll stuff it and it will be done. We both learnt blanket stitch at school. It has come back to me. My owl is purple and blue. It has chevrons of blue metallic thread on the tummy and button eyes.

Carol and I walked home together until we said goodbye at the start of Blackbird Leys bridge. Occasionally when I say goodbye to Carol it feels like decades ago at the end of a school day. Today it felt like that.

I put my mini Lindt Lindor balls in the Christmas woodland scene biscuit barrel. I have decided that this will be used to store the Christmas chocolate. I will get some more Cadbury chocolate mousse snowmen and I will ask Malc to take a couple in to Donna to thank her for the felt owl pattern.

Wednesday 19th September
At this point in September Christmas really wakes up. It's been dormant in the summer, although not for me! I finished reading *A Cotswold Christmas* compiled by John Hudson. It had no index so you didn't know what was coming next. It had some bits I've already read but are well worth re-reading (extracts from Laurie Lee and Jilly Cooper) and some local things I've never heard of.

Ken has given us a large cauliflower. Malc gave him some courgettes. We had Bolognese pasta bake with added courgette slices for dinner.

Thursday 20th September
I began reading *Calm Christmas and a Happy New Year* by Beth Kempton. I have a good chance of a calm Christmas this year. It is Val's turn to do Christmas dinner and I will not be working in a food shop in the run up to Christmas. I will stroll slowly up to Christmas, enjoying all the detail of it. Some Christmases have blurred past me.

Malc and I went to Lidl when he got in from work. We wanted pesto and goats' cheese focaccia but there weren't any. We spent forty pounds on mostly random stuff that doesn't make an actual meal! I thought he was going to spend thirty pounds on a leg of ham but thankfully he thought better of it. We should have waited until tomorrow morning to go to Lidl.

Nicola phoned. She's entered a competition to win a year's supply of crisps. She was pleased because she got a free face pack in Holland & Barrett with O2 Priority. She said Holland & Barrett doesn't smell like health food shops used to. She used to like Sunstore in Newbury because they did Beauty Without Cruelty make-up. She had a lovely gold eyeshadow that I borrowed once or twice. When I got off the phone I added gold eyeshadow to the snowman tin of gift ideas.

Friday 21st September

This morning Malc and I lay in bed until it got light with no alarm clock and no urgency. Then Malc said 'My onions need me' and got up. I went to see Mum. I had tomato soup and a roll with her for lunch. I mildly nagged her again about getting an alarm in case she falls. She said she doesn't intend on falling.

This afternoon I finished making my felt owl. It is quite good. It's not as neat as Donna's but Donna has made lots of them. I am going to adapt the pattern and make a robin next.

Saturday 22nd September
Mum rang this morning to say Norwich was on *Homes Under The Hammer*. I cut out the brown body, black legs and red tummy for the felt robin I'm making. I have loads of little black buttons for eyes and plenty of stuffing. I just need some yellow felt for the beak.

This evening we went out to Dorindos Mexican restaurant with Val and Henry. The food was great and you can try on a big Mexican hat. Malc enjoyed trying on the hat, Henry didn't. I would have expected it to be the other way round. It made me think of the episode in *The Good Life* when Tom makes hats out of newspaper and Margot wants the one made out of *The Daily Telegraph*. I had chilli con carne, Val had prawn tacos, Malc and Henry had steak. For pudding Malc and I had mango and coconut cheesecake and Val and Henry had churros.

Val gave me three books she got in her local charity shops; *The Virago Book Of Christmas* edited by Michelle Lovric, *The Little Book Of Christmas Joys* by Brown, Brown and Peel and *The Perfect Christmas* by Rose Henniker Heaton. I said that having a pile of unread Christmas books brings me joy. Henry said if you have a garden and a library, you have everything you need. Malc said those were wise words but he'd also like a bathroom and bedroom. I said a kitchen would also be useful. Henry said it was Cicero who said a garden and a library is everything you need. Val said she hoped Cicero wasn't an architect or an estate agent.

We told Val and Henry about our day out at Southsea. Malc said we could all go one Sunday before it gets cold and he doesn't mind driving. Val is going to look at their calendar and get back to me.

Sunday 23rd September

Malc harvested the pears from the pear tree. He said astronomical autumn starts today. I love this time of year. The only thing I don't like is getting a cold bum in the shower. Malc has put the heating on timer so it'll come on in the morning if the house is cold enough. When I think of the dusty coal fires of my youth I go over to the radiator and give it a little grateful pat.

We went to Hobbycraft in Botley this afternoon so I could get some yellow felt. Unlike some husbands, Malc never questions my wants. Gail once bought a Bedazzler and Len was scathing about it. I bought some red foil cupcake cases as well as the yellow felt, they will be great for Christmas cupcakes. When did we stop saying fairy cakes and start saying cupcakes?

Monday 24th September

Malc and I went to Swindon shopping. It was stressful on the way there because it was hard to find town centre parking. We went to the outlet centre and parked there then got the bus to the town centre (which was very easy).

In Swindon town centre Malc got shoes in Debenhams, pants and socks in M&S (he's bought his first pair of briefs rather than trunks, he may like them and buy briefs from now on, or it may be just a briefs encounter!), foot cream in Boots and *Plebs* series 4 on DVD from HMV. We had coffee in a non-chain coffee shop. I had a caramel shortcake and Malc had a sausage bap. On the wall it had painted 'Quality is doing it right when no-one is watching - Henry Ford'. I bought a book in the British Heart Foundation shop called *A Wiltshire Christmas*.

I know being from Oxford I am supposed to dislike Swindon on a football rivalry basis. It is hard to be impartial. I have to say the town centre is quite bleak and does little to endear itself to one. However, people might say that about Templars Square in Cowley. I don't think they could say that about Oxford. To give Swindon its due, the statue of Isambard Kingdom Brunel is very good. Also it cost twelve pounds to park all day which is cheaper than Oxford or Reading.

The McArthur Glen Designer Outlet Centre is swankier than the town centre. We smelt a lot of candles in the Yankee Candle shop until our noses got confused. We had a big browse in the Lindt shop. They have enormous foiled chocolate Santas. We used to say Father Christmas more, now we seem to say Santa. We tried the mango and passionfruit tea in Whittards. It is full of sugar and very nice. The Cadbury shop has what they say are bargains but everything is the same price as B&M. We're spoiled with our B&M, it's a very good one.

We got KFC fillet burger meals for dinner and planned an evening of drinking tea and watching the new *Plebs* DVD.

Tuesday 25th September

Today is three quarter Christmas, in three months it will be actual Christmas! This morning I finished making my felt robin. I have hung it next to the owl I made up in the loft conversion by the Christmas tree and decorations. This afternoon I baked a chocolate Swiss roll and decorated it with chocolate icing, icing sugar and a little robin thus transforming it into a Yule log.

Wednesday 26th September
Malc bought a stonking great spaghetti squash home from the allotment this morning. He's not sure about his new M&S briefs. He thinks they're a bit snug and he might stick with trunks. We had a slice of Yule log for lunch today. I had to eject a big spider from the bath.

Thursday 27th September
I met Val in town. Val and Henry can come to Southsea this Sunday. Val said she's really looking forward to it and she hasn't seen the British seaside for ages. We walked up St Giles and then down Little Clarendon Street to Central Living. Val bought some heart shaped spoons which are a wedding present for a friend of Henry's. It is his third marriage. They are lovely spoons.

We had lunch in Branca. My main was chicken Kiev and green beans on potato rosti (I'd have preferred a potato waffle but when in Jericho…). Val had chicken tagine. We shared a dessert of chocolate nemesis with ginger ice cream and it was extremely good, intensely, richly chocolatey like a Cadbury mousse snowman.

We looked round some shops after lunch. I got some berry bon bon hand cream in The Body Shop. My hands will smell Christmassy!

Friday 28th September

We went to Notcutts garden centre today. There were three peacocks indoors by the bird food. One of them was trying to peck open a massive bag of sunflower hearts. A shop assistant had to shoo them out. Fancy having that in your job description!

Malc looked at the plants and pots outside while I had a big browse of their Christmas department. There was a huge amount of shortbread. We had lunch in the restaurant. We both had steak and ale pie and mash. Malc said there was a lovely lot of cyclamen and maybe he should get some and put them in a pot for some winter colour in the garden. I got the sense you get after many years of marriage that he wanted to be encouraged so I did. We chose three plants; red, bright pink and pale pink and a pale blue pot to put them in.

Nicola rang, she has entered a competition to win a year's supply of pies and a year's supply of ECCO shoes. At first I thought it was one competition for both pies and shoes, but it is two separate competitions. Nicola said she will give Nan the shoes if she wins. I told her we had a good pie today. She said retirement sounds like great fun. I said it is! I told her I am still keeping this diary and it was a very thoughtful present and I am using it to record my cheerful keeping of Christmas. She said she is planning some Christmas storytelling events in the library.

Saturday 29th September

I finished reading *Calm Christmas and a Happy New Year*. It's a bit different to the Christmas books I've read before. The author has this idea of a Christmas constellation, which is the bits which are most important to you. It's the sort of book Nicola might like, she's quite introspective. Maybe I should buy everyone a Christmas book for Christmas this year? I feel like I could recommend Christmas books to people now I've read so many.

Sunday 30th September

We had a great day out today in Southsea with Val and Henry. Val bought Waitrose Butter Mintoes for us to suck in the car. Henry said taste wise they are akin to the Murray Mint. He was not wrong. We all had chips for lunch on the South Parade Pier then went to the castle (which was quiet compared to two weeks ago). We saw loads of cannons and a model of Henry VIII. Val took a picture of Henry next to his famous namesake! She said she knows which one she'd rather be married to!

Next we went to the D Day Museum (Henry and Malc's choice) in which the most moving exhibit for me was short films of recent interviews with elderly veterans. We owe them a debt of gratitude that can never be repaid. All those young men who never got to become fathers or enjoy a Christmas with their loved ones, or exist for their allotted three score year and ten.

We went to the Clarence Pier where we spent lots of two pees in the two pee falls machines winning keyrings and other novelties (Henry said it made him think of Noel Coward's diary in which he goes to the casino and has some good wins).

We had burgers for dinner in Wimpy. Malc dropped Val and Henry home at half past eight.

September reckoning, have I kept Christmas all September? The year has turned its face towards Christmas and it has been a truly lovely month. I wish I could keep my life at this point and no-one I love would grow old or frail. We've had super family occasions; David's birthday and days out with Val and Henry have been highlights. Also Bognor.

My Christmas gift ideas are coming along nicely. I've had the gift of a free jigsaw from a man at the boot sale, cauliflower from Ken, chocolates from Carol and books from Val. I've made a Yule log which was absolutely delicious! I've sewn a felt owl and felt robin, who are maybe not very professional looking but it was fun to reacquaint myself with the blanket stitch I learned at school. I have honoured Christmas in my heart and home this month.

October

Monday 1st October

I like it when a new month begins on a Monday, it's tidy. Other months sprawl and are untidy, starting mid-week. It's like when Easter straddles March and April rather than sitting neatly in one month or the other.

I retired eight months ago, and I still appreciate not being woken up by an alarm clock. Today is the start of my eighth month of retirement. Am I making the most of it? I think so. I am very content right now.

I started reading *The Virago Book Of Christmas.* It's an anthology and all of the writers in it are women.

Tuesday 2nd October

Today I had a practice at making some Christmas cupcakes which I might make for the care home Christmas Bazaar (or fayre or fete or whatever they call it this year). I made plain sponge cupcakes in red foil cases then iced them with a big triangular swirl of green icing to look like a tree. I topped the tree with a star made of marzipan (very fiddly, I need practice or to find some ready-made stars) and decorated it with mini Smarties to represent the baubles. I popped round to Carol's with one for her and one for Donna and she called me a clever thing!

Wednesday 3rd October

Tonight we went to the theatre to see Dave Gorman with Val and Henry. We had a drink in The Grapes before the show. It has gone back to being a more traditional looking pub. For a while it had pallets on the walls and a stripped back industrial look. Henry said it was like drinking in a skip, although I'm sure he doesn't know that from experience. Henry says an alcoholic drink is a wonderful prelude to some clever comedy.

Val had some minced beef in her bag! They had popped to M&S before meeting us. She had a Waitrose order this morning and they didn't deliver the Aberdeen Angus minced beef for the cottage pie she's going to make. Val got me the M&S Christmas gift guide.

Nick Doody was the support act for Dave Gorman. He did some funny material about Lidl. Henry has never been to Lidl! Val has only been a couple of times. Dave Gorman was great, he did two found poems. I adore his found poems. We were all in stitches. After the show Henry and I bought books and got them signed! I got the *Found Poetry* book. There are twenty found poems from the comments section of news stories.

It was a great evening. We ate ginger nuts in the interval that Val had got from M&S when she was getting mince. When we got home Malc and I had a hot chocolate in bed and I read the M&S Christmas gift guide. The women in M&S nightwear never look tired. They don't take their make-up off before bed, Joan Collins says you should.

Thursday 4th October
I've had a lazy day of reading. I read all my new Dave Gorman book then I read a bit by Sue Townsend in *The Virago Book Of Christmas*, from her Adrian Mole book. Nicola loved that book. We all watched the telly programme, it was very, very funny.

I went to the Co-op and got beef to make a beef casserole for dinner. Sitting next to Val's minced beef last night has made me want something beefy! Nicola rang. I reminded her of Adrian Mole. She reminded me that Malc used to sing a song about do you want some Christmas pud to the tune of Take That's 'Back for Good'. Nicola said she has come to realise that it is unlikely she will marry Mark Owen. Nicola has shown no interest in marrying anyone else. She said she has got a lovely copy of *The Nutcracker* to read from in the library for a Christmas story event. I have never read *The Nutcracker*.

Friday 5th October

Val has ordered the turkey crown for Christmas Day dinner from Waitrose, to be delivered on Saturday 22nd December between one and two in the afternoon. It is ridiculous to have to order it eighty-one days before Christmas but it is necessary. Val said the delivery slots for Sunday 23rd December have all gone already.

I went to see Mum. She has bought a new dressing gown in Primark. I'm surprised, she is usually firmly M&S for nightwear. She was with Bridget and I think Bridget egged her on. For dinner we had leftover beef casserole and mash. A new series of *Have I Got News For You* starts tonight.

Saturday 6th October

This morning I ordered Malc more vests and pants (trunks not briefs) from M&S online at his request. He went out to the allotment. At lunch time he bought the last of this year's spaghetti squashes home. We had our usual Saturday bacon sandwich. I listened to Trans-Siberian Orchestra while I did some ironing. Their 'Christmas Canon' is one of the most beautiful Christmas songs ever. It almost makes me cry but I can't explain why and I'm not generally a big crier. Even Malc said it was stirring. Perhaps I'll buy Gail one of their CDs for Christmas. She quite likes music and could do with some moments of joy.

Sunday 7th October
I made a lightly fruited cake which came out well. When I make the Christmas cake this year I might deviate a bit from the traditional very heavily fruited recipe. It should still have some wonderful decoration and a strong taste of marzipan.

Monday 8th October
I woke up at half past six, got up for a wee, then went back to bed. Not having to get up at a particular time to go to work is still a novelty after so many years of employment. It's a wonderful privilege to have a day stretch ahead of you in which you don't have to spend eight and a half hours of it doing something you'd rather not do. I used to get at least one headache a week when I was working. I've had very few headaches since I retired.

I did some ironing while watching *Still Open All Hours*. Ironing is something I'd rather not do so I only do half an hour sessions. They have no new plots on *Still Open All Hours*, but people like familiar stories.

I read a bit by Elizabeth Goudge in *The Virago Book Of Christmas* that was set in Oxford and was about watching a play; 'They knew how to enjoy themselves on

Christmas Eve, did these people of Oxford, and they were doing it'. A lot of books are set in Oxford. I sometimes feel sorry for other lovely cities like Coventry. If I wrote a book I wouldn't set it in Oxford.

Tuesday 9th October

I decorated the cake I made on Sunday with white icing and large yellow marzipan stars. I met Carol for coffee and she gave me a crocheted Christmas pudding! It's very neat. It has tiny dark brown sequins on to represent the raisins! It has a cream-coloured topping, felt holly leaves and red bead berries.

We watched *The Great British Bake Off*. It was vegan week. We had a slice of the cake I decorated this morning.

Wednesday 10th October

I browsed an Oxfordshire County Council website called www.pictureoxon.org.uk which had some photos of 1960s Christmases. There was one of a Round Table Santa I liked especially.

Tom knocked on our door this evening wondering if Malc could show him where the stop cock is. We both went round. Their stop cock is in the same place as ours. Tom and Tamsin are aiming to do their own home improvements except for the big stuff like a new boiler. Malc told Tom to give him a shout if he needs to borrow any tools.

Thursday 11th October

I got the Boots Christmas gift guide today. I made a cup of tea and sat and flicked through it. There are a lot of hand cream gift sets. I hope Mum gets more biscuits than hand cream this year. I don't buy much in Boots at Christmas now because I can never find the third thing I want in their three for the price of two offer.

I read a bit by Agatha Christie in *The Virago Book Of Christmas*. I like this quote; 'Colonel Johnson, Chief Constable of Middleshire might be of the opinion that nothing could beat a wood fire, but Hercule Poirot was of the opinion that central heating could and did every time!' I totally agree with Poirot about central heating. Maybe Poirot, like me, sometimes pats radiators gratefully.

Friday 12th October
I popped round to Mum's and took her a slice of cake. Mum said she and Bridget are thinking of going to Woodstock Christmas Market later this month.

When I got home there was a parcel from M&S at the back door. It was Malc's vests. We're still waiting for his pants. Nicola rang, she asked if I'd seen that the Boots Christmas gift guide was out.

Saturday 13th October
Today is windy and rainy and so mild we haven't got the heating on. I sewed a bag out of garden fleece for protecting Malc's camellia from frost. I embroidered a simple flower on it with a yellow middle and pink petals. Malc said it was jolly. I have plenty of time this year for extra flourishes. Malc buys a roll of frost protection fleece because it's cheaper than the frost protection bags, but he likes the bags because they are easier to slip over the plant then attach to the pot, so I make bags of the perfect size out

of the roll of fleece. It's nice to help Malc with something in the garden, which is firmly his department.

I chased up Malc's pants with M&S. They said they will send a replacement because we should have had them by now. We started the jigsaw this evening. When we are finished we will have a picture of a robin looking at a slice of Christmas cake. We found the straight edge bits and put a few together.

Sunday 14th October

I went in Wilko today and got some Malteser reindeer and Cadbury chocolate mousse snowmen. I put them in the Christmas woodland scene biscuit barrel I got in Bognor. I browsed advent calendars. I overheard someone planning to buy the Thornton's Continental advent calendar now and eat it now because the advent calendar is cheaper per hundred grams than a box of Thornton's Continental is. There are a lot of financially savvy people in Cowley (not including the people who use Bright House to get their sofa obviously).

Malc and I have done the top row and a side row of the jigsaw.

Monday 15th October

A Monday morning on which you don't have to get up for work is a wonderful thing. This time last year I was leaving my warm bed suddenly when my alarm clock rang, catapulting myself into the dark, tearing myself away from dreams and to my responsibilities. Sometimes now I lay in bed and imagine the things I'd like to do with the day, I go on imaginary shopping trips, or cook elaborate recipes in my head.

I popped in to see Mum today and took her a Malteser reindeer. She said she'd not had one before. She was wearing a new blue jumper with pearls on from Bon Marche. She said she fell in love with it. She gave me the advice she always does at this time of year, never pick blackberries after the middle of October, because the devil has tinkled on them. I said the blackberries round by us ripened weeks ago and are over now so the devil will have to relieve himself elsewhere. She said the seasons now aren't like the seasons used to be. She said Christmas goes on for much longer than it used to. We agreed this was a good thing. I asked Mum if she wanted an advent calendar this year. She said yes, why not? She said she's thinking of becoming more frivolous in her old age!

Tuesday 16th October

For dinner Malc and I went to the Oxy Oriental for no reason other than we fancied it. We heard two different people have 'Happy Birthday!' sung to them. We both had some little wobbly puddings. We had a mango one, a pistachio one and one we couldn't identify the flavour of. It's Danish week on *The Great British Bake Off*. We watched it in bed. I felt a bit Christmassy, snuggled up, having eaten lots of nice things and knowing we didn't have to be up early in the morning.

Wednesday 17th October

This morning Malc is making noises commensurate with having eaten too much at Oxy. He sounds like a balloon deflating. We finished the bottom row and other side row of the jigsaw so now the outline is complete. We made some progress in the bottom left corner. I had to eject a big spider from the bath, this is a sign of autumn. We went to Sainsbury's this afternoon to add air to the car tyres and while Malc was bending down doing the back rear left tyre a leaf fell off a tree and onto the inch of his bum crack that was visible due to him bending right over. It's as if the tree was trying to protect his modesty!

Thursday 18th October
I've been giving a lot of thought to a festive duvet cover this week. Would Malc like sleeping under jolly penguins in hats and scarves? Or should I buy the snowflake print one I've seen? There is a navy one with a silver star print in M&S that's quite nice too but it doesn't scream Christmas, it's subtle.

I finished reading *The Virago Book Of Christmas.* It's a very original anthology with a lot of writers I've never read before. I must remember to thank Val for getting it and see if she'd like to read it. It made me wonder if women write about Christmas differently to men.
Nicola phoned. She hasn't found any competitions to enter this week to win a year's supply of anything. She says grocery shopping is boring and it would be good to have some things that you had a whole year's worth of.

Friday 19th October
I read *The Little Book of Christmas Joys* by Brown, Brown, and Peel. It's a gorgeous book with a metallic plaid cover that looks like gift wrap. It's from Tennessee and lists 432

things to do. I first noticed it was American at the eleventh thing to do; 'Find out what's on everyone's Christmas wish list when the family is together at Thanksgiving'. I love the idea of 'Bake Christmas cookies while a Johnny Mathis Christmas album plays in the background'. I also liked 'Have a special place to display the Christmas card from the farthest distance away'. The card we get from farthest away is from Joyce Matthews, who I went to school with, and who trained as a hairdresser (she did both Nicola and David's first haircuts), and who moved to Australia two decades ago. We've exchanged Christmas cards every year since. I love getting Joyce's card in December. I try to find an especially English looking card for her, maybe some sort of Cotswold looking church or high street scene.

There was the sensible but not fun 'Mail in warranty cards promptly', which Malc is very good at and also 'Don't use the words 'I'm on a diet' during the holidays'. Gail is the only person I know who does this, but actually, if she is on a diet I don't see why she shouldn't say so.

The recommendation of 'Don't forget, no matter how many Christmas photos you take, next year you'll wish you had taken more' made me sigh. I wish I had more photos of my Dad. Henry is the person who takes the most photos in our family.

Saturday 20th October

Can you believe that none of the four Johnny Mathis Christmas albums include 'When a Child Is Born'? I don't know which to buy. Nicola when she was small thought this song was about her because we all used to sing it to her!

We went to collect a parcel from the delivery office (Malc calls it the get it yourself office) and the postman gave us two parcels! One was Malc's M&S pants that should have been delivered ages ago with his vests and the other was his replacement pants. The vests were left in the back garden, by the back door, which is fine. Why did they not bother bringing the pants too? It's a mystery.

I've still made no decision re: the festive duvet cover. I've looked at George at Asda, Matalan, Debenhams, Wilko and Dunelm. I began reading *Remembering Christmas* by Anne Harvey. It has the shortest extracts of any anthology I've read. If most anthologies are a selection box, this one is a tin of Quality Street. There was a good poem by Colin West called 'The Father Christmas on the Cake'. It's about a Father Christmas cake decoration that complains about being in a cupboard for most of the year. I have moved my Father Christmas cake decoration to sit on the Christmas book shelf.

Sunday 21st October

I had a very long online pant conversation with M&S. I explained that both the original pants and the replacement pants were at the delivery office yesterday. The eventual outcome is free pants for Malc and apologies for the inconvenience.

I made my first ever Groupon purchase. I got pork scratchings advent calendars for Henry and Malc for £12.50 each instead of £15. I'm going to Christmas shop carefully and early this year.

Malc came home from the allotment and said that a new allottee is organising a Christmas party for their allotment site and the next nearest allotment site. There is a poster about it on the shed and tickets will be on sale soon. I asked Malc if he wanted to go and he said he didn't know.

Monday 22nd October
We did quite a bit of jigsaw today. The picture is two pieces deep all the way round and we've done the whole bottom left quadrant which is Christmas cake. We had beef burritos for dinner followed by a chocolate snowman. We watched *Still Open All Hours* and *Upstart Crow*. It's been a lovely Monday.

Tuesday 23rd October
I met Lauren for lunch. They are advertising for seasonal staff. Lauren said she told Mr Barker she was meeting me for lunch and he said to ask me if I fancied going back for Christmas! It is nice to be asked but even nicer to be able to decline with thanks. Lauren is doing well in her studies. Dylan is still with his girlfriend, they have been together for six months now. He is on time a bit more often than he used to be and Mr Barker says 'Kicked you out of bed has she?' which the new supervisor tells him is inappropriate. The new supervisor has finally taught Dylan to change till rolls. Lauren said it's lovely to meet me for lunch and have a little moan because I understand the situation and know all the players in the little work dramas. She asked what I've been doing and I told her about the jigsaw then felt a bit old. Lauren's lunch break was quickly over. We said we'd meet before Christmas.

This afternoon I read a good bit by Frances Hodgson Burnett in *Remembering Christmas*. It was about being at a party but not quite feeling that you're at a party. Some Christmas celebrations I lose myself in, like shopping with Nicola, other ones I feel like I'll start to get into the spirit soon but then never quite do and it's time to go home and you feel you've wasted an opportunity.

Wednesday 24th October
Malc and I went to Reading today. We had lunch in Bluegrass Steakhouse on Gun Street. I had a beef burger with mac and cheese on, Malc had a chicken burger. We had cherry flavoured barbecue sauce. Malc was in a thoughtful mood. He said if we had lived a hundred years ago it would have been rare for people of our class to travel thirty miles to the nearest big town. We would have mostly stayed in our village and visited the neighbouring ones we could walk to. Sometimes I think Malc would like living a hundred years ago but I wouldn't.

We got a Moomin advent calendar for Nicola in Waterstones. We got some Turner's Assorted Chocolates from Poundland for Mum. Mum usually gets these and they are always chocolates she recognises, but the last bag she bought had chocolates in she couldn't identify so she wanted another bag from somewhere else to see if these are no longer famous chocolates (they used to be essentially Roses mis-shapes). I got *The Nutcracker* written by E.T.A. Hoffman and illustrated by Maurice Sendak from the BHF shop. Malc got a mustard colour jumper in M&S. We had a big browse in John Lewis. Their Christmas decorations department is lovely. It's a good mix of traditional and modern. Before we set off for home we had a cupcake and a coffee in a café at the Oracle shopping centre.

Thursday 25th October

I rang Witney M&S to see if they had an XL mustard colour jumper in stock (according to the internet they had one), but they didn't actually have one. I'm glad I checked. Malc accidentally bought a size small in Reading yesterday and this jumper has sold out in Oxford. Mustard is the big colour this season.

I made chili con carne for dinner and put cocoa powder in it for the first time ever. Malc didn't notice anything different. Nicola rang, she said Asda are selling a chocolate orange Viennetta this year. I'm not sure I'll like it but I want to try one. She has entered a competition to win a family trip to Lapland! Nicola wouldn't want to just stay in one small village. David already spends a lot of his time at Bicester Village. How wonderful it would be if we all went to Lapland. If this diary of mine was a film it would happen. But it's just the ramblings of a retired woman trying to keep cheerful and enjoy her freedom.

Friday 26th October

Malc and I went to Witney this morning. He took back his size small mustard jumper to M&S. He exchanged it for a red one. When I say he took back his jumper, I mean he stood close by while I returned it. He's oddly shy in shops. Malc got a nice leaf print shirt in White Stuff, it was pricey so he had to be persuaded to splash out.

The clock in Market Square had stopped which seemed quite fitting. Witney does not change much. Bakers

Butchers were doing a roaring trade. There was a newish shop called Lily's Attic which wasn't an attic at all, it was on the ground floor. I'd have liked there to be a shop on the top floor called Lily's Basement, but there wasn't. We had a browse in Lakeland and I got some gold cupcake cases.

We had fish and chips for lunch at Yarnton garden centre. Then Malc looked at the plants and I looked at the Christmas lights and decorations. They have snow globe lanterns with carol singers inside that light up and play a tune.

Malc and I did some jigsaw. We've done more than half now. We have a robin and some Christmas cake done and just the top part to do which is the cake icing and red berries on twigs against a snowy sky.

Saturday 27th October

I went to the Sandy Lane Royal Mail collection office and collected a parcel first thing. I was in when they first tried to deliver but they still put a 'Sorry we missed you' card through the door rather than ringing the doorbell! It was my first Groupon order, two pork scratchings advent calendars, for Malc and Henry. I still need to get an advent calendar for David, Val, Mum and me.

I went to see Mum. I took her the Turner's Assorted Chocolates I got her in Reading. She opened them and said it was the same as the previous bag so she'll stop buying them. I am going to teach her to online shop with Iceland. She insisted on showing me some new cereal called Oatiflakes. I don't think it's actually new, I think she's just noticed it. She said Woodstock Christmas Market was good yesterday. I didn't realise it was a one-day event. I will go next year.

We did more jigsaw, there is about one-fifth left to do. We give each other a cheer when we put a piece in its place.

Sunday 28th October

British Summer Time Ends. This morning Malc went round putting all the clocks back by one hour. I spent my extra hour finishing reading *Remembering Christmas*.

Val came round for coffee. She has tried to persuade Mum to get a wearable personal alarm and Mum told her she'll get one when she's ninety. This is progress of a sort, she'll be ninety in March next year. Val and I went round Cowley Centre shops. Val was very impressed with the Christmas chocolates, sweets and biscuits aisle in B&M. I got some cranberry sauce. It is coming up to the cranberry sauce eating time of year. Val got some orange and lemon slices jelly sweets for cake decorating. We looked at the books in the British Heart Foundation shop and I got *Scrooge's Guide To Christmas* by Richard Wilson.

I made a roast dinner for our evening meal. Malc gets a bit glum at the onset of winter. It takes him a little while to adjust to more time indoors. He has got winter occupations, he has a little pile of almost finished crosswords, he plays his guitar a bit more and he has gardening catalogues which he reads.

Monday 29th October
I started reading *The Perfect Christmas* by Rose Henniker Heaton, it was written in the 1930s for the well-to-do. Sometimes I dream of being the well-to-do, but I am very happy with my lot. Malc read a bulbs catalogue. He says he'll only do hyacinths outdoors because they smell too strongly. I agree.

We finished the jigsaw. We're going to leave it on the table for a while, it's a very cheery robin and Christmas cake picture. Maybe I should get another one? It might help Malc with his getting used to winter blues. Malc noticed that we can now see St Luke's Record Office from our back bedroom window. Every autumn it comes into view when the trees lose their leaves.

Tuesday 30th October
When I went round to see Mum today she didn't answer the door because she was asleep in her chair. I have keys so I let myself in. She looked peaceful and old. I went out of the room again and came in the front door much more noisily. Mum said she didn't sleep well last night. I made us both a cup of coffee. Mum said her friend who has gall stones will feel better in the summer. Old people say this sort of thing. I have never been to the doctor and been prescribed summer. I had a moment of feeling sad about the passing of time. Everyone I love is getter older.

Tonight is the final of *The Great British Bake Off*. Everyone in it is good enough to win. Nicola likes Kim-Joy best. I've been looking at the Lego Star Wars advent calendar for David. If I get the Lego Star Wars advent calendar for David it will be more expensive than the

Moomin calendar I got Nicola. Malc and I always try to treat Nicola and David the same.

Wednesday 31st October
I had to Google what a cotillion is when I was reading *The Perfect Christmas*. It's a kind of dance for four couples. I bought the Lego Star Wars advent calendar for David. I will buy Nicola a second advent calendar with chocolate because her Moomin one is just pictures. I can even things up with their Christmas presents if there's still a discrepancy. I looked at Hotel Chocolat advent calendars, I might get one for Val.

October reckoning, have I kept Christmas all October? It's easier to keep Christmas in the ber months because Christmas more naturally pops up. I've read some Christmas books and also the Boots and M&S gift guides. I've made Christmas cupcakes and a lightly fruited cake. I've had a night at the theatre which to me always feels like a Christmas treat because the first time I ever went to the theatre it was to the pantomime.

My lovely family have given me joy this month. Val has ordered the turkey for Christmas Day. Malc and I have done the festive jigsaw. My friend Carol has given me a crocheted Christmas pudding.

I've listened to the wonderful music of Trans-Siberian Orchestra. I've viewed old Christmas photos on the council's website. I've thought about advent calendars. I've eaten chocolate snowmen. October has had lots of jolly elements but I feel like I can have an even firmer grasp of Christmas in November!

November

Thursday 1st November

One of the present suggestions for women in *The Perfect Christmas* is Pyrex. Malc says I should get a job for the Pyrex marketing board because I'm always saying how good it is.

A poem in praise of Pyrex;
Clear, trusty and unrusty,
but don't buy too much or it'll get dusty.
Crumbles, cottage pies and pasta bakes,
Go in the oven then on your plate.
Happy in the fridge with foil on top,
Pyrex, Pyrex, don't ever stop.

However, I won't be buying Pyrex for any women this year. There was a shift at some point, maybe in the 1970s, when women were encouraged to want something for themselves rather than for the kitchen. You can still buy kitchenware as a Christmas gift if you know the person you're giving it to really likes cooking.

I'm aiming to have done a lot of my Christmas shopping by the end of this month. Every year I see newspaper columns or people on magazine programmes like *The One Show* saying how Christmas has become too commercial. I think it's okay to buy things, as long as you don't take it too far, going beyond your budget or buying things for the sake of it rather than with a reasonable sense of confidence that the recipient will like it.

Friday 2nd November

Things you're reminded repeatedly to have enough of in *The Perfect Christmas* are soda water, stamps and cigarettes. Nowadays we have lots more mixers for drinks, can send emails and know that smoking is bad for people. I had a vision of a room full of people in the 1930s all smoking, drinking and writing in a wood panelled room in a big house. Imagine if you could pop back in time to look at other Christmases? In the 1950s I imagine crepe paper garlands, Meccano for the boys and dolls for the girls. In the 1960s I imagine shiny foil decorations, make-up for the girls and records for the boys. In the 1970s everyone's wallpaper would be lurid and Abba would be playing on a music centre in the background. You could watch Walkmans being unwrapped in the 1980s and see computers appearing in the 1990s. The one thing that would be common to all Christmases would be Christmas spreading like a soft glow, taking over your mind and body, like that Ready Brek advert.

Malc and I went to the big Tesco and got ingredients for dinner. We're having burritos, at Malc's request. He doesn't usually want to shake things up at dinner time so I'm being encouraging. I've had burritos with Nicola at Las Iguanas. Malc and I have never had burritos together before. We have plenty of time to choose and make our evening meals now. I used to be so tired by Friday when I worked full time that I either wanted soup or takeaway for dinner.

Saturday 3rd November

I'm not aiming to make this Christmas better than the last one, I'm aiming to make it equally as good. Adverts that encourage us to have the best Christmas ever are setting us up for disappointment. Christmas is like a rock formation, each year gets added to the ones before.

This evening we're going to a bonfire night party at Val and Henry's. They've been having this party for decades. After this party the next big family events are Malc and I's birthdays and then Christmas. We take Mum to the party and Val fusses about her being warm enough. We only have sparklers now. Until 1994 Henry set off fireworks then he read about some research that showed letting off fireworks caused an increase in persistent organic pollutants so he stopped. Val cooks jacket potatoes and hot dogs and invites the neighbours.

Sunday 4th November

We had a lovely evening at Val and Henry's. Mum has got a new hat. It's from Damart and is red with a flower on it. I wore my long black velvet skirt and a blouse which is black with blue glittery swirls. I think I wear this every other year to the bonfire night party! We drank hot chocolate. Henry has bought a new coffee machine that uses pods. Val doesn't know how to work it yet. Val and Henry's neighbours with the wine cellar got their wine cellar into the conversation twice, once on arrival when handing Val a bottle and saying 'a little token from our cellar, in thanks for your hospitality' and once when saying they recently discovered a great wine with a chocolate note and simply had to add a few bottles to the cellar. Mum and I overheard them saying to some other, newer neighbours, 'All our toilets are Villeroy & Boch' and Mum whispered to me, 'You can shit just as well on an Armitage Shanks for a fraction of the cost!' I heard Malc say 'I've had good nduja in Bognor.' We all stood in a circle with our sparklers. We could see a lot of fireworks going off in the sky around us. The air smelt of excitement. There were lights all aglow and faces all aglow. It reminded me of when you have people round a Christmas tree.

This afternoon I fell asleep on the sofa with my book and awoke just after five to the sound of chopping. Every so often Malc thinks he should do more around the house and become what he calls a new man (he has been saying this roughly twice a year since 1977, when Nicola was tiny and I was overwhelmed and exhausted by my first go at motherhood). Malc has been to the local Co-op and bought things to cook dinner. We're having paprika chicken, mashed potatoes and carrots. Malc never checks the cupboards before shopping. He bought more paprika and butter rather than using what we've got and had to pay for a bag because he forgot to take one with him. I would like his new manning to include cleaning the toilets but it never does.

We watched a Louis Theroux documentary before bed called *Love Without Limits*. It was about polyamory. I do not think I could cope with two Malcs and I don't think he could cope with two of me! But each to their own.

Monday 5th November

I finished reading *The Perfect Christmas* and now I know how to glacé a chestnut. Malc and I went to Asda at Wheatley to get a chocolate orange Viennetta. David came for dinner. He has tomorrow off work. We had hot dog and chips followed by chocolate orange Viennetta (we like it) and then went out in the garden and had a sparkler. David

wrote rude words in the air with his. It ran out after bollo so Malc let him have another one to write cks with. He does indulge that boy.
Nicola sent me a message saying it's fifty days until Christmas!

Tuesday 6th November
I asked Malc what he wants for his birthday. He said he didn't know. It is only a week away. Why is full of the joys of spring a phrase and not full of the joys of autumn? Today is a lovely autumn day and I am full of the joys of autumn. I read some of Richard Wilson's *Scrooge's Guide To Christmas*. There are pictures of him making a hat out of a *Daily Telegraph*. The headline on the paper is 'Blair wins by a landslide'. Both Malc and I voted for him then regretted it when he took us to war with Iraq.

Val rang to suggest we do a London Christmas shopping trip soon. I said yes please! She is booking us a nice hotel for the eleventh of November. Val asked what she should get Malc for his birthday. I said I wasn't sure and she said how about a Notcutts voucher and a tin of fancy biscuits? I said that would be perfect. I asked if she had any ideas of what I can get Henry for Christmas. She said Glenlivet Captains Reserve Whiskey is going down well with him at the moment. I added a bottle to my online grocery shop. I watched a video on YouTube of the L'Occitane advent calendar being opened. I'm thinking of getting this for Val.

Wednesday 7th November

Lauren served me in the shop today, she's looking well. I was buying brandy butter icing topped mince pies, easy peeler satsumas and brie and cranberry flavour tortilla crisps (a special Christmas invention). The Christmas stamps are out. It's post boxes in the snow this year.

I read a funny bit in *Scrooge's Guide To Christmas* by George Bernard Shaw about how much he dislikes Christmas. He lays it on a bit thick and he says we have to buy things people don't want for Christmas. If George Bernard Shaw had shopped earlier and communicated better he could have avoided this.

Malc asked if I want to go to an allotment Christmas party. Ken has been buttonholed by the woman organising it. She works part time organising events and thinks it would be nice to provide an opportunity for allottees to meet socially at a time when they aren't busy on their plots. I said I'll happily go if Malc wants to go. Malc's face was inconclusive.

Thursday 8th November

Mum has lost her digital camera at Blenheim Palace. I told her to find the box and I'll help her order the same again because she knows how to use the one she has. Is her losing her camera just the sort of absent mindedness anyone can briefly experience or is it a sign of dementia? I don't want to think too much about this but also want to be realistic.

I went to collect a prescription for Malc but it wasn't there yet. It goes from our doctor to the pharmacy but the woman in the pharmacy said their driver quit this week so there is a delay. I did a bit of Christmas shopping.

I got a whiskey glass for Henry from Asda with jolly Santas on it. I also bought a festive Christmas duvet cover, it has a photographic bauble print all over it. I didn't find anything exciting for Malc's birthday although I did get him some chocolate covered Brazil nuts. Maybe I'll get him a jigsaw.

Malc was late home from work. He had been talking to bereaved relatives in the car park. There is always a waiting list for care home places and Malc always feels terrible for the relatives who have to clear the room of their loved one swiftly. Sometimes he helps if they are struggling. Sometimes he goes away and comes back with a cup of tea for them. I am glad I married a kind man.

Friday 9th November

I have bought Malc some mini bark chippings, compost and winter pansies for his birthday. We went to Notcutts today and I told him I'd pay for whatever he wanted for his birthday and that was what he wanted.

I overheard a couple in the food section dithering over buying a Bakewell tart. She said 'It's a bit of an indulgence, but we haven't had one for ages.' Then he said 'The one in Tesco is half the price.' Then she said 'The doctor told you to go easy on this sort of thing.' Initially I'd thought they were probably on a tight budget but then the health concern came into play. I've noticed that it is expected in marriages of long standing that the wife looks after the health of the husband. Older people will give me advice about Malc's health if they find out he's had heart trouble but they won't say it to him. I find this maddening.

I browsed the Christmas cards. There were some lovely Raymond Briggs Father Christmas ones. There were also some lovely ones by the RSPB. I checked when I got home and I have plenty of Christmas cards. I've got ones with Christmas trees from WH Smith. I've got robins wearing scarves and town scenes with Santa's sleigh overhead, I've got some luxury Woolworths ones Malc rescued from a skip, plus a few cards left from last year, so almost fifty. I have put them on the table downstairs and when the mood takes me I shall begin to write them.

I suggested to Malc that we should start celebrating his birthday now and spread it out so we had fish and chips from the Littlemore Fish Bar for dinner. While he went to get the fish and chips I ordered a jigsaw online for his birthday so he has a surprise to open on the day. I got one of a summer garden.

I read a bit in *Scrooge's Guide To Christmas* where it is suggested that putting on a CD of Christmas carols sung by Russ Abbot would make your guests want to leave. This wouldn't happen round here, we all love Russ Abbot. We've got both his fun books up in the roof room.

Saturday 10th November

Malc and I popped round the shops to get his prescription this morning. We saw Gail outside Holland & Barrett. She said she is giving up smoking with Nicorette. She said she tried with just willpower but felt permanently furious. Most of her customers in the bookies smell of fags.

I changed the bedclothes to the new festive bauble print bedclothes. The bedroom looks jolly! I will be sleeping under the new duvet cover tonight then tomorrow night I'll be sleeping under a hotel one in London!

Malc is watching *The Matrix* which no longer is convincingly futuristic because of the CRT monitors and old mobile phones. How quickly the future becomes the past!

Sunday 11th November

Christmas shopping trip to London with Val.

Val picked me up just after eight and we got on the Oxford Tube at Thornhill Park and Ride. Today is Remembrance Sunday so London will be busy. We are both wearing our poppies.

We went to McDonalds when we got to London because not a lot else was open yet on Oxford Street and we needed a wee. We both had a cheeseburger and a cup of tea. Then we looked at Selfridges Christmas window displays. The theme is Selfridges Rocks Christmas and they have borrowed guitars from Bernie Marsden. I like it, but some people have said it's not very Christmassy. We walked up Oxford Street and looked at the Christmas decorations. We walked along Carnaby Street and admired their Bohemian Rhapsody themed décor. This is a film which has just come out about Freddie Mercury's life. We looked at loads of restaurant menus before choosing Browns for lunch. I had beef roast dinner (mostly good; slightly undercooked parsnip). Browns was decorated for Christmas with red and gold baubles on green foliage. I felt like I was in Christmas.

We checked into our hotel, the Victory House Hotel on Leicester Place, just off Leicester Square. The room was quite grey and geometric patterned. It was nice. After we'd dumped our bags we walked to Covent Garden. We had a matcha tea and vanilla ice cream from Milk Train. We looked round the Christmas Market at Leicester Square. It's like all Christmas markets; wooden things, hats, German sausage, star shaped light shades. We went to the Japan Centre on Piccadilly Circus. Val got some mango flavour Pocky. Then we went back to the hotel to have a rest for an hour before dinner.

We went to Caffe Concerto for dinner. Val had scones and I had Black Forest gateau. We just eat whatever we fancy in London. I indulge my sweet tooth! After dinner we went to the cinema and saw *Bohemian Rhapsody*. It was very good. Malc has got *Queen's Greatest Hits* on cassette still.

We sat on Leicester Square after the cinema and watched the world go by. We spotted Eddie Izzard, in high heeled boots and a pink and black anorak, looking truly fabulous.

Monday 12th November

As usual I slept erratically in unfamiliar surroundings and without the comforting shape of Malc to the side of me. I woke up too hot at two a.m. I woke up at four forty-five a.m. to the sound of luggage being dragged along the corridor outside my room. While lying awake I thought about what I'll buy people for Christmas. Val and I tend to do a lot of looking and not that much shopping. I got up at seven. I sat by my window having a coffee and watching people smoke outside the Premier Inn opposite. I wondered how Gail was getting on with not smoking. I hope she succeeds this time. It's a shame you can't give people the things they really want for Christmas at our age like younger knees, better eyesight or hearing that still works when the kettle is boiling. The Christmas lights hung from the trees in Leicester Square were still lit. You have to stay overnight to watch London wake up. It's worth being a bit tired for.

Val and I went for breakfast at Breakfast Club in Soho. She had disco fries, I had Cabbie's breakfast. We hummed along to the tunes playing in the background. Then we went back to the hotel, checked out but left our overnight bags with reception and got the tube to Borough and went to Borough Market. We ate loads of little bits of free sample food. I got Malc an apple muffin. Val bought some satsumas. We saw the Golden Hind. We walked across Tower Bridge and back. We got the tube back to Leicester Square and had a walk round Chinatown. It began to rain so we went to Waxy O'Connor's for a drink.

We collected our bags, said farewell to Leicester Square and made our way home. I'm going to have an early night tonight. I have had a lovely trip to London with Val. We didn't buy much but we got some good ideas. I feel I can start my Christmas shopping in earnest now!

Tuesday 13th November

Today is Malc's birthday, which he likes to keep fairly fuss-free. He is sixty-nine years old today. He went to work as usual for a Tuesday. Next year his birthday will be a Wednesday so he won't be at work. Before he went I gave him his surprise gifts from me. He seemed pleased with the chocolate covered Brazil nuts and summer garden jigsaw.

I had a lovely lazy morning reading *The Nutcracker*. I'm surprised Nicola is reading it at a story time because she doesn't like stories where part of it is a child's dream. She and David used to complain about books that did this. I went out this afternoon and got a ginger and lemon loaf cake. When Malc got in from work we had a slice of cake and he opened his present from Val and Henry, which he said was very generous (fifty pounds to spend at Notcutts and some Belgian chocolate biscuits). Mum had got him some socks he likes with a comfort top and a nice card with a garden shed on. Nicola rang, she has got him a subscription to *Garden Answers* magazine and will visit at the weekend. David remembered to send a card. We'll see him at the weekend too. Viv and Eric sent a lovely card. Malc said Donna did him a cake at work and all the residents sang happy birthday to him.

We had pizza for Malc's birthday dinner. He said there are good offers on a Tuesday.

Wednesday 14th November

Malc started his new birthday jigsaw today. We had a slice of ginger and lemon cake mid-morning. I finished reading *Scrooge's Guide To Christmas.* It's important for the people who love Christmas to remember that not everyone agrees.

I've asked David to get me a L'Occitane advent calendar for Aunty Val, I remembered there is a branch where he works at Bicester Village. You need your head and your heart for Christmas preparations. I just need an advent calendar for Mum now, and one for me. It's wonderful having plenty of time to do my Christmas preparations.

Thursday 15th November

I started reading *A Wiltshire Christmas*, compiled by John Chandler. I read that you should use a wooden spoon to stir your Christmas pudding mixture because the manger was made of wood. This is quite convenient, most people would use a wooden spoon anyway. Malc said I have now read so many Christmas books I could become a Christmasologist.

For dinner we had cottage pie and I made snowmen figures in the mash on top. They had real carrot noses, peas for eyes, scarves made of red pepper and hats made of aubergine. Malc said it was the jolliest cottage pie he had ever eaten.

Malc has given Ken the money to get us two tickets to the allotment Christmas party on December 12th. We will meet Ken's wife. Malc wondered if she will have hairy ears too.

Friday 16th November

Malc and I went to the Hungry Horse Tandem pub in Kennington and had lunch. I had macaroni cheese and chips, Malc had chicken tikka masala. We took photos by the Christmas tree! On the way home we went to big Sainsbury's so Malc could choose a birthday cake for Sunday when the family are round. We got a large chocolate cake. I adore ganache.

Saturday 17th November

I popped round to see Mum. She has given a library book to a charity shop by mistake. She doesn't know what to do. She went back to the shop but they couldn't find the book. I told Mum to go to the library and come clean about it.

Mum said Ros over the road drew her curtains at quarter to four yesterday, which is a bit early and a waste of daylight. Margery down the road with the wooden windows and big extension is moving to a bungalow, her legs have become unreliable. Mum is looking forward to watching *Strictly Come Dancing* tonight.

Malc and I had cheese on toast for lunch followed by chocolate Yule log. Malc did some jigsaw while I read on the sofa. According to *A Wiltshire Christmas*, you should keep the fat from your Christmas goose because it's good for bruises. I have never eaten goose.

Sunday 18th November

Nicola came over and picked David and Mum/Nan up on the way. David has a rare Sunday off. All the shops at Bicester Village will be rammed from now until Christmas David says. Then it's the January sales and people returning unwanted Christmas gifts.

Val and Henry joined us and we had an Indian takeaway in honour of Malc's birthday. Mum tried a bit of my peshwari naan and liked it. Whenever she tries a new mouthful of Indian food she thinks it will be very hot and spicy. There was lots of talk of my approaching birthday (in five days I will be sixty-six years old) and of Christmas. I'm going to visit Nicola in Coventry on the sixth of December and we'll go Christmas shopping. She's going to book the day off work. Henry said I seem to have taken to being retired like a duck to water. Val said that's because women have so much to do round the house that when they retire they haven't actually retired in the same sense men do. I changed the subject. Val has a bigger house to keep clean than I do.

Monday 19th November

This morning Malc said he had celebrated his birthday adequately and asked me what I want for my birthday. I couldn't think of anything. Malc said his blood runs cold at the thought of having to surprise me! He suggested we take a run out to Yarnton garden centre in case there's anything there I'd like. We had a lovely browse. They have a lot of Christmas decorations. I don't even want a present, just knowing Malc would like to get me one is enough and knowing that thankfully our budget is not too tight is a gift. Our budget is not too loose either, but it is comfortable at the moment.

We went to Asda and I saw a lovely Christmas jumper with Christmas trees on so Malc bought it for my birthday. He also bought me a selection box because I was eyeing them up when we were queuing to pay! He seemed relieved when he'd done his husbandly birthday gift buying duties.

I like drawing the curtains on a dark winter night. It is out there and we are in here. I like writing this diary, it keeps me focused on the good stuff.

Tuesday 20th November

The postman delivered a brushed cotton winter nightdress I'd bought for Mum online so I took it round to her. When Nicola took her home on Sunday she set the heating timer for her so it stays on longer. Mum said on Sunday she'd been getting up in the night feeling cold, going downstairs and filling a hot water bottle then struggling to go back to sleep. She'd forgotten how to set the timer which is a worry. It's also a worry her filling hot water bottles with boiling water while half asleep. I ordered the nightdress on Sunday night as soon as everyone had gone home. Despite being eighty-nine years old and sleeping alone Mum was keen that her nightie not be frumpy and made of Winceyette. Mum said she is sleeping better since Nicola adjusted the timer so the heating stays on for longer.

Nicola rang to confirm she's off work on the sixth of December. I am really looking forward to our Christmas shopping trip. Coventry is the perfect size for a day of shopping. Nicola is pleased because she got a free pack of Christmas cards from WH Smith just for having her phone contract with O2 Priority. She chose a winter hare design and will send them to her pagan friends at Yule. She has entered a competition to win a year's supply of clotted cream. I asked how often she buys clotted cream now and she said never.

Wednesday 21st November

While Malc did the crossword this morning I looked in the snowman tin of present ideas and made one big list from the little bits of paper I've put in there this year. Some ideas are general and some are for specific people.

General Christmas present ideas; homemade hampers, homemade coconut ice, tutti fruitti ice cream, homemade marzipan veg patch for Malc, homemade marzipan fruits for everyone else, cheese selection, Christmas books.

Malc; rhubarb and ginger jam, tree fern, Roman things.
Nicola; book token, cross stitch, lilac Broderie anglaise dress, gold eyeshadow, Hobbycraft voucher.
David; chocolate Angel delight, Drifters, Vivienne Westwood tie.
Mum; golden lily print item, aniseed balls, Christmas thimble.
Henry; mint humbugs.
Viv; Ulster Weavers tea towel.
Eric; Floral Gums.
Gail; Trans-Siberian Orchestra CD.

I have no specific ideas for Val or Carol but both of them are easy to buy things for and most years I buy them something quite early on in my Christmas shopping. If I buy David an expensive tie I can make Nicola's presents up to the same value with a book token and Hobbycraft voucher.

I will start adding new ideas to the snowman tin in January next year. I think it's been a success. I'm not going to buy anyone ice cream because it's just too impractical to wrap and put under the Christmas tree but today I have ordered Viv two tea towels (one with a sheep design for everyday use and one with gingerbread men for Christmas use).

Thursday 22nd November

I met Carol and we went to Wetherspoons. It is decorated for Christmas with a green, gold and fir cones theme. It looks rather fabulous! Carol insisted on treating me to lunch for my birthday tomorrow. We had chicken burger and chips for a change from fish and chips. Carol bought me some lovely chocolates from Hotel Chocolat.

We looked round the shops after lunch. It is still a novelty for me to be able to look round the shops on a Thursday afternoon rather than working in one of them. Retirement feels like winning a time lottery. I had an email from Iceland telling me I can have free custard slices or a cheesecake, because it's my birthday soon. They only cost a pound, but I actually like custard slices quite a lot so I got some. I also got a Thornton's Continental advent calendar for Mum and one for me.

I was just getting in from the shops and Tamsin next door was just going out. She is pregnant! I'm so happy for her and Tom. She was beaming from ear to ear when she told me. I caught her smile and grinned for at least an hour after. I made some chocolate chip fairy cakes ready for the care home Christmas bazaar on Saturday and while waiting for them to cool I finished reading *A Wiltshire Christmas*. There was only one county boundary change mentioned, unlike in *A Berkshire Christmas* when it sounded like places were constantly shifting between counties. I decorated the fairy cakes to look like Christmas trees.

Malc came home and asked what I fancy for dinner. We had cheese on toast. He said Donna is already decorating the care home for Christmas so it looks nice for the bazaar on Saturday. Also, Donna said you never know how long the residents will reside for, so why not decorate early? Malc and I ate the chocolates Carol bought me, they were fancy and delicious. I had a birthday card in the post from Gail and one from Viv and Eric.

Friday 23rd November

I am sixty-six years old today. I'm grateful for every one of the days I've lived so far. There is a famous quote by John Barrymore 'A man is not old until regrets take the place of dreams'. I think a woman is not old while she can still be bothered to put on mascara and a sparkly jumper.

For breakfast Malc and I had the last of his chocolate birthday cake. My big birthday celebration will be tomorrow night when Nicola and David, Mum, Val and Henry come round for dinner.

Malc asked how the birthday girl would like to be entertained today. He needed some screen wash so we went to Halfords in Botley. Then we looked in Homebase which is closing down on the 14th December. There was a load of scruffy stuff left. They had loads of cheap Christmas trees and boxes of baubles. There is something beautiful about a whole box of baubles. I got a bit mesmerised staring at some shiny gold ones, I could see myself reflected in them. Next we went to big Sainsbury's and I chose my birthday cake. I picked a Christmas fruit cake and we got some Wensleydale with cranberries because Henry likes to have cheese with Christmas cake.

We called in on Mum at lunchtime. We ordered fish and chips and ate it in Mum's front room. Mum said it was a lovely bit of fish. I have never eaten fish and chips with

Mum without her saying it was a lovely bit of fish. I don't know if we're always lucky with fish or if her fish standards are low. Mum gave me a sterling silver heart necklace from M&S for my birthday. She said she's noticed I wear different necklaces since I've retired. This is true, I have time in the morning to get dressed and choose a necklace. I used to only think about putting on a necklace if I was going out in the evening or to London with Val.

As well as being my birthday, today is also black Friday. I donated £20 to Homeless Oxfordshire, a local charity. Homes cost too much money in Oxfordshire, rent is excessive and people can easily get into arrears if they have a bit of bad luck and no savings or family to help them. We need more affordable housing. My children can't afford to live where they grew up.

Saturday 24th November

I decorated the cakes I made for the Christmas bazaar first thing this morning then Malc dropped them off to Donna at the care home on his way to the allotment. Ken wants some help spreading horse manure.

Malc came home at lunch time with a big bunch of pink and yellow alstroemerias for me from Ken for my birthday. I put them in a vase by the fireplace. They remind me of Battenberg cake and are a very thoughtful gift. I can forgive Ken for making my husband smell like a badly kept stable.

We got to the Christmas bazaar at two-thirty and it was in full swing. There were just a few of my cakes left for sale, I shall get some more red foil cupcake cases from Hobbycraft, Carol said they give the cakes the look of luxury. Carol was running the tombola as usual. Malc won a woolly hat that looks like a Christmas pudding! He put it on and everyone admired it. He didn't keep it on long, it is very warm in the care home. I won a golden lily print cake tin. I was more delighted than I've ever been at a tombola prize! This will be a perfect Christmas present for Mum, she likes tins and this particular print. Donna was in charge of the book stall. I got two books, *Hark!: The Biography Of Christmas* by Paul Kerensa and *Christmas At Thrush Green* by Miss Read. We stayed until the end of the bazaar at four to see some members of a local choir sing Christmas carols. They sang 'Away in a Manger', 'God Rest Ye Merry Gentlemen' and 'Deck The Halls'. I can't wait to deck my halls in a week's time!

Malc gave Carol a lift home. We went in for a cup of tea and a biscuit. Carol opened a box of M&S extremely chocolatey biscuits. She said we were a special occasion! She said she'll let us know how much the bazaar makes. Donna wants to take the residents who are able to go to a matinee of the pantomime. She has also arranged for a local theatre group to come in and perform for the residents.

When we got in Malc fired up the computer to order food. I had checked in advance what everyone wanted from House of Tim. I could have guessed what people would have. Mum and I had sweet and sour chicken balls, Nicola and Val had chicken chow mein, Henry had duck in orange sauce, David had chicken foo yung and Malc had the chicken curry. It will stain if you get it on you (we found this out with his beige summer trousers) so he ate it with a tea towel on his lap.

Nicola, David and Mum arrived first. David had changed a light bulb for Mum on the landing. She said it went ping last night. I am wearing my new necklace from Mum today. Val and Henry bought me a holly, ivy and fir cones wreath for the front door! Val was going to buy me birthday flowers but saw the wreath and decided to get that instead. I often see them on the doors of fancy houses and point them out to Val but we've never had one. Also, Val has got us tickets to see *The Nutcracker* in High Wycombe in January 2019! And she gave me some Heston Blumenthal chocolate and cherry crumble mince pies she saw in Waitrose.

Nicola made me a Fimo birthday cake and gave me a Fimo kit to make little Christmas trees. There is a silicone mould and she said it's nice and easy. David had two phone calls from the temporary Christmas staff he's training during the evening, one because a customer demanded to speak to the manager (David isn't the manager but sometimes pretends to be if it's easier than getting the actual manager) and another because they forgot how to set the shop's burglar alarm so they rang him at twenty to nine! He forgot to bring my present but having him here is all I want.

Everyone sang 'Happy Birthday!' to me. I cut my birthday Christmas cake. Henry was delighted there was Wensleydale to go with it. He said Epicurus himself couldn't be better provided for. David said 'Who's he when he's at home?' and everyone laughed.

I don't mind my birthday being close to Christmas, it feels like a practice for it. I like sharing a birthday month with Malc. Val and Henry left at ten-thirty and took Mum home. Both Nicola and David are staying over which makes it feel like Christmas or the past when they both still lived at home.

Sunday 25th November

I cooked bacon and sausages for sandwiches for everyone's breakfast this morning. It's lovely eating all together as a family. Nicola took David to work then went back to Coventry. As she left she reminded us it was one month until Christmas Day!

I decided to take advantage of some black Friday weekend online offers. I got a hot chocolate and a slice of birthday Christmas cake then settled myself at the computer. I ordered a jar of Floral Gums for Eric, aniseed balls for Mum and mint humbugs for Henry from A Quarter Of. I got Malc to help me choose a Vivienne Westwood tie for David. Malc said all his ties don't add up to the price of that one tie! Malc has five ties, none of them purchased in the last couple of decades. One of them is a black tie for funerals. There is a lemon yellow with grey stripes one which was from Fosters Menswear (the most recently purchased). Malc also has a purple tie, a brown knitted tie (very horrible but he has an inexplicable attachment to it) and the tie he wore on our wedding day which is brown, orange and cream with an eye-watering sort of circular pattern. It matched the colours of Carol's bridesmaid dress. I only had one bridesmaid because Val, Gail and Viv were already married and in those days if a woman was already married she couldn't be a bridesmaid.

We walked to the Sandy Lane West delivery office to get a parcel (it was the tea towels I ordered for Viv).

Malc said we do as many miles as the postmen do to get our parcels but he is exaggerating.

I read some of *Hark!: The Biography Of Christmas*. There was a quote from Juvenal, a Roman poet. I read it out to Malc who loves the Romans 'two things only the people anxiously desire – bread and circuses'.

Food and entertainment are both very Christmassy. If I get stuck for gift ideas I'll pick one or the other of these. Thanks Juvenal!

Monday 26th November

We had a Heston Blumenthal chocolate and cherry crumble mince pie for our elevenses today. It was too dry on top and would have benefitted from some buttercream.

The bulb went in Malc's bedside lamp last night so we went to Sylvester's for a new one. Malc likes to buy bulbs from Smith & Low or Sylvester's. I got a Thunderbirds mug for David for Christmas in Sylvester's, they have some wonderful old things. We went to the Co-op and got some squirty cream to accompany Heston's mince pies and some sprout flavour crisps.

I watched some videos of people's Christmas villages on YouTube. I ordered a brushed cotton nightie for Mum for Christmas, she likes the one she has. I read in *Hark!: The Biography Of Christmas* that King Henry II served crane (the bird, not the building site vehicle) at one of his Christmas dinners and had entertainment from a man called Roland The Farter!

Tuesday 27th November

This morning I wrote and posted a Christmas card to Joyce Matthews in Australia. I told her how much I'm enjoying being retired and that I'm going Christmas shopping with Nicola in Coventry and to *The Nutcracker* with Val early next year and that everyone is well and that I hope she has a super Christmas and to let me know if she's coming over to England and we can have coffee or lunch and a catch up.

I went to the Littlemore Post Office to buy some Christmas stamps. Outside the shop next door was a chap I strongly suspect to be a Littlemore Hospital patient. He asked me for forty-four pee and told me he had saved the world then drew my attention to a sign he's done saying he saved the world from nuclear war using maths problems and lighter fuel. I said 'Impressive!' which seemed to please him and then I went to the Post Office. Forty-four pee seems a small price for saving the world.

I ordered a jigsaw of Roman Britain for Malc for Christmas and a Roman numerals pencil tin which he can keep his plant labels in.

I read in *Hark!: The Biography Of Christmas* that twenty-seven is the average number of mince pies eaten per person in Britain in the Christmas period.

Wednesday 28th November

Malc and I went to Hobbycraft today. We got a cross stitch set for Nicola of an owl in a Santa hat and a gift voucher. I dithered for ages over a spray of fake snowberry with glitter then bought it. Malc said it was still my birthday month so I should treat myself.

We had brie and turkey croissants for dinner, followed by a Heston chocolate and cherry crumble mince pie with squirty cream. Malc finished doing his birthday summer garden jigsaw.

In *Hark!: The Biography Of Christmas* I read that it was Gordon Selfridge who invented the how many shopping days to Christmas phrase we hear so often.

Thursday 29th November

I met Carol for coffee and a look round the shops. We went in WH Smith and went upstairs which has been shut for years and is now open as a clearance outlet. They still have the old beige carpet upstairs. The downstairs and actual stairs has a new blue carpet. There was a lot of stationery going cheapish, they had some nice notebooks. We went to TK Maxx and I got a lovely metallics eyeshadow palette for Nicola and a silk peacock feather print scarf and a black velvet evening bag for Val. I'm glad I've now read *The Nutcracker*. TK Maxx had a load of them and a really huge selection of panettone. Carol said she'd never had a panettone. We walked home together, chatting about our plans for this Christmas.

I made sausage casserole for dinner which went down very well with Malc. It's wonderful being able to start cooking dinner at three o'clock and do something from fresh ingredients.

I finished reading *Hark!: The Biography Of Christmas*. In 1923 Big Ben was heard on the radio in a Christmas broadcast, but until then only people in London would have heard it! Our Queen sits on the same chair her father and grandfather sat on to do the Christmas message.

Friday 30th November

I got the Christmas tree out of its box ready to decorate tomorrow morning. I took all the boxes of decorations from the roof to the lounge. My little diary writing nook is much less cluttered, but only briefly. I took Woolly Willy the knitted snowman downstairs and sat him on the sofa. I said to Malc 'Have you seen my Willy?' and we both giggled!

We went to Lidl. It was surprisingly quiet. We got goat's cheese and pesto focaccia, lots of marzipan, desiccated coconut, condensed milk, dark chocolate lebkuchen with apricot jam inside, iced lebkuchen, Christmas pasta, stollen, and two packets of spekulatius spiced biscuits.

I started reading *Miracle on 34th Street* by Valentine Davies.

November reckoning, have I kept Christmas all November? November is mine and Malc's birthday month and is bonfire night party month so we've had some great family get togethers. I enjoy Malc's birthday as much as my own. My birthday lunch with Carol was very pleasant (and a bit festive due to the pub's decorations). It was fab to go round the local shops with Carol and to listen to Christmas carols, with Carol, at the care home bazaar. Without the people you love Christmas would be meaningless. It was wonderful to be with Val in Browns and enjoy a roast dinner in such wooden, well-decorated surroundings which could have been olden days London if it wasn't for people looking at their phones.

My Christmas book reading has been very entertaining this month. If I don't know what to do with myself I get my book and I read until I do know what I want to do. Reading a book takes you out of yourself.

The festive duvet cover makes me smile every time I go in the bedroom. I like wearing my Christmas jumper with Christmas trees on from Malc for my birthday.

I thought I'd have all my gifts bought and wrapped by now and all my cards done but I have time aplenty. By the end of November Christmas starts to seem tantalisingly close. I'm going to linger over my preparations and enjoy every little bit of it.

December

Saturday 1st December
Today is the first day of advent and the first day of meteorological winter. I got up at seven-thirty, leaving Malc gently snoring. I decorated the Christmas tree until ten then stopped for a cup of tea and a mince pie. It takes ages to hang all the baubles.

I took two bags of stuff to the BHF shop (continuing the great retirement declutter project) but when I was in the BHF shop I bought a bag of stuff; a book, *The Christmas Star* by Eva Ibbotson and a jigsaw called A Winter Song with some birds singing outside a lovely big house. I got three packets of chocolate flavour Angel Delight for David from the Co-op, it's a silly stocking filler but he'll like it. Angel Delight should do a Christmas flavour, maybe mince pie and custard or stollen flavour. I'd buy it. I'm a sucker for novelty Christmas fare.

I showed Malc the jigsaw I got. It has two robins on the front. Malc said jigsaw manufacturer's don't seem to realise how odd it is to see more than one robin, if you do they are a breeding pair and that's not the sort of thing you see happening on a jigsaw.

Malc and I had cheese and crackers for lunch. Malc had some pate too. I have never taken to pate. I had my Thornton's advent calendar chocolate and Malc had his pork scratchings. Door one is now open, we are firmly in the festive season. I finished decorating the tree then put all the Christmas knick-knacks out.

Malc hung the wreath on the front door while I supervised. Tom and Tamsin came out while we were doing it and admired it. We invited them in to look at the Christmas tree. Tamsin said it was a joyful sight. Tom said it was nice and straight.

Sunday 2nd December

When I came downstairs this morning I was delighted by the decorations. I love the first part of December where the house seems transformed. I switched the tree lights on and ate my breakfast in front of it. I like un-focusing my eyes so the lights go all fuzzy and indistinct, and it could be any Christmas tree anywhere, then re-focusing and being in the right here, right now of this particular Christmas.

I read some of *Miracle on 34th Street* and liked this bit especially; 'this is the imagination. And once you get there you can do almost anything you want'. I'm blessed with a good imagination. I was a bit of a dreamy child compared to Val. You can let your mind wander in the quiet bits of working in a shop. I used to be called Little Dolly Daydream by the assistant manager in my first job.

I thought about all the Christmas preparations I have plenty of time to do this month; a bit of Christmas shopping, writing Christmas cards, gift wrapping, posting Eric and Viv's parcel and food shopping. It's Val's turn to host on Christmas Day this year so my food shopping can be a bit less than last year.

Malc passed wind in the kitchen and apologised because it smelt of pate. This is quite a festive occurrence but I don't want to encourage it in the kitchen. Malc made us coffee and walked round the tree admiring it. He pointed out that we have four robins and you usually only see lone robins.

We went to TK Maxx in the afternoon and I got a fancy chocolate panettone to give Carol for Christmas. We went to Sainsbury's and I got lots of Drifters for David and an extra packet so we could have one with our coffee when we got home. We saw Ken outside Shoe Zone. He said he was after some new wellies. When he'd gone Malc said Ken sometimes wears wellies when there's no need for wearing wellies. Malc said Ken will probably wear wellies to the Christmas party.

Monday 3rd December
I wrote all my Christmas cards today. I like this bit of festive admin. It's lovely being able to do it during the day this year instead of squashing it in the evenings and at weekends. There are pressures and pleasures of Christmas, you have to make sure the pleasures outweigh the pressures, which is hard when you work full time. The words joy, love and peace get used more at Christmas but so do the words stress, expense and bother. I'm truly enjoying my first Christmas of liberation from paid employment.

Malc has learnt to cook omelettes. The chef at the care home has tutored him. We had a cheese one for lunch. It was very good. Mid-afternoon we went to Tesco for some salt and pepper bread and overheard someone say loudly and angrily 'pea and ham is the worst soup.' I disagree, I think mushroom is the worst soup.

For dinner I cooked chicken casserole with carrots, potatoes and leeks (all grown by Malc's fair hands, he says we are a team, he does the growing and I do the cooking). Cutting leeks makes me think of green and white crepe paper. You don't see crepe paper used for streamers as much as you used to. I wonder what is the most popular decoration to hang just below ceilings? There is foil garlands, paper chains, tinsel, and crepe paper streamers. It's probably foil garlands now.

Tuesday 4th December

I posted my Christmas cards this morning then went to see Mum. She has lost all her wooden spoons. She said she hides her Barclaycard under a saucepan before going to bed. She has got a mayonnaise jar full of two pence pieces in the kitchen cupboard. She is becoming odder as she gets older. Young children are also odd, it's two sides of the same coin. Young children haven't been taught how not to be weird yet and old people don't care any longer if you think they're weird.

I watched some telly with Mum. The blue team won on *Bargain Hunt* with a profit of £108. We had some tomato soup for lunch. We watched a bit more telly, Christopher Biggins is spending Christmas in Oxfordshire with his Godchildren.

When I left Mum's I bumped into Joyce Matthews! You don't expect to see people who live in Australia. She is only here in England for one more week and is going up north tomorrow. She asked if I had time for a quick coffee. I said yes so we went to Wetherspoons. The coffee machine was broken so Joyce said let's have a Christmas drink and we had a Tia Maria. Then we had a Baileys! Joyce had her own salon in Australia which she sold this summer. She loves living there but misses her family here. She asked after Malc, Nicola and David.

On our way out of the pub we saw Gail's husband Len. I said hello to be polite. Joyce had to rush off. What followed was a bit of a heavy conversation. I'll write it in full because I want to check I didn't say anything I shouldn't have and it's left me feeling a bit disconcerted.

Len: I suppose you think I'm a bit of a let-down?

Pam: Pardon?

Len: I suppose you think I'm a bit of a let-down? As a husband, for your friend.

Pam: It doesn't matter what I think, it matters what Gail thinks.

Len: I've not always been the best husband.

Pam: Then try a bit harder now. Len, I know you can do the right things if you want to.

Len: I do want to, it just comes out wrong sometimes.

Pam: Have the difficult conversations, tell her you won't cheat on her again and she can rely on you, she won't believe your words but over the course of years she'll come to believe your actions.

Len: I don't think we've ever had such a heavy talk.

Pam: I don't think we've both ever been tipsy in Wetherspoons together in the middle of the day.

Len: That's true.

Pam: Keep at it, try again tomorrow, that's all marriage is, that's the big secret. Make her a cup of tea, clean up after yourself, ask how her shift at work was. A marriage can always be improved if you've got the patience.

Len: I've got some patience.

Pam: Right, I've got to go and put the dinner on. Merry Christmas Len.

Len: Merry Christmas, and thanks Pam, you're a good woman.

My face was red when I left the pub. Len was half cut so he probably won't remember our conversation tomorrow.

Malc does not think it romantic that Elizabeth Taylor and Richard Burton married twice, he thinks they overreacted when they got divorced the first time. I'm glad neither Malc nor I are an overreactor.

We watched *UK's Strongest Man* and then went to bed quite early.

Wednesday 5th December

I finished reading *Miracle on 34th Street*. It's a lovely story about believing in the unlikely and magical. I'm not sure a court case is very Christmassy but there was a court case in it. You can choose to believe something that makes you happy even if there is no proof of it, like that everything happens for a reason or conkers keep spiders away.

I made a big batch of coconut ice today to give people for Christmas. When it cooled I put it in the clear gift bags with a poinsettia print I got from Lakeland. It looks lovely, even if I do say so myself.

Mum rang to say Pam Ayres was on *Celebrity Antiques Road Trip*. The other team went to Fanny's Antiques in Reading. We've driven past there many times but never been in. I mentioned it to Malc and he said we'll go next time we're in Reading. I love him for always being amenable to my plans.

Nicola rang this evening to say she'll meet me outside Cov Station tomorrow morning, she always shortens Coventry to Cov.

Thursday 6th December
I had an email from ERNIE. I have won £25 on the Premium Bonds! What a great start to a Christmas shopping day! I got the train to Coventry and met Nicola. Today is St Nicolas's Day, so I took her a chocolate Santa. I've got a head start on my Christmas shopping (I just need to make marzipan fruits and vegetables and buy Nicola a book token so her present adds up to the same as David's) so we did Nicola's shopping.

Nicola told me about Whamageddon, it's where you lose if you hear Wham's 'Last Christmas'. I have not heard it yet this Christmas so I am still in the game. We looked round Coventry's indoor market, it's a lot bigger than Oxford's Covered Market and not as old. It was voted Britain's favourite market a few years ago. When we were in there I heard someone say they were parched. I haven't heard this expression for a long time. Nicola and I had a cup of tea and a jam and cream finger doughnut at one of the market cafes.

We went to M&S and Nicola got a mustard colour jumper for Malc for Christmas. Mustard is a very popular jumper colour this year. She also got a tin of biscuits for Nan. She's getting David Lego from the internet. We went to TJ Hughes and she got Aunty Val some red leather gloves (I know she used to have a pair which she loved, but she lost one). Nicola said she'll get Uncle Henry a book.

We had burritos for lunch in Las Iguanas. It was quite busy. The women at the table nearest us both had bags with rolls of gift wrap sticking out. It's lovely to sit in a restaurant or pub in December and absorb all the Christmas anticipation.

After lunch we looked at Lady Godiva. I got a book in the Oxfam bookshop; *Inventing the Christmas Tree* by Bernd Brunner and Benjamin A. Smith. The assistant was very friendly. Nicola goes in there a lot.

We walked past the Library where Nicola works and saw the poster for the Christmas story time she's organised. I said when I read *The Nutcracker* it reminded me that she and David used to complain if I read them a story in which part of the action was a dream. Nicola said she ignores that bit of any story and just says it happens at night. The people who believe in magic will believe it and those who don't will think it's just a dream. But, is it ever fair to say just a dream? Our brains are amazing for making dreams happen. I don't know the science exactly but chemicals make pictures in our minds that seem real.

I got the train home just after four o'clock. I love being on a train. I love that my daughter wants to spend a precious day off work with me.

Friday 7th December

I'm enjoying reading *Inventing the Christmas Tree.* It was written in German and translated, the writer or translator has a lovely turn of phrase; 'As the days began to lengthen, the sun flaunted its victory over winter'.

Malc and I went to buy some Christmas gift wrap from WH Smith. We got three rolls (there is no point buying less, it's three rolls for the price of two). We got snowflake pattern, Christmas tree pattern and Merry Christmas in curly writing pattern. Christmas gift wrap does the magic job of turning things into presents, it makes them presentable. It makes a stack of colourful parcels under a tree become Yuletide treasure.

Saturday 8th December
Here's another lovely bit from *Inventing the Christmas Tree*; 'Christmas was considered a magical time in which the normal rules of everyday life – indeed, even the rules of nature - were suspended'.

I donated twenty pounds to BookTrust. It's a charity Nicola told me about. They send books to children who are vulnerable or in care at Christmas. Reading is such a key skill and such a great pleasure.

Sunday 9th December
I didn't write much yesterday or the day before which I think is because it is not hard to keep Christmas when you're in December, in good health, and have more free time than you've had for decades! It has occurred to me that this diary could be a useful resource for me in the future when my Christmas spirit is flagging and being retired has become my default state rather than still a novelty.

I wrapped half of the Christmas presents I've bought. I like the paper from WH Smith because it has a grid on the back allowing you to cut it neatly. Malc and I picked Mum up in the car and we went to Val and Henry's for lunch.

Val showed me a round robin letter from Audrey Wilson who we went to school with. Round robins get a lot of stick for being boastful, and this one did have moments of that, but you want to know people are doing well. I'm not sure if the main purpose of it is to provide news to the wider family and friends or for the writer to convince themselves that their family has lived a good year, or both. As someone new to keeping a diary this year I have sympathies for the yearly round robin writer.

Val did a buffet lunch, she said she wanted to try out a few new recipes and we make good guinea pigs because we'll be honest! Mum tried some pesto penne pasta and pronounced it a bit greasy. A neighbour had given Val some fancy pesto as a thank you for feeding their cat at short notice for two days. Val made Wensleydale and cranberry scones (delicious), pear tarts with Stilton and walnuts (lovely) and cauliflower and cumin fritters (Malc and I liked them, Mum not so sure). There were also plenty of Val's usual buffet items, including mini pork pies which Val always gets because she knows Malc likes them.

Mum said she hasn't bought Bridget a present yet and wants to get her something special and thoughtful. I offered to help her order something from the internet. Mum uses email and a couple of websites (Amazon, Damart) but doesn't understand that practically every shop is also online, it's always a surprise to her when I suggest she buy something online.

Monday 10th December

I sat in front of the Christmas tree today and read *Inventing the Christmas Tree*. It said 'the tree inspires a quietude, reflectiveness and joy'. I completely agree.

The allotment Christmas party is this week, on Wednesday. I asked Malc what he's going to wear and if he wanted a new shirt. Val has a lovely new dress from Roman Originals, she showed it me yesterday, it's navy blue with diamante on the top half and a sort of tiered, triple layered bottom half. The dress is also available in black and I bought it this morning hoping it'll turn up on Wednesday for the party. I will wear it with a cream shrug. Val has good taste in clothes, she always looks elegant. Val says you should avoid anything too complicated and never wear a hanky hem or a one shoulder dress. I sometimes wear knitwear that needs de-bobbling and sometimes wear my clothes a bit too big. For reasons of economy, when I was a child, Mum would sometimes dress me in clothes that were a bit too tight. Since then I've tended to overcompensate.

The allotment party is local, in a community centre. I said we could get the bus but Malc wants to drive. He said he might want to make a quick getaway, which sounded like he might be planning something nefarious but knowing Malc it is because he has limited patience for small talk in a loud room.

We went to Notcutts because Malc wanted some twine. We had a piece of cake in the café. Malc had lemon drizzle and I had Belgian chocolate and we each had a forkful of each other's to try it and I had a sudden moment of being delighted I had a Malc to share cake with. We overheard someone say 'That can wait until after Christmas now'. There is a point in December where I put things on hold until after Christmas, I'm not sure when this starts. It might be later in the month now I'm retired.

For dinner I cooked chili con carne. Malc and I watched a Netflix film called *Dumplin'* about a girl who is a bit fat and enters a beauty pageant.

Tuesday 11th December

I went round to Mum's this morning to help her choose something for Bridget for Christmas. On my way I nipped to WH Smith and got two copies of the *Radio Times* Christmas issue, one for me and Malc and one for Mum. Mum flicked through it trying to find out when *The Sound of Music* is on. Mum always notes when people are the same age as her, and Christopher Plummer from *The Sound of Music* is the same age as her. It is sad that at eighty-nine there are less people around who are her age. I think age used to be more important than it is now. Both Mum and I wondered why WH Smith is so keen to sell you a big bar of chocolate for a pound. Every time you buy anything they ask if you want a big bar of chocolate for a pound. They can't be making that much profit from their chocolate badgering.

Mum put her glasses on and we browsed the internet for something for Bridget. We narrowed it down to something for the garden (Mum said Bridget loves her garden) then chose a round wall plaque of a big tree from www.crocus.co.uk. Mum was very grateful for my help. She is a very grateful sort of a person and has passed this on to Val and I. I hope I've passed it on to Nicola and

David. I think I have, they don't act entitled (which I notice is what people say now instead of spoilt).

This afternoon I made marzipan fruits and vegetables. I ate quite a bit of marzipan while I worked. The carrots and peas in pods came out especially well, the sprouts and beetroot are okay, I gave up trying to do sweetcorn and did spaghetti squash instead but may squash these squash and make another yellow vegetable only I can't think of one right now. The fruits I did were orange, pear, lemon, apple, strawberry and banana. I've put them all in a tin and I might try and make little cardboard punnets or weave little baskets for them. I am not currently what you would call a creative woman but maybe I'll become one!

I love hearing Malc's key in the door. This evening he did some of the birds singing outside a big house in the snow jigsaw while I finished reading *Inventing the Christmas Tree*. I read that real Christmas trees can be fed to polar bears, elephants, camels, llamas and mountain goats. The goats don't surprise me, they'll eat anything. Nicola got her anorak chewed at Cotswold Wildlife Park and has given goats a wide berth ever since.

Wednesday 12th December

I got cupcakes with reindeer on from the Co-op this morning so Malc and I had festive elevenses. My new floaty party dress with diamante arrived at lunch time and is a good fit. We watched a bit of the lunchtime news. Teresa May is having a vote of no confidence today. By nine p.m. she'll might not be prime minister (but she probably will be).

At nine p.m. we were in the thick of the allotment party. We sat at a table of six with Ken and his wife Rose (short for Rosemary, but she was nearly called Primrose and is glad she wasn't. I told her I'm not keen on my middle name Dorothy) and Luke and Matt who both have plots on the same allotment site as Malc and Ken. Luke and Matt are a bit younger than Ken and Malc. For a while something about the names Luke and Matt was prickling my memory and I thought of Matt and Luke Goss of Bros who Nicola had a brief liking for and then I remembered that the birth of Jesus is mentioned in just two of the gospels; Matthew and Luke. I have gained a lot of Christmas knowledge this year!

I overheard a man at the next table say, loudly, 'My wife's name is Joan, it rhymes with moan' and I thought I bet she's glad when he buggers off up the allotment. There were about equal numbers of men and women in attendance, in a variety of clothes, though tending towards the informal. Ken didn't wear his wellies and Rose doesn't have hairy ears. I met the woman who organised the party, she's called Daphne. She came to each table before dessert and introduced herself. I thanked her for organising such a nice event. The community centre looked great with loads of fairy lights round the room.

The food was very good indeed. The community centre has a kitchen and they did magic in there. My salmon mousse was the nicest I've ever had (this was probably prepared earlier rather than in the community centre kitchen). The main course, turkey roast dinner, was super and the vegetables were local. The dessert was a brownie that tasted like a mince pie with chocolate ice cream. We pulled crackers and wore our paper hats. I was glad we came. Matt and Luke were chatty and so was Rose. We talked about our Christmas plans. Matt has a daughter who is five years old and is asking a lot of questions about Father Christmas.

After dinner a band played, the drummer of the band has got an allotment. They were a covers band and played Mudd's 'Tiger Feet', Abba's 'Does Your Mother Know That You're Out', an Oasis song which I used to hear coming out of David's room, Tom Jones' 'Delilah' (which makes me think of Bognor), some songs I don't know and they finished with Slade's 'I Wish It Could Be Christmas Everyday'.

A DJ did a disco after the band. It was mostly modern music I haven't heard. Luke told us we were hearing Kings Of Leon 'Sex On Fire' and I saw Malc blush. Then it was Taylor Swift's 'Shake It Off' apparently. I lost Whamageddon and went to Whamhalla (this is the game Nicola told me about whereby you see how long you can go in December without accidentally hearing Wham's 'Last Christmas'. It doesn't count if you choose to listen to it and cover versions don't count. The DJ played it. I have done well to get half way through advent).

We left at eleven-fifteen and gave Ken and Rose a lift. Malc said he'd had a pleasant evening. Malc needs to be coaxed sometimes to do something different, for tonight's party it wasn't me doing the coaxing, it was Ken. Ken said they should attend tonight because Daphne was trying hard to make the allotments more successful. When Ken first said this Malc replied that a successful allotment has big onions, not a party, but he's changed his tune. We saw some lovely Christmas lights in people's gardens on the way home.

Thursday 13th December

I got up this morning when Malc got up for work so I could make him coffee and toast while he was in the shower. He didn't stir when his alarm clock first went off, I had to kiss him on the cheek and say 'Up you get party animal!' We didn't get to sleep until after midnight!

I went to the Littlemore Post Office and sent Viv and Eric's parcel. I overheard a woman telling her friend she'd bought a quiche that was disappointing. It was brie, bacon and cranberry but the pastry was too thick and it was not flavoursome. I thought if all she's got to moan about is a quiche disappointment then she is truly blessed.

I met Lauren for lunch. We exchanged Christmas cards. I bought a little cuddly penguin for her daughter Daisy who is three. I told Lauren about the marzipan fruits and vegetables I've made. She suggested getting some green shredded tissue to use as grass. I asked how everyone who works in the shop is. Dylan has got a tattoo he's hiding from his mum. He's still with his girlfriend. Mr Barker has started talking about retirement and when he does the new supervisor's eyes light up. Phil has got a corn which is giving him gyp. There are some temporary Christmas staff one of which is good and keen and the others Lauren said are decidedly average. I love chatting to Lauren and miss working with her. We revert to the same level of intimacy effortlessly despite only seeing each other every few months instead of most days.

This afternoon I lay on the sofa, in front of the Christmas tree, reading *Christmas at Thrush Green*. It's a fictional place near Oxford. Some of the people sound a bit snobby; 'Joan shuddered – there was a lion and a unicorn, turned slightly inwards. It was one thing to have such resplendent statues on the gateposts of a stately home, but not a house built between the last two wars!'

I walk past a flat by Minchery Farm shops that has a chandelier, you can dream big and have nice things in a small dwelling, there's no law against it.

Friday 14th December

I went for a walk first thing when it was dark and the day was fresh and new. I love being outside in the dark at this time of the year. It's pleasant to watch the sun slowly rise. The shortest day is approaching and the wheel of the world will turn and I feel calm and happy about my place in it. I took Malc a cup of coffee in bed when I got home. I watched Malc slowly rise. I try to remember on Wednesdays and Fridays that he was at work the day before and may want to do quiet things at home.

I Googled how to make a simple basket out of cardboard. Twenty minutes later I had the first of the baskets I need for the marzipan fruit and veg I've made. Malc and I went to The Works and I got some green shredded tissue to use as grass. I already have some clear cellophane. I will package my marzipan produce when Malc is at work on Tuesday.

I read a bit of *Christmas at Thrush Green* and someone in it put on a headscarf because it was raining. I can't remember the last time I saw a woman in a headscarf but when I was growing up there were busloads of them everywhere.

We watched *Have I Got News For You* with Gary Lineker presenting. I think he's rather attractive and he has lovely manners.

Saturday 15th December

Today I am doing one of the few Christmas preparation jobs I don't enjoy. I am defrosting the freezer. We have a combined fridge/freezer, not because we want one, but because that's what space there is in our fitted kitchen (which otherwise is jolly nice, with terracotta, olive and cream-coloured tiles, pale green walls and wood effect work surfaces).

I emptied the freezer and most of the fridge, putting the food outside because it's cold. The milk is by the back door. Malc said he'll keep an eye out for local cats attempting to pilfer it. I went through the *Radio Times* Christmas issue with a yellow highlighter pen marking what I'd like to watch then Malc did the same with a blue highlighter.

At six o'clock the freezer defrost was complete. We ordered Domino's pizza for dinner. I chose cheeseburger topping (instead of my usual pepperoni). It was good except the gherkin was sliced too thickly.

Sunday 16th December

Malc went to the allotment this morning to pick some Brussels sprouts and saw Ken who has invited us to dinner with him and Rose on Wednesday. It was Rose's idea. She said keen gardeners are at a bit of a loose end in winter.

Malc and I got the bus to town. We're meeting Val and Henry today at the Christmas market. We got off on the High Street because the bus was too hot. I think the heating must have been stuck on. I do not think we'll get a white Christmas. We have not had one since 2010. We looked round the Covered Market which is lovely at this time of year, it's like being in the olden days. The Cake Shop is a truly wonderful sight. Then we went to Blackwells and I got Nicola a book token. My Christmas gift shopping is now complete.

We met Val and Henry by the Christmas tree at the Broad Street Christmas Market (which was bustling). We had some mulled wine. Val and I had churros. Malc and Henry had big German hot dogs. While we were eating a silver band played carols. It sounded wonderful. I especially enjoyed 'God Rest Ye Merry Gentlemen' and 'Once In Royal David's City'. I had one of those realisations that I was in a perfect moment of Christmas. I'd have liked to freeze the scene and put it in my pocket and keep it forever as a place I could go back to, but I suppose that is what keeping this diary is.

Monday 17th December

I've got the middle-aged satisfaction of having almost nothing in the freezer. I need the space for Christmas food. The freezer is the emptiest it's been for a long time and contains one Magnum ice cream, a bag of Quorn mince (Nicola has been vegetarian then not vegetarian more times than I can count) and thirty fish fingers.

I finishing reading *Christmas at Thrush Green*. They had a dinner party and didn't eat until nine. That wouldn't suit me and Malc at all. Nicola rang, she got a free Chocolate Orange in WH Smith with an O2 Priority offer. She asked if I was going to watch the *Inside the Factory* Christmas special on at nine. They are going to the Quality Street chocolate factory. This is my kind of telly programme.

Tuesday 18th December
Last night Malc and I watched Quality Street being made. This morning I got up early and went to Tesco and bought a tub of Quality Street and a tub of Roses. I have been wondering which two of the four chocolate selections to get for ages (they are on offer, two for £7). Roses and Quality Street have the longest history, Heroes (available since 1999) and Celebrations (available since 1997) are Johnny Come Latelys to the Christmas food shop. We once had a misprinted shelf label in the shop I worked in which read Cadbury Herpes!

Malc went to work and I packaged my marzipan fruits and veg in little woven cardboard baskets with green tissue paper grass and wrapped them in cellophane so they stay fresh. It is one week to Christmas and I am not overwhelmed with things to do, as I have been in previous years (mainly when Nicola and David were young).

I met Carol for lunch and we gave each other gifts. I gave her a panettone and she gave me a poinsettia. It is beautiful and I'm concerned about looking after it properly. Malc said he'll water it the right amount, and to get a good result it'll need to be put in the dark overnight from September next year to part way through December. He said 'Leave it to me' and I felt a sudden surge of love for

Malc, like I had once when we had to sit apart on a train and I wasn't feeling well when we got on and twenty minutes into the journey he came to see how I was, and when I saw him walking down the carriage towards me I almost cried.

Tonight we watched a programme presented by Howard Goodall about Christmas carols.

Wednesday 19th December

Malc and I bought Christmas pudding, Pringles, mince pies, white wine and marzipan in the Co-op this morning. Every basket I peeked into had either mince pies, mulled wine or a chocolate selection box. We already have a Christmas pudding but I sort of panicked and got another one. In the years when I host Christmas dinner I have to remind myself that I'm just feeding seven adults for one day. On Friday we'll get our Christmas online shop. I have amended it many times. A Parcel Force van delivered a box from Viv and Eric at lunch time. We've put it under the Christmas tree.

I made some marzipan fruit and vegetables to take to Ken and Rose's as a thank you for dinner and some spare ones as well, just in case I think of anyone else who'd like some. Before making them I Googled what percentage of the UK likes marzipan but was unable to get a clear answer. I did discover marzipan pigs are given as gifts to bring good luck. We are also taking white wine, chosen by Malc.

We spent the afternoon lazing in front of the telly, watching *Elf*. Then I put on a nice green velvet dress and Malc put on a clean shirt and we went to Ken and Rose's for dinner. Rose opened the white wine straight away and said she loves marzipan and she'd never seen such perfect miniature fruits and vegetables. Rose said she had thought the allotment party would be full of people talking about turnips and peat free compost but she was pleasantly surprised and had especially enjoyed chatting with Malc and I.

They had a real Christmas tree which was decorated with red, gold and silver balls. Among their Christmas cards there was a card saying happy Corbmass with a Jeremy Corbyn style Santa on it. This was from Ken's brother who is political.

Rose cooked us pork and apple sausages, honey glazed parsnips and sweet potato wedges. The parsnips were grown by Ken. He is going to try to grow sweet potatoes next year. Rose is retired now but she used to work in a bank. Ken said she never brought her work home with her unfortunately.

For dessert we had raspberry Santa hat profiteroles and custard from M&S. It was so lovely to have dinner cooked for us. We got home at eleven, full of sausage and happiness. We've invited Ken and Rose to come to us for dinner early next year.

Thursday 20th December

Today is the last day I can amend my online shop before it is delivered tomorrow. I think I have captured all of the likely things people will want to eat, based on previous Christmases.

I went to Gail's for coffee. I hope she likes the Trans-Siberian Orchestra CD I got her. She put it by her pile of Christmas cards. She said she hasn't got round to decorating the tree or putting the cards up yet. I offered to help. She said 'Really?' and I said I'd enjoy it. We chatted while we strung cards and hung baubles on her four-foot tree. It was a pre-lit one but has stopped working. Gail said Len has been a bit different lately. He made her a cup of tea when she got in from work yesterday and asked how her shift was. I said people can and do change, not easily and not quickly, but gradually and with effort. Gail said it's always been an effort being married to Len. I asked if it was worth the effort. She said it might turn out to be, she doesn't know yet. Len has asked Gail what she wants for Christmas but she hasn't told him. I said he'll never know if she doesn't tell him.

I saw Tamsin on my way home. She is in her second trimester now. I asked how she was feeling and she said she had sore breasts and then she blushed. I hope I don't appear to be a prude, I'm not, I can cope with people saying sore breasts at me from noon to night if necessary. I said I'd had that with Nicola. With David it was the indigestion which got me. I asked Tamsin if she was ready for Christmas. She said almost but she still didn't have anything for Tom. They had agreed early in the month not to get each other anything and save their money for the baby. Then a week ago Tom had changed his mind and said they should get each other something, so Tamsin thought of two books she'd like (she gave Tom two book titles in case he couldn't get one of them). But he has given her no ideas. Tamsin looked down at the ground and said 'He says he doesn't want a fuss but he is making all the fuss' and I realised she was on the verge of tears. I said 'Has he got an electric screwdriver and does he like marzipan?' She said he loves marzipan and he has got a cheap set of screwdrivers but they aren't electric. I asked Tamsin if she was busy and she said no (at this time of year people often have a great big to do list), so I invited her to pop in for a minute because I couldn't remember the brand name of the electric screwdriver that Malc has and raves about.

Tamsin and I had a cup of tea. She took a photo of Malc's screwdriver then looked it up on Amazon and ordered one which will be delivered before Christmas. I gave her some marzipan fruits and Tom's gift was sorted. She was very grateful and I told her to give me a knock if there is ever anything she thinks Malc and I can help with.

Today is Malc's pay day so he suggested we get Chinese for dinner. Malc had beef in black bean sauce and I had sweet and sour chicken balls. I invented a song; 'Eating balls at Christmas' which can be sung to the tune of Chris Rea's 'Driving Home For Christmas'. Malc called me a silly sausage. I said if you can't be a silly sausage at Christmas then when can you be?

Nicola rang. She has won some after dinner mints in a competition on Twitter! She said she has asked for them to be posted here because she won't be in for the postman and we can eat them at Christmas while watching the telly. We always set snacks out on the breakfast bar for Christmas grazing.

Friday 21st December

The Christmas online shop arrived and had just two missing items (crackers for cheese and pate). Malc suggested we go late this evening to the Tesco and M&S retail park. This is a good suggestion. Supermarkets can get a bit horrible at Christmas. Being retired and semi-retired we can choose when to go shopping.

The Christmas number one was announced today. It wasn't 'Eating Balls at Christmas' by Pam Dickens. It's a charity single raising money for The Trussell Trust who run food banks and is a cover of Starship's 'We Built This City', but with rock and roll changed to sausage rolls, and the rest of the lyrics altered too, made by a blogger called LadBaby. I am not quite sure what a blogger is but well done to him.

We went to the chip shop to get lunch. In the queue behind us was a woman on her phone to someone. I heard her say 'money is nice, but it's more important to enjoy the holiday together' and then she said 'there will be other opportunities for doing overtime but we won't get this Christmas again.' Next she said 'Why phone to ask if you knew what I was going to say', and then 'Don't be like that' and then we got our cod and chips. When we got home a red 'Sorry we missed you' card had been put through the door by Royal Mail.

In Eva Ibbotson's 'Vicky and the Christmas Angel' I read this lovely bit; 'the chrysalis which had been growing inside Vicky all these days broke open and Christmas, in all its boundless and uncontrollable joy, broke out'.

At eight o'clock we went to M&S and Tesco. We got crackers for cheese, venison pate, a cooked ham, and a pack of four dips. Christmas music was playing and Christmas jumpers were being worn and we had time to browse because we don't have to get up early.

Saturday 22nd December

After breakfast we went to collect a parcel from the Sandy Lane West delivery office. On our way a DHL man asked us to take in a parcel for next door but two. Malc said why can't Royal Mail work out this clever system? The parcel is probably the after dinner mints Nicola won, we're not expecting any other parcels. We have already done all our shopping and we've had a lovely big box from Viv and Eric.

I accompanied Malc to the allotment where he harvested Brussels sprouts and parsnips which we then took to Val's. Malc showed me Ken's plot, it's very neat. Malc's carrots have had an attack of the wire worm recently. When we got to Val and Henry's Val had just finished putting away the Waitrose delivery of our Christmas dinner. She got everything she ordered but forgot to add brie. Henry said he could nip out for some brie later. He made us coffee and opened a tin of Belgian biscuits.

Val and Henry are going for dinner tonight with Henry's work colleagues. Most of them are anti-Brexit, but one is very pro-Brexit and Henry says woe betide anyone who sets him off about it. Val said she's got enough to think about today without remembering things not to talk about at dinner. Henry said Brexit gives him indigestion. He has gone off talking about it, much to Val's relief.

The traffic was slow on our way home. Our neighbours opposite (he drives a taxi and she is a pharmacist) gave us a box of McVities Victoria chocolate biscuits. This is very neighbourly. We gave them some marzipan fruits.

We watched the *Vicar of Dibley* Christmas special where she has three Christmas dinners.

Sunday 23rd December

I ate my breakfast while looking at the Christmas tree with the lights on. It seemed this morning as if sitting in front of the tree filled me with the energy I needed for some pre-Christmas housework. I hoovered the stairs (my least favourite part of the hoovering). I cleaned the upstairs toilet and the downstairs toilet. I will now do minimal housework until after Christmas.

I popped round to Mum's. I took some mince pies but Mum already had two packets. We had a mince pie from the pack with the shortest date and a cup of tea. Bridget's Christmas present has arrived and is lovely. Mum has put a red bow on it and will give it to Bridget tomorrow. Mum has got lots of tins of biscuits from friends and neighbours.

I called in to Templars Square. I am happy to no longer work in retail at Christmas. I overheard someone say there was no mulled wine left in the Co-op. I love having done all my Christmas shopping. It has been a doddle this year with plenty of time to think and shop.

I went in Yours and bought a black scarf with silver snowflakes. It's a last-minute gift to myself. Women of my age were brought up to put other people's needs before our own but we need to resist this sometimes. Our needs are as important as those of everyone else. The sales assistant asked me if I was ready for Christmas. I said I was very ready, bring it on!

The film *Up* was on today. The start of it made me shed a tear. We watched *Still Open All Hours* which yet again had a plot in which Granville pretends a foodstuff is an aphrodisiac in order to sell lots of it. This time it was mince pies.

We watched *What We Were Watching* and it was about Christmas 1988. Malc said in 2048 we will be watching *What We Were Watching* Christmas 2018. If I live until 2048 I will be ninety-six years old. I did not point this out to Malc. I don't want us to think about our mortality today.

I finished reading Eva Ibbotson's *The Christmas Star*. It was so charming I wished it was longer.

Monday 24th December

Nicola arrived this morning and is staying until the day after Boxing Day. She opened the parcel of after dinner mints she'd won. There were some with a fondant centre and some with honeycomb in dark mint chocolate and there were also some orange cremes and some coffee cremes. We ate some of coffee cremes (delicious!) then put them on the breakfast bar with the other Christmas snack foods (Mini Cheddars, Cheese Footballs, mince pies, dry roasted peanuts, salted peanuts, nuts still in their shells, shortbread, dates, tangerines and Pringles).

Last year I was busy cooking on Christmas Eve but this year is Val's turn so she'll be up to her elbows in turkey crown, pigs in blankets and stuffing balls. I offered to do some of the cooking but Val said she had it in hand.

Nicola went out to see Fiona and Darren. Malc watched *Scrooge* (the Alistair Sim version). I wished everyone on Facebook Merry Christmas because it's the done thing nowadays. I love seeing pictures of people's trees and Christmas jumpers. I remembered these words by Elizabeth Goudge; 'They knew how to enjoy themselves on Christmas Eve, did these people of Oxford, and they were doing it'. She didn't add 'and posting about it on Facebook while wearing matching pyjamas'.

I am re-reading *A Christmas Carol.* I wonder how many other people around the world are reading it right now? Sometimes Christmas feels like a big human connectedness.

Tuesday 25th December
The 12 days of Christmas begin today!
It's hard to capture Christmas in words but I will try, or my name's not Pamela Dorothy Dickens! Today is my 66th Christmas. I've seen Mum on all of them, Val on most of them (she was delayed coming back from holiday once and a few times they've seen Henry's family on Christmas Day), Nicola and David on most of them (there has been the occasional year when they had partners whose families they spent Christmas with) and this is Malc and I's 45th Christmas together.

I got up at seven and cooked some bacon (there were nine slices in an eight-slice pack, it's a Christmas miracle!) and made Malc, Nicola and I a bacon sandwich. Malc said he loves waking up to bacon.

We are all due at Val and Henry's at eleven. Malc and I went to get Mum/Nan and Nicola went to get David and will meet us at Val and Henry's. The roads were quiet. We saw a man wearing a Santa hat on Barns Road.

We got to Val and Henry's first and settled Mum in a chair with high arm rests brought in from the conservatory. She finds it easier to get up out of a chair like this. Henry took her photo, then grouped the rest of us round her and took another snap. Asked how he was today Henry said 'I am positively fervent about the festivities', which is nice. Our Henry has a lovely turn of phrase.

David arrived looking a bit tired but perked up when Aunty Val made him a fancy coffee from a pod. We all got a drink and then exchanged gifts. I got a lovely big page a day diary from Nicola. I think I will keep up this diary next year. I got books from everyone and a jigsaw called The Christmas Library from Malc.

We ate dinner at the table, just after two. I remembered that last year when I did the cooking the challenge of getting everything hot at once caused me to be snappy with Malc. Then I forgot that and looked round the table at everyone in their Christmas clothes and Christmas mood.

We had cauliflower cheese but we know it's not really part of a roast dinner, we just like it. Val said some people on mumsnet.com got very cross about it last December. We had turkey and ham, loads of roast potatoes, parsnips, carrots, sprouts, stuffing balls, Yorkshire puddings, gravy and cranberry sauce. We pulled gold crackers and we all wore our paper hats. My favourite cracker joke was; How does Christmas Day end? With the letter Y!

We had a big pause and a bit of telly before we had our Christmas pudding. We watched *The Queen's Christmas Broadcast*. Her Christmas tree was mostly decorated in gold and was very tasteful. Then we watched part of *Carry On Up the Jungle*. Then we sat at the dining table again and had Christmas pudding. Nicola, David and I had ours with honeycomb flavour ice cream, Val, Mum and Malc had custard, Henry had brandy butter. We left at six and took Mum home, while Nicola took David home (he has to work tomorrow). Val sent us all home with neatly packaged leftovers. When we got in Malc rang Viv to wish her and Eric a Merry Christmas. She said the tea towels we sent her are already in use.

Nicola got back just after seven and we had some nibbly bits (cheese and crackers, ham, coleslaw and crisps) for dinner. We watched the Christmas episode of *The Good Life*. It has been a classic Christmas Day. I'm so lucky to spend it with the people who have my heart. Before she went to bed Nicola asked why does Christmas Day go so fast?

Wednesday 26th December

Today is the second day of Christmas!

I got up at eight. For breakfast I had trifle, a banana and four squares of Cadbury Fruit & Nut chocolate. It took me ages to decide what to eat out of all the available options.

I think Christmas Day goes so fast because of the anticipation of it. You'd expect something which has been mentioned with increasing frequency since September to be a bit longer lived. It was the industrial revolution that shrunk Christmas from twelve days to just one. I am having a retirement revolution and having the full twelve days again! I wish everyone could have twelve days off.

Nicola got up at nine. She said David really liked his tie. She had two stuffing balls dipped in salad cream, some paprika Pringles and a chocolate reindeer for breakfast. We sat about with the telly on. Malc got up and had some Weetabix for breakfast. He said he'd eat more decadently later in the day. He went to the allotment for some fresh air. Nicola went for a shower and came back smelling of Body Shop vanilla marshmallow body lotion. She's always liked getting new smellies for Christmas.

We had smoked salmon and scrambled egg for lunch. Nicola and I walked to Templars Square shops. Most shops were open but B&M and the jewellers were shut. We browsed the Christmas decorations on sale in Wilko. We overheard two women talking about their Christmases. One of them said it feels like a storm has passed. The other said she feels like a task has been accomplished. She went on to say no one fell out this year and no one was ill this year.

We went to the Co-op for milk and big oranges. The woman who served us wished us a Merry Christmas and was chatty. She said everyone has been buying bread and milk. I said we had enough Pringles to last until February. This is a slight exaggeration. We saw a youngster learning to ride a bike on our way home. When we got home Malc made us a cup of tea and we all had a slice of Christmas cake.

We had bubble and squeak for dinner. The fridge is still very full. We watched *The Morecambe and Wise Show* Christmas special from 1971. Nicola said she feels like Christmas is a bubble of time outside time.

Thursday 27th December
Today is the third day of Christmas.
Nicola left this morning. Then I spent a couple of hours reading. I got some great books for Christmas;
A Royal Christmas by Louise Cooling from Mum.
A Tudor Christmas by Alison Weir and Siobhan Clarke from Val and Henry (and also *The Xmas Files The Philosophy of Christmas* by Stephen Law from Henry. A colleague of his was giving it away, so Henry said it's not exactly a present, but I think it is, it doesn't matter that someone didn't pay for a thing, it's that they thought of you).
A Stocking full of Christmas Stories by Pat Thomson from Nicola.
Christmas in Wales Edited by Dewi Roberts from David.
On one of the twelve days of Christmas I will spend all day in bed or on the sofa reading. Going back to bed to read is a huge pleasure available to me now I'm retired.

After lunch (cold sausage and soft cheese sandwich with cranberry sauce) Malc and I got the bus into town. We went to the Roman bit of the Ashmolean Museum. There were Roman farms in Oxfordshire. We also looked at the silver gallery and the Egyptian things.

Tonight we watched the first heat of *World's Strongest Man*. Laurence Shalei of Swindon was eliminated. Whilst we in Oxford have a longstanding football rivalry with Swindon, I am still sad to see Big Loz going out so early in the competition.

Friday 28th December
Today is the fourth day of Christmas.

I weighed myself this morning. I am eleven stones and two pounds. Usually I'm a few pounds under eleven stones. At this point of Christmas the telly is nagging at you to go on a diet so often it makes you wonder if you need to. I wrote birthdays and anniversaries on next years' calendar. There is a whole blank year ahead. I've been retired for ten months, when Dad died he'd been retired for eleven. I want to make it to the end of February and have been retired for a year, then I'll stop worrying about history repeating itself.

David came round for dinner. We ordered Domino's pizza then went to the Vue Cinema to see *Aquaman*. It's a very comfy cinema but the price of snacks is astronomical. David has been busy at work. He said he's never seen a Boxing Day like it at Bicester Village, but prices in the shop he works in are the same now as before Christmas, so people aren't getting a bargain.

We gave David a lift home after the film. David thought the under the ocean characters in *Aquaman* needed more development so you cared about them and believed there would be a war with the surface people. David likes to talk about films, I sometimes wonder if he should have been a film critic like Barry Norman, but he never really liked doing his English homework, or any homework for that matter. His dream job is building Lego models but he says it's a very competitive field.

Saturday 29th December

Today is the fifth day of Christmas.

For breakfast I had toast with pineapple jam and some paprika Pringles. I ate it in front of the Christmas tree which I will take down in a week. We're at the stage of

Christmas where the fridge is starting to have some space in it again. There are very few Klippits food bag clips left in the jar I keep them in because we have a lot of open, half-eaten packets of food.

I met Val in town and we spent the day shopping and lunching. It was very pleasant. We walked more than six miles according to Val's phone. Val got a dress in Debenhams. We had lunch at The Alchemist. I had fish and chips (the fish with black batter is fabulous) and Val had katsu chicken curry. I looked at all the Christmas decorations in shop windows and in town (we are a bit too tasteful in Oxford in my opinion, we have just white lights) because in a week they will be taken down.

Malc and I tried to watch yesterday's *World's Strongest Man* (we didn't see it because we were at the cinema) but our Virgin TV box kept crashing. Then Malc Googled *World's Strongest Man* to try and stream it and accidentally found out who won. Then I looked to see who won (Björnsson, also known as The Mountain from *Game of Thrones*) because I don't like big secrets in a marriage.

Malc and I went to bed with a hot chocolate and the knowledge we don't have to be up early in the morning.

Sunday 30th December
Today is the sixth day of Christmas.
I popped round to see Mum. We finished a tin of lemon shortbread. Our conversation was mostly about Christmas. Mum's friend Bridget had a good one with her son and family. Bridget's daughter-in-law, who it has been established makes an effort to be agreeable, bought her a really lovely dressing gown with a passionflower print,

made a sherry trifle and always remembered to put the subtitles on when they were watching telly. Ros over the road had a house full for three days and her nephew was seen smoking outside frequently. He's currently unemployed but is hoping to become a bin man. We started a tin of chocolate chip shortbread biscuits in the shape of West Highland terriers.

When I got home Malc was dozing in front of the telly. He had the *Haynes Explains Christmas* book on his lap. I got my book and made a cup of tea and settled on the sofa. Malc woke up and had a hankering for toad in the hole so that's what I made for dinner.

Monday 31st December
New Year's Eve.
Today is the seventh day of Christmas.
When I was a younger woman I used to get in a bit of a tizz at the end of the year. Before Malc and I were married I worried that he'd never ask. Then before we had Nicola I worried I'd never fall pregnant. Then when we had Nicola and I stopped working I worried about money. Then we had David and I was too tired to worry for a few years and I realised just because it's New Year's Eve it doesn't mean you have to re-evaluate your entire life, you could do this on any day of the year.

For lunch I had the last of the paprika Pringles, a Lindt chocolate bear, an orange and some cheese straws. Malc had the last of the sour cream and onion Pringles, a mini Babybel cheese, some Twiglets and a slice of toast with Marmite. We went to Halfords in Botley so Malc could get a kit to make his car headlights clean again. Then we walked round Oak Furniture Land, one of the less exotic lands I've visited. It smells very nice. A small boy was repeatedly opening and shutting a drawer.

I helped Malc clean his headlights on the driveway. Tom and Tamsin wished us a Happy New Year, they are going out to her parents for the evening. Tom has eaten all his marzipan fruits.

Val and Henry came round to us at six to see the New Year in. Henry described Christmas Day (already a week ago!) as a splendid day of cheerfulness with his clan. We got fish and chips from the Littlemore Fish Bar. There is some good telly on tonight but *University Challenge* clashes with *Terry And June*.

Val and Henry left at a quarter past midnight, and here we are in another year.

December reckoning, have I kept Christmas all December? It has been a piece of cake to keep Christmas all December, much easier than any other month of the year, especially tricky February or sunny August.

Christmas is the ultimate expression of the phrase 'This too shall pass'. We prepare and anticipate, then it ends, not returning to give you another go at having the kind of Christmas you want until a whole year later. Christmas is about the good coming back. You can carry a little bit along with you all the time, but it's extra powerful when shared with other people in December.

On telly the question of what's most important about Christmas is often discussed. We know it's not the presents (pleasing though they are, and fun to give and receive). It's not the food (delicious though it is). It's not the tree in the house (which is a pretty reminder of the season and helps put you in the right frame of mind). It's not the wearing of bright new clothes (fancy though it makes you feel). It's not especially the date of the twenty-fifth of December (traditional though this has become).

The most important thing about Christmas is being together, now, and the always continuing warm concern and care for the wellbeing of each other. The substantial hope that your fellow human beings and your friends and family will prosper and enjoy good health (physical and mental).

I think I have kept Christmas all the year, and I think you can too if you've read this book.

Printed in Great Britain
by Amazon

62384786R00188